Kelly pushed herself away from her desk and walked to the table. She crossed her arms over her chest and then wondered what type of body language she was conveying to the detective. No doubt Nora Wolman was scrutinizing every nuance of Kelly's reaction and speech pattern and how she moved her body. She uncrossed her arms. She had nothing to hide or be defensive about. "I really don't see how that relates to Maxine's murder."

"I'm the detective. Let me be the judge of what relates and what doesn't."

"Fine. Bernadette's vision was of a man being murdered. She said the dress was connected to the murder."

The detective's lips started to form a smile but stopped short. "You went to see Mrs. Singer to ask her if she murdered her husband wearing the dress in question?"

"Something like that. Detective Wolman, I didn't kill Maxine. I didn't have anything against her."

Wolman stood. "But you had something against Bernadette Rydell?"

"No, I never said I had anything against Bernadette."

"But do you?"

"No!"

"The two women were similar-looking. Miss Rydell is costing you business. I've heard some of the talk. You could've mistaken Miss Lemoyne for her cousin when you snuck in."

"I didn't sneak in. I was asked to come over, and the door was unlocked. I didn't kill Maxine…"

Books by Debra Sennefelder

A Resale Boutique Mystery
Murder Wears A Little Black Dress

Published by Kensington Publishing Corporation

Murder Wears A Little Black Dress

A Resale Boutique Mystery

Debra Sennefelder

LYRICAL PRESS
Kensington Publishing Corp.
www.kensingtonbooks.com

LYRICAL UNDERGROUND BOOKS are published by
Kensington Publishing Corp.
119 West 40th Street
New York, NY 10018

All Kensington titles, imprints, and distributed lines are available at special quantity discounts for bulk purchases for sales promotion, premiums, fund-raising, educational, or institutional use.

Special book excerpts or customized printings can also be created to fit specific needs. For details, write or phone the office of the Kensington Sales Manager: Kensington Publishing Corp., 119 West 40th Street, New York, NY 10018. Attn. Sales Department. Phone: 1-800-221-2647.

Lyrical Underground and Lyrical Underground logo Reg. US Pat. & TM Off.

First Electronic Edition: January 2019
eISBN-13: 978-1-5161-0893-0
eISBN-10: 1-5161-0893-0

First Print Edition: January 2019
ISBN-13: 978-1-5161-0896-1
ISBN-10: 1-5161-0896-5

Printed in the United States of America

For my niece Jennifer Ciombor who always keeps it fashionable.

Chapter 1

"How do you explain this? The tag says my dress has been marked down by seventy-five percent. There appears to be a mistake."

Kelly Quinn turned her head to the raised voice of the woman standing at the sales counter. She held a midi-length floral dress with cap sleeves in one hand while her other was propped on her hip.

"Irene, you know the store's policy on markdowns," Pepper Donovan answered with a smile. She always had a smile, except for when Kelly announced she was making changes to the consignment shop.

"How on earth am I supposed to earn any money? Martha never put merchandise on sale," Floral Dress Lady countered.

As Kelly made her way across the shop, she was well aware her grandmother didn't do a lot of things, and that was why, in the past few years, the shop's earnings had steadily declined.

"Good morning. I'm Kelly Quinn." She extended her hand, but it was received with an intense glare. She pulled her hand back and braced herself for an unpleasant conversation. "What seems to be the problem?"

"Seems? Dear child, there doesn't *seem* to be a problem. There *is* a problem. My dress has been marked down to an unreasonable amount of money. Please explain to me the reason for your decision."

Kelly bristled at being called a child. She'd just celebrated her twenty-sixth birthday three months ago and, up until forty-five days ago, she had a full-time job with a well-laid-out career path and her own apartment, albeit it tiny, in the West Village of New York City. How many children could say that?

"I was just reminding Irene of the store's pricing policy." No doubt Pepper was trying to remind her new boss about the agreement every consignee signed. She was younger than Kelly's late granny but still old enough to feel she should be in charge.

Kelly didn't need to be reminded. She was familiar with the document, as well as many other documents pertaining to the shop. The past few weeks had been filled with reviewing papers, meeting with lawyers, and sleepless nights because of her new acquisition.

"When you consigned your clothing, you signed an agreement, which stated how merchandise is priced. After seven weeks, merchandise is marked down by seventy-five percent," Kelly said.

"I see." Floral Dress Lady stretched out her arm, and the dress dangled from its hanger while she admired it. "So, this lovely dress that cost me way more than the original consigned price is now a mere ten dollars?" Her brows arched, and her glare intensified.

This isn't good.

"It's important to keep turning over merchandise. Especially out-of-season clothing." When Kelly had gone painstakingly through every item in inventory, she found a bunch of spring/summer clothing that should have been cleared out months ago. "When customers see new stuff, they tend to buy more. This translates into money for our consignees." Kelly hoped the explanation would appease the woman.

"Except for this consignee. Why don't you do a better job of selling your merchandise so it doesn't become old?"

No appeasement there.

"I'm sorry, I didn't catch your name."

"Kelly, this is Irene Singer." Pepper jumped back into the conversation. "She's been consigning with us for a while."

Irene Singer gave Kelly a stern nod as if her name should have meant something. It didn't.

The bell over the front door chimed, prompting Kelly to glance over her shoulder. More shoppers. She needed to wrap up this dispute over the pricing.

"Ms. Singer, unfortunately I can't change the price on the dress as per our policy to mark down accordingly based on length of time in inventory, but I'm going to give the dress back to you." Phew. She managed to say all that in one breath, and it actually sounded like she knew what she was saying. "Let me just snip off the price tag."

Irene Singer's eyes widened. "I don't have a use for this dress, which is why I consigned it."

There wasn't going to be any appeasement with the woman whatsoever. Frustration bubbled in Kelly. She hadn't worked a sales floor since fashion school, and after graduating, she didn't think she'd ever be back to arranging displays, restocking inventory, or handling cranky customers. Yet, there she was. The new owner of the Lucky Cove Consignment Shop soon to be renamed Curated by Kelly Resale Boutique. The name change reflected Kelly's vision for a trendy consignment shop for locals and tourists.

"Irene, look, you consigned with us to get some cash. Let us sell the dress. After all, you did say you have no use for it," Pepper said.

Kelly admired Pepper's genius in using Irene's own words to try to bring the woman around to reason. Her years of experience working in the shop shone, and Kelly was grateful to have her on her team. Her team of two.

Irene was silent for a moment. "Fine. A little extra cash will come in handy." She dropped the dress on the counter and, without as much as a goodbye, she marched out of the shop.

Kelly exhaled a relieved breath. "Thanks for your help."

"No problem." Pepper's gaze drifted to a spreadsheet Kelly had created with a list of items in the home furnishings department to be marked down. Her head shook as she scanned the list of every item stuffed into the small addition of the building. No doubt, she was second-guessing Kelly's decision to stop selling home items and focus solely on fashion and accessories.

"She's wound kind of tight."

Pepper looked up from the spreadsheet. "You'll learn how to handle the tough ones. You're right about Irene. But she wasn't always like that."

Before Kelly could ask what happened to turn Irene bitter, Pepper reached her hand over the counter and touched Kelly's arm. "We didn't finish our conversation earlier."

Kelly's stomach constricted. They'd been having a lot of conversations, and none of them were easy.

Pepper gave her new boss a pointed look over the rim of her glasses. "I still don't understand why you need to change the name. It's been Lucky Cove Consignment since the day your granny opened the shop."

Kelly had been on the receiving end of that look, which she dubbed the "Pepper glare," since she made the decision to stay in Lucky Cove and keep her late granny's consignment shop. She broke eye contact and considered how to tell Pepper one more time the reason for the name change.

"Granny did her thing and now it's my turn."

When would the explanation sink in for Pepper? She hoped soon. Kelly gave her granny props because she knew what her thing was.

Kelly? She didn't have a clue anymore. Her life plan went right out the window the day she carried a cardboard box out of the buying offices of Bishop's Department Store. At least she'd had the foresight to wear a Rebecca Taylor floral dress she had scored for sixty percent off and Marc Fisher's lace-up sandals she found for seventy percent off. Yes, on her last day at Bishop's, she had looked as good as she did the working girl's walk of shame—the trek from desk to exit for the last time with her entire career stuffed in a box.

Kelly's heart seized when she thought about that morning. Everything she'd worked for was gone. Poof. Just like that.

"You can do your thing without changing the shop's name," Pepper countered.

Kelly sighed. She now understood how hamsters felt on their wheels. Around and around and around and nothing changed.

"I have muffins!" Liv Moretti announced as she breezed by the sales counter on her way to the office.

Kelly's nose wriggled. Pumpkin spice muffins. Her favorite. She stepped back from the counter, releasing herself from Pepper's hold, and followed her best friend to the back of the store.

They entered the staff room, which used to be the original kitchen in the colonial house before it was transformed into the clothing store. Granny turned the kitchen into a multipurpose space for meal breaks and office work. A desk was tucked into a corner, and a file cabinet stood where a hutch used to be. The tile floor was dull with chips and cracks from years of use, and there was a draft around the sink window. Definitely not a pretty space, but it was functional.

Liv opened the pastry box. The heavenly aroma of freshly baked muffins turned Kelly's souring mood bright again. Liv was a genius in the kitchen. Good baking genes ran in the Moretti family, while good eating genes ran in Kelly's family. She grabbed a muffin and sank her teeth into the moist, tasty treat and savored unapologetically.

For the past week, Liv had been coming to help mark down merchandise and always brought treats from her family's bakery. Kelly should've had more resolve, because the skinny jeans she pulled on at the crack of dawn were already a little tight around her waist, thanks to her overindulging. She attributed it to stress eating, and once she settled into her new role as a shop owner, she'd be more in control. At least, she hoped so.

"You know, this is kind of fun." Liv reached into the box and plucked out a muffin. She took a bite as Kelly watched in amazement. Somehow Liv managed to stay lean, despite the fact she was surrounded by cakes, cookies, and cupcakes all day long. At nearly five seven, her lithe frame was reminiscent of Audrey Hepburn. Her dark auburn hair was styled in a pixie cut, and she favored skinny pants with bateau neckline tops. Good thing she was Kelly's bestie or else Kelly would've hated her.

"Fun?" Now it was Kelly's turn to give a look to Liv. Fun was bargain hunting in the city. Fun was meeting up with friends for cocktails. Fun was sleeping in. Kelly had been doing none of those things.

She'd been operating on limited sleep since Granny's funeral. She was used to working long hours at Bishop's, especially during Fashion Week when she had to keep up with her buyer as they crisscrossed New York City to attend shows. But owning a retail store? That was a whole new level of sleep deprivation.

"You'll see. Once you're all settled, you'll see for yourself how much fun it is to own your own business."

Kelly took another bite of her muffin while she tried to identify the "fun" part of owning a business. So far she hadn't come across anything remotely considered fun, only a lot of hard work.

"I guess the upside is no one can fire me." Kelly walked to the refrigerator and pulled out two bottles of water. She handed one to Liv before opening her bottle. "The downside is there will be no customers."

"Stop! You're going to have customers. There are a whole bunch out there now." Liv gestured to the swinging door that led to the shop.

"What if the regulars hate what I've planned for the shop? Pepper does. What if I can't get enough new customers? What if I let Granny down?" Kelly's mind raced with every negative scenario that could possibly play out. She took a long drink of water to cool her jets. She needed to remain calm and confident. What was the old saying? Don't let them see you sweat.

"Hey, you. I'm sure your grandmother would approve of what you're doing."

"You really think so?"

"Yes, I do."

"I had a run-in with Irene Singer. Do you know her?"

Liv gave an exaggerated nod. "Everyone knows Irene Singer."

"What's her deal?"

"Her husband died and she took it hard." After another swig of water, Liv screwed on the lid and set the bottle down. "I'm here to help with the sale. I better get out there. And you should too."

"Bossy much?" Kelly glanced at her fitness tracker, which doubled as a watch, and, given the number of sugary sweets she'd been eating, she should revert the tracker back to its basic function—counting her calories and steps—or her skinny jeans would never fit.

Liv chuckled. "Habit."

Kelly led the way out of the staff room. The shop's layout was choppy. None of the original walls were removed when the residence was turned into a retail store. Liv and Kelly arrived in the area that used to be the living room.

"Who's that woman?" Kelly asked.

A tall, willowy blonde stood beside a circular rack. Her golden hair cascaded down her back, skimming the Victorian-inspired tiered maxi dress with lace inserts and delicate flutter sleeves in creamy white she wore. Her skin was porcelain, and her gaze was fixated on the black lace dress she held. She was a woman who could wear lace and not look dowdy.

"Bernadette Rydell. Lucky Cove's resident psychic." Liv's tone was cynical, and she usually didn't do cynical. "She talks to dead people."

"Seriously?" Kelly swung her head around to look at her friend.

"She does readings out of her cottage on Gull Drive. My aunt Eloisa gave me a gift certificate for one last Christmas," Liv said.

Kelly's mouth gaped open. The Morettis were all about holy water, rosary beads, and fish on Fridays. They didn't do psychics. "No!"

"My mother almost had a stroke when I opened the envelope. You know how she is. She sees psychics as the devil's handmaidens."

"I know. What was her sister thinking?"

Liv shrugged. "Eloisa has always been out there on the fringe. I think she wanted to push my mother's buttons."

Kelly laughed. She enjoyed Liv's family. When Eloisa and Geovanna, Liv's mother, got together, they were a hoot. They were sisters who loved big and fought even bigger. But, at the end of the day, they always had each other's backs. A twinge of sadness flicked inside of Kelly. She doubted she'd ever experience that type of relationship with her own sister again.

"Did you have the reading?" Kelly asked.

"No. No way. I don't believe in that stuff. Oh, there's Carly. Let me see if she needs any help." Liv dashed away, leaving Kelly alone, mesmerized by Bernadette.

The psychic, if she really was one, had a unique aura around her. Kelly couldn't quite put her finger on it. While not able to pinpoint what made Bernadette intriguing to her, she did realize she needed to stop lurking and welcome the woman to her shop.

Her shop. That still sounded weird to her. She never thought in a million years she'd own a business, much less a consignment shop. Yet, there she was. Bernadette turned and caught Kelly staring. *Not cool, Kell.* Bernadette probably thought Kelly was some kind of stalker. Time to act like the professional she was supposed to be.

Kelly smiled as she set forward to introduce herself. She extended her hand. Hopefully, Bernadette would receive her better than Irene Singer did earlier. "Hello, I'm —"

"Kelly Quinn." Bernadette shook Kelly's hand. Her grip was firm. "Very nice to meet you." Her dark eyes with flecks of gold held Kelly's gaze. "I'm sorry for your loss. Your grandmother is at peace now. She wants you to know that. She's…she's proud of you and your decision."

Her granny was proud of her? All the weight that had been crushing Kelly's shoulders eased up for a moment. Her granny was proud of her. *Wait.* Did Bernadette just read her?

"I see you two introduced yourselves." Liv returned with an armful of clothing. "Carly wants me to hold these for her while she checks out the back room."

Kelly nodded absently. She was entranced by Bernadette, who still held on to her hand.

"Passing over to the other side is often a welcome relief for people." Bernadette's voice was soothing and confident.

"Would you like to try the dress on?" Liv asked Bernadette, gesturing to the garment draped over the psychic's arm.

Bernadette blinked. "Oh, yes." She let go of Kelly's hand and gave Liv the dress. "I was immediately drawn to it."

"The dressing room is right there." Liv turned and walked just a few feet to pull back a curtain and hung the dress in the small space outfitted with a mirror and a stool. Bernadette followed and stepped into the dressing room. She pulled the curtain closed.

Liv returned to Kelly's side. "Cat got your tongue?"

"What? No."

"Don't tell me you're falling for her routine? Lucky Cove is small and people talk. Especially about your granny. There's nothing she can tell you she couldn't have learned from the gossip mill."

Kelly wouldn't agree that she was *falling* for Bernadette's routine, but she was curious. Her first summer as an intern for Ralph Lauren, a fellow intern went to see a psychic in the East Village. Kelly nearly choked on her latte when she found out Bethany forked over a thousand dollars for readings. For a fashion student working only for course credit, that was a lot of cash.

Later she found out the psychic turned out to be right about several things. She nailed the cheating boyfriend, an awesome job opportunity at Tory Burch, and a health scare that landed Bethany in the hospital. So maybe there was something to psychic readings. Who was Kelly to judge?

"You're falling for it. I can see it in your eyes." Liv shot Kelly a stern look she'd picked up and honed from her mother. "This could all be some kind of prank to drum up business for her and her soothsayer cousin. Halloween is just a few days away."

Before Kelly could respond, Pepper came up beside her and leaned close to whisper, "Camille just called and gave me a heads-up your uncle is on his way over."

"Good grief." Kelly rolled her eyes. Her uncle Ralph had been hovering around the shop since the day Granny's will was read, and not because he wanted to lend a hand to help Kelly. Manual labor wasn't her uncle's thing, but underhanded business maneuvers were his specialty.

"Do you think he's up to something?"

Kelly shrugged. "He's always up to something. Unfortunately, because he's executor, I have to deal with him. Can't Camille keep him in the office?"

Camille was Pepper's sister-in-law and Ralph's secretary. Both women shared a mutual dislike of the man, as did most normal people.

Pepper shook her head. "No can do. He's already left."

The dressing room curtain swept back, and Bernadette stepped out wearing the black dress. Kelly struggled to find a word to describe how amazing Bernadette looked, because she was blown away. Stunning was the first word that popped into Kelly's head.

Bernadette had pulled her long hair up into a messy bun to show off the scalloped eyelash-trimmed lace bateau neckline, which showcased her elongated neck. The bodice and skirt of the dress, intricately sewn pieces of fabric and lace, skimmed her lean torso and hugged her hips, and the scalloped lace hem gave a tease of her long legs.

Kelly stepped forward. "It's beautiful on you."

"Kelly's right," Liv agreed.

"Exquisite. The dress is meant for you," Pepper said.

"I can't see how you wouldn't want to buy this dress. If it looked that good on me, I'd buy it in a heartbeat." Kelly wasn't trying for a hard sell. She really meant the compliment.

Though, Bernadette didn't look as excited about the dress as Kelly felt. Bernadette's face should have been all lit up. Women knew when they looked darn good in a dress. Heck, Kelly had done her fair share of happy dances when she'd found a dress her body rocked. But not Bernadette. The expression on her face was void of any emotion.

"If I were twenty years younger, I'd buy the dress." Pepper laughed. Both Kelly and Liv knew Pepper meant thirty years younger, but what woman didn't want to shave a decade or two off?

"You don't like it?" Kelly's brows furrowed.

Bernadette hadn't moved since coming out of the changing room. She stood there as if frozen in place.

"We'll find you another dress," Pepper suggested.

Bernadette shook her head and then shut her eyes. She swayed as she dragged in a deep breath. "There's something wrong. Wrong with this dress."

Kelly, Liv, and Pepper exchanged looks. There wasn't anything wrong with the dress. It was perfect.

"I feel it. It's happening far away." Bernadette's soft and lyrical voice captivated them.

"If she starts to levitate, I'm outta here," Pepper quipped.

"I'll be right behind you," Liv agreed.

Bernadette's hand flew up and pressed against her chest. And her eyes opened suddenly; her gaze was set dead ahead. "There's a man. I see a man. He's far away."

Kelly, Liv, and Pepper looked around the shop. There weren't any men. In unison, they asked, "Where?"

A chill skittered along Kelly's spine. This was getting weird. "What's going on?" she whispered to Liv, who replied with a simple shrug.

"Do you think we should call someone?" Pepper asked.

"Who?" Kelly looked around, and customers started to turn their attention to the sideshow playing out in front of the dressing room. This wasn't good for business.

"An ambulance," Liv suggested.

"Let's just get her changed out of that dress and out of the store." Kelly stepped forward and stopped when Bernadette stretched out her arm, her palm facing Kelly.

"No! No! No!" A look of stark panic flashed in Bernadette's eyes just before she screamed, "He's dead," and then she collapsed to the floor.

Chapter 2

"Holy crap!" Kelly rushed to Bernadette and dropped to her knees beside the unconscious psychic. What just happened? One minute Bernadette was trying on the dress, and another minute she was seeing a dead man and then, bam, she was on the floor. Kelly's mind raced as adrenaline pumped through her body. "Call 9-1-1!"

Pepper dashed to the sales counter, knocking over a display of mini-pumpkins as she reached for the phone. Meanwhile, all heads in the shop swiveled to see what was going on. Double holy crap! This wasn't how the first day of the big three-day sale was supposed to go. Customers weren't supposed to faint or see dead people. *Focus, Kelly, focus on the unconscious woman.* "Bernadette, can you hear me?"

"Is she breathing?" Liv asked.

Kelly nodded. She was. Thank God.

"What do we do?" Kelly wished she'd taken a first aid class. She'd had plenty of chances over the years, but something more interesting always came up, like brunch or a sample sale. Maybe her sister wasn't completely wrong about her. Lesson learned. The next first aid class she saw offered she'd sign up for.

"I don't know." Liv pulled her cell phone from her back pants pocket and swiped it on.

"What are you doing? Pepper just called 9-1-1."

Liv typed and talked at the same time. "I'm Googling what to do with an unconscious person."

"Why not just ask Siri?"

"Good idea."

"I wasn't serious."

But the situation was getting serious. Shoppers closed in around them, whispering, and not one of them offered to step forward to help. It looked like Kelly wasn't the only person who hadn't taken a first aid class.

"Bernadette!" a voice from the crowd called out. Heads swiveled again, toward the voice. "Oh, no!"

Kelly's breath caught when she looked in the direction of the voice. *Bernadette?* It couldn't be, but the woman looked just like Bernadette. Same height, same hair color, same aura. The only difference was the doppelganger was wearing a flowy burgundy caftan beneath a knitted sleeveless black duster and her blond hair was pulled up into a high ponytail.

"I sensed something was wrong." The woman broke through the crowd and hurried to Bernadette's side. She stroked her hand across Bernadette's cheek.

"Who are you?" Kelly asked.

"I'm her cousin, Maxine Lemoyne. She must've had a vision."

"This has happened before?" Kelly glanced to Liv, but she was still Googling answers about what to do with an unconscious ghost whisperer. No help there.

"A side effect, if you will, of being gifted." Maxine gently shook her cousin's shoulder and whispered her name in an attempt to rouse Bernadette, who stirred and, within a few moments, opened her eyes. "She's back with us."

The crowd let out a collective breath of relief.

"What...what happened?" Confusion crossed Bernadette's face.

"You passed out." Kelly stood and swatted at Liv's hand. "You can stop Googling. She's awake."

Liv flashed a sheepish look as she returned her phone to her back pocket. "Thank goodness. Is she okay?"

Bernadette stood with the assistance of her cousin. "It happened again, didn't it?" She wobbled a little as she found her footing and rubbed the back of her neck.

"Do you think you should get up? Maybe you should wait for the ambulance." Kelly heard sirens approach, which was a welcome relief.

"No, no. I'm fine. Maxine is correct. I...I had a vision. I saw a man. A man was...murdered," Bernadette said, and the crowd gasped.

Triple holy crap! Did Kelly hear Bernadette correctly?

"Murdered? Who?" a woman from the crowd asked.

Confirmation. Kelly did hear Bernadette correctly.

It was time to break up the crowd and get them back to shopping while Psychic Girl took her vision to some other store. "Why don't we go into the staff area for some privacy?"

"The dress is haunted?" another woman asked.

"You're selling haunted clothes," a third woman chimed in with not so much a question but a statement and started the crowd buzzing with speculation.

"No wonder everything is on sale," another woman added to the hysteria.

Good grief. Kelly was going to lose a whole bunch of business if she didn't do some damage control. But what? She scanned her memory, but nothing from her Retail Management 101 class had prepared her for haunted merchandise. Damn!

"She's okay, everybody. Why don't we give her some room?" Pepper made her way through the shoppers and gingerly yet firmly shuffled them away from Bernadette. "She's going to be fine."

"I need to take this dress off now. The murder is connected to this dress," Bernadette declared.

Kelly and Liv stared at each other. They had to be thinking the same thing. "You're saying a woman wore that dress when she murdered a man?" A part of Kelly was scared to hear the answer.

"Yes." Bernadette's hands wound around her neck to begin unzipping the dress.

"Who was the woman? Who was the man?" Liv asked.

"I need to get this dress off. The energy is too disturbing." Bernadette pivoted and raced to the dressing room, pushing past the shoppers who still gawked at the scene of the alleged supernatural visitation.

Kelly chewed on her lower lip. The shift in the mood of her shoppers was disturbing. They were too busy talking about Bernadette and not busy shopping.

The sirens stopped just before the boutique's front door swung open, bringing in a sweep of autumn air and Officer Gabe Donovan. He bypassed the biggest crowd of shoppers the store had ever seen. Too bad their attention was diverted to the psychic who saw a vision of murder.

"Who collapsed?" Gabe scanned the crowd as he turned down the volume on his radio.

He'd been a cop for three years, and since Kelly only came back to Lucky Cove for holidays and brief summer vacations, she wasn't used to seeing him in uniform. To her, he'd always be Pepper's goofy son.

"Hi, hon." Pepper waved her son over. "Bernadette Rydell. She had a vision."

"Officer." Maxine intercepted Gabe and lifted a palm. "I'm Bernadette's cousin. We don't need any assistance. She's fine now, and I'm taking her home to rest."

Gabe gave Maxine a once-over, and Kelly noticed the suspicious look in his baby blues. Even though she'd seen him a handful of times on the job, she'd never really seen him in action. His chin lifted, his shoulders squared, he took a wide V-stance, and he propped his hands on his hips. He was in full cop mode.

"Your cousin should be evaluated by a doctor. An ambulance is on the way." Gabe's tone was firm.

Maxine's gaze lingered on Gabe before she spoke. "Thank you for your concern, but that's not necessary." She turned her head away from Gabe with a snap.

Gabe shifted his attention to Kelly. "What happened here?" A hint of annoyance sliced through his tone.

"She fainted after she tried on a dress." Since Gabe was in the boutique on official business, Kelly decided to keep her answer brief and concise. She didn't think he'd appreciate the finer details of the dress or how amazing Bernadette looked in it.

Liv inserted herself between Gabe and Kelly. "Gabe, you're right about her going to the hospital. She might've hit her head when she landed on the floor."

Hit her head? What would that mean for the boutique's insurance? Kelly could feel the premiums skyrocketing, and the last thing she needed was a lawsuit. The way some juries came up with crazy compensations for injuries could land her beyond broke. They couldn't blame the shop for accepting a dress with a murder attached to it for consignment, could they?

"There's no need for me to go to the hospital." Bernadette had exited the dressing room and handed the dress to Kelly. "What happened wasn't your fault. I assure you I'm fine and I won't be suing you."

How did she know Kelly was thinking about a possible lawsuit?

"It's a hazard of my gift." Bernadette confirmed Kelly's fear that the woman was reading her mind, making her even more uneasy.

Maxine wrapped a protective arm around her cousin. "We should leave. I'll make you some tea when we get home." She shuffled Bernadette out the door, and the chime of the bell announced their exit.

"Well, talk about a performance." Pepper came up to Gabe's side. She rose up on her tippy toes and gave him a kiss on the cheek.

"Ma, I'm on duty," Gabe said. "You're right, Bernadette is definitely something else. Now I have to file a report."

"Then you should take a pumpkin spice muffin to go. We have a few left." Liv turned and dashed to the staff room. She'd had a crush on Gabe forever.

"How's the sale going?" he asked.

Kelly took a moment to scan the boutique before answering. The incident seemed to thin out the shoppers. "It was going well until Bernadette had her vision and fainted."

Pepper raised a finger and was about to say something when the boutique's telephone rang and she excused herself to go answer it at the sales counter.

"How's your uncle handling your decision to stay and keep the shop open?"

Kelly rolled her eyes. It was an involuntary reflex whenever her uncle or his third wife was mentioned. "Not well. If this place ever burns down, make sure he's at the top of your suspect list."

Gabe laughed. "I'll keep it in mind."

"Here you go." Liv rushed back with one of her muffins in a plastic bag and a napkin. "Baked fresh this morning." She beamed.

When she returned she had a new application of her favorite shade of lipstick and added a hint of color to her cheeks.

Gabe accepted the muffin. "Thanks. This will make report writing a lot easier." He smiled. Tiny lines creased around his pale blue eyes, and a blush crept across his face. He had a crush on Liv! Why hadn't Kelly seen it before?

"Bernadette is flighty. My neighbor went to her for weeks." Pepper had returned to the group and touched the dress Kelly still held. "She told my neighbor her daughter would get pregnant by the winter. And sure enough, she did. I'm not saying I believe, but who knows?"

"Glad to hear you don't believe, because they're scam artists preying on insecurities and vulnerabilities," Gabe said.

"You sound so cynical." Where had the boy Kelly used to know gone? The boy who did silly, spontaneous things that landed him in the principal's office on a regular basis? The jokester who never failed to make her laugh?

"It's a fact. I better get back on patrol now since everything's okay here. Love you, Mom." He kissed Pepper on the cheek, and she walked him to the door.

Pepper then returned to the sales counter and rearranged the pumpkins she'd knocked over earlier.

Liv's gaze followed Gabe, and she sighed when the door closed. Lovesick. That's what she was.

"Why didn't you tell Gabe about Bernadette's vision, about what she said about a murder?" Liv asked.

"You heard him. He's not going to believe her vision."

"You do?"

"Probably not."

"Do you want me to rehang the dress?" Liv reached out for the dress.

"No. I don't think I'm going to put this back out just yet."

"Why not?"

"I want to check the records and see who consigned the dress."

"What does it matter? The vision wasn't real. It was all staged. A stunt." Liv tilted her head sideways. "Come on, don't you think it was odd how Maxine just happened to appear in the shop at the exact moment Bernadette had her vision and collapsed?"

"Possibly." Kelly's curiosity was piqued. Could there be something connected to the dress? As crazy as it sounded, there could have been a crime committed. And a murder at that.

Kelly glanced at the dress. Liv and Gabe were probably right. But what could it hurt to check? She padded through the boutique to the staff room and went directly to the desk, where she dropped the dress and then sat.

On her first day in the boutique as the new owner, she had spent eight hours sorting through all the paperwork and had begun transferring all the data into her laptop.

Granny and Pepper hadn't jumped on the computer bandwagon and had managed all records on paper. She couldn't blame them. Because of the nature of the consignment business, it was contrary to the normal inventory and accounting systems, which couldn't handle consigned inventory effectively. That was why many shops used manual processes. She had two top-priority tasks to tackle—finding an inventory system and a new cash register that would tie into the inventory system.

Until then, she created a database that should make it easier to track merchandise, but it meant she had to be extra vigilant in monitoring what came in and what went out, because reconciling inventory would easily become a nightmare.

Since her one-day organizing binge, the top of the desk was cleared and a desktop organizer sat to her right, with all the pertinent files she needed to access. She'd set out her pink polka dot pencil holder and her heart-shaped mouse pad she used on her desk in Bishop's buying office. They'd been stuffed into a cardboard box her work best friend, Julie, handed to her along with a handful of tissues on her last day of work. Humiliation and hurt reduced her to a ball of tears, but she hadn't had the luxury of time to pack up her belongings. No. Serena Dawson wanted her out of the building ASAP.

Kelly shook off the memory that seemed would never fade. But it'd been only forty-five days, so maybe she needed some more time.

While she waited for her laptop to power up, she reclined. Her gaze landed on the photograph of her, her parents and her sister, Caroline. They were all gathered together in front of Radio City Music Hall after coming out of the Christmas Spectacular show. Kelly was twelve and Caroline was fourteen; they were all smiles. She'd kept the photograph on every desk she ever worked at, from her bedroom to her dorm to Bishop's and now there in Granny's shop.

A little ding drew her attention back to her computer and away from her past.

She straightened up and tapped on a few keys and accessed the inventory information. She scanned for the black lace dress. Given the state of the boutique when she took over, the dress could have been consigned within the past three months or six months. Whatever policies the boutique had when it first opened were most likely gone by the time she took over the reins. Granny was old and Pepper was just one person.

There it was! Black lace dress, size six. And the original owner was...Irene Singer.

"Interesting." She patted the dress. Liv did say Irene's husband died. Was it possible Bernadette's vision was of Mr. Singer dying at the hands of his wife?

Kelly took a mental step back. The thought sounded crazy, and if she shared it with anyone, they'd think she was certifiable.

But what if it wasn't crazy? She pressed her lips together, eyeing the dress. What if it really happened? Someone could get away with murder.

Kelly shook her head, hoping to shake out those crazy thoughts. She closed the program and powered off her laptop. She needed to get back to the sales floor and rehang the dress and try to salvage her three-day sale event.

She stood and scooped up the dress. With a purposeful stride, she headed to the door but stopped mid-step.

What if what Bernadette saw was true? What if she wasn't a scam artist? After all, she was right about Pepper's neighbor's daughter, and the psychic Kelly's intern friend went to had been right about her life.

Kelly twirled around and walked back to the desk. She grabbed her camel-colored suede tote bag, one of Bishop's private label bags inspired by a Lanvin shopper tote, and shoved the dress into it. There was only one way to settle the matter once and for all.

Liv poked her head into the room. "Hey, is everything okay?"

Kelly nodded. "Yes. I have an errand to run. On my way back, I'll pick up lunch for us."

Liv pushed the door open wider. "What are you up to?"

"What makes you think I'm up to something?" Kelly swung the tote bag over her shoulder after digging out her designer sunglasses. Luckily, she'd had an employee discount, which enabled her to purchase both items so her budget wasn't completely blown. The thirty percent off everything was what she missed the most from her previous job.

"I can just tell. You should know your uncle is out there." Liv hitched a thumb in the direction of the door.

Kelly huffed.

"Better he shows up now than earlier when Bernadette was still here," Liv stated.

"Good point."

Liv's gaze landed on Kelly's tote bag. "Where exactly are you going?"

"Out. I'll be back soon." Kelly snagged her gray leather moto-jacket from the coat hook and slipped it on.

"You didn't answer my question."

"Don't be a worry wart. And thanks for the heads-up. I'll use the back door." Kelly smiled as she slid on her sunglasses and breezed by Liv. She wiggled her fingers in a wave as she disappeared into a small space that was used as a mudroom back in the day.

Liv sighed. "I want a grilled veggie wrap! And don't do something stupid!"

Chapter 3

Don't do something stupid. Liv's parting advice after her lunch order repeated in Kelly's head as she stood on the front steps of the Singer house. The simple pale green ranch house was nestled among other similar-looking homes in the mature neighborhood. There weren't any fancy cars or heated in-ground pools or gardeners maintaining gardens in this section of town. No, what was found on Belle Flower Lane were homes of hardworking people who settled there for a life of ordinary. The exact thing that sent Kelly headed to New York City on the Long Island Expressway after she graduated high school. She didn't want a life of ordinary. She wanted something more.

Caroline had called it running away. Her mother had called it being foolish. Her father had called it irresponsible. But Granny had called it brave. Granny had always had her back and loved her unconditionally.

Standing on the concrete front steps of the Singer home wasn't what she came for, so she needed to either press the doorbell or walk back to her car. *Pick one, Kell.*

Just as Kelly pressed the doorbell, a barking dog drew her attention away from the white door decorated with a harvest wreath. She turned toward the yapping and found Irene Singer standing on the sidewalk, holding a leash to a Yorkshire terrier. Irene was frowning, no surprise there. She removed an earbud, which was attached to her cell phone secured in an armband. Dressed in a pair of yoga pants and a zipped-up fleece hoodie, Kelly could now see Irene's slender frame that had fit into the little black dress. Irene's severe bob was pulled back into a loose ponytail; she looked ten years younger with a slight flush to her cheeks.

"What are you doing here?" Irene walked along the concrete path to the front steps with her little dog leading. "I wasn't expecting company." "I hoped I could have a moment of your time." "If it's about what happened at your grandmother's shop…I mean your shop, there's nothing to talk about." Irene pulled out a key from a hidden pocket in her yoga pants.

"It's not. It's about something else that happened after you left." "Bernadette Rydell's incident? I heard all about it. She's crazy. Psychic? Ha!" Irene shook her head as she unlocked the door. After she pushed the door open, the dog trotted in, and she then turned to face Kelly. "Since you're here, you might as well come in."

Not exactly a welcoming invitation, but Kelly accepted it. She followed Irene into the small house and, with no foyer area, she stepped right into the living room. The furnishings looked comfortable, especially the dark brown recliner angled in front of the television.

"You have a lovely house."

"It's home. Has been since I married." Irene bent over and unleashed the dog, who then approached Kelly and sniffed her. "His name is Buster."

"Buster? He's cute." Kelly moved to pet him, but he started yapping again. She pulled her hand back. Like owner, like dog.

"Please, sit." Irene gestured to the sofa as she walked to an upholstered chair and sat. "What can I do for you, Miss Quinn?"

Kelly moved to the sofa and sat. "Kelly, please."

The sofa was piled with needlepoint pillows in all shapes and sizes. She barely had enough cushion to sit on. Trying to get comfortable by readjusting a pillow behind her, she grabbed hold of something small. She removed her hand and took a look.

Packing peanuts?

"Sorry." Irene stood and took them from Kelly. "Buster is always finding stuff and then hiding it." She disappeared into the kitchen for a moment and then returned. She must have disposed of them in the trash can. "You were saying?"

Finally, as comfortable as she was going to get, Kelly said, "Bernadette had her episode when she tried on a dress. She said when she put the dress on she saw a man who was dead. She believed he was murdered."

Irene stared blankly at her.

"I checked our records. The dress was consigned by you. It's a black lace dress with a bateau…ballet neckline."

Irene gasped. "I was wearing the dress when I received the call about my husband's accident."

"Accident?"

"Yes. He was on his way home. He was in Maine for a fishing trip." Tears welled in her dark eyes. "The trip was unexpected, but it was only a short one because it was our wedding anniversary. We were going out to dinner when he came home." She dabbed away a tear before she dipped her head.

"How awful." Kelly glanced at the recliner. She guessed it was the late husband's chair. Her dad had one. And so did her grandpa.

"It was. I was expecting to celebrate, not think about funeral arrangements."

"Did you purchase the dress new or was it a consignment?" There was a chance Irene wasn't the original owner of the dress and the previous owner could have been wearing the dress in Bernadette's vision.

"New, of course. Why are you asking about the dress? Wait, do you believe my husband was murdered?" Irene lifted her head slowly, and her glare landed on Kelly. It was as harsh as it was earlier that day. "Oh, now I see... You came here to ask if I killed Eddie. This is outrageous. You have some nerve, Miss Quinn. This crazy woman said she saw a murder while wearing my dress? You immediately thought I murdered Eddie?"

"Irene, I apologize for upsetting you. But once Bernadette had her vision, my store cleared out faster than a Rebecca Minkoff sample sale."

"And that gives you the right to come into my house and accuse me of murder?" Irene stood.

"I didn't accuse you of murder. I'm trying to find out if there's any validity to what Bernadette said."

"Then you should go talk to her." Irene stalked to the front door and opened it. "I never wanted to see the dress again, so I consigned it. Goodbye, Miss Quinn."

"I'm truly sorry I upset you." Kelly walked past Irene with her head still hung low. The moment she crossed the threshold, the door slammed shut and she winced. "Really sorry," she murmured.

She descended the concrete steps and walked to her car. She slid into the driver's seat and started the ignition. At least she knew the owner of the dress wasn't a murderer. A good thing. Right? It explained why the dress had no damage or stains. Otherwise, it would have been present at the cleanest crime scene ever.

Her cell phone blared Liv's ringtone. She dug into her tote bag and pulled the phone out of the back pocket. "What's up?"

"Where are you?"

"I'm heading back to the shop now. I'll pick up lunch."

"Seriously. Where are you?"

"Belle Flower Lane." Kelly cringed in anticipation of Liv's reaction.

"You went to see Irene Singer? Oh, my lordy. It was her dress? Are you insane? That's like poking the bear with a short stick."

"Tell me about it."

"Well, did she do it?"

"No."

"Of course she didn't do it. Her husband was killed in a car accident in Maine on their anniversary. Everybody knows about it."

"Not everyone," Kelly said quietly in her defense.

Liv let out an exasperated sigh.

"Why did you call me?"

"Bernadette called here looking for you. She's upset. She says she needs to see you immediately. Since you're over at Irene's house, you can head over there before picking up lunch."

"Did she say what's wrong?"

"No. She sounded rattled."

"Good grief. How's business?" Her question was met with silence. That wasn't good. "Liv, please tell me the boutique is packed with bargain hunters." More silence. Kelly gritted her teeth. More evidence word had spread quickly about Bernadette's little show in the boutique.

"I'm sure it's just a temporary lull," Liv said quickly.

"It better be." The sinking feeling in Kelly's stomach was the fear of her inheritance going down the drain. The boutique wasn't much, but right now it was her only hope for an income. "Can you text me Bernadette's address?"

"Sure. Don't forget my veggie wrap."

The line went silent, and a moment later Bernadette's address came through as a text. Kelly started the ignition and pulled out of the parking space. At the intersection, she made a left turn onto Island Road, which eventually would lead to Gull Drive and hopefully to an explanation of why Bernadette created the scene at the boutique and what she intended to do to repair the damage she caused.

Kelly's eyes grew wide as she navigated her car up the gravel driveway as Bernadette's home came into view. A Gothic Revival Victorian cottage. It took her a few seconds to remember. Once she did, a smile crept onto her lips.

This was where the old witch lived when Kelly was a kid. She wasn't sure if the spinster had had any magical powers, but the old lady sure enjoyed fueling the speculation she did. The house was popular for trick or treating, and then sadly became popular for vandalism when the homeowner became too old to defend her property.

With her car shifted into park, Kelly leaned forward, resting her forearms on the steering wheel, and stared at the cottage. If shabby-chic and Halloween had a baby, it would be Bernadette's cottage.

From its steeply pitched roofline with a gable to its ornate multipaned windows to the front porch decorated with intricate woodwork, the weathered cottage was mysterious and inviting at the same time. She attributed the welcoming vibe to the abundance of sunny yellow mums scattered across the covered porch, while the mysterious feeling that emanated from the house came from the dark gray paint and heavy gingerbread trim that draped the house.

She cut the ignition and grabbed her tote bag off the passenger seat. She pushed open the car door and stepped out. She had to hand it to Bernadette, the psychic, ghost whisperer, whatever you wanted to call her, had the perfect setting for contacting the dead.

Kelly couldn't help but wonder if there was a black cat lurking around.

As she adjusted her tote bag, she inhaled a deep breath of chilled sea air. Her moment of bliss lasted barely a moment. She wobbled. High heels and gravel didn't mix. Shoot! She'd probably just scraped a heel.

Ruining a pair of Stuart Weitzman booties wasn't a good thing because, even on sale, they cost a small fortune.

She tossed a glance upward. "What else can go wrong?"

She huffed out a breath and continued to the front porch. She climbed the three steps and walked across the painted floorboards to the front door. She looked for a doorbell and when she didn't find one, she raised her hand to knock. Her knuckles had barely touched the wood door as it creaked open slowly. Finding a door unlocked and open wasn't too unusual in Lucky Cove, especially off-season. It was that kind of place.

"Hello! Bernadette? It's Kelly Quinn." She stepped inside. The small entry hall consisted of a closet on one side and a staircase on the other side. The once-polished wood floor was now scuffed and dull. The entry hall was open to the second floor, and a petite crystal chandelier hung above, catching the early afternoon light from an upper window. She stepped farther into the house and called out again. Still no response.

She passed through the simple eat-in kitchen to arrive at the entry of the living room. Plush, upholstered furniture was arranged in front of the fireplace. A perfect spot to settle in on a cold, late autumn night. Kelly almost forgot how much she loved those nights when the Atlantic was riled up and darkness blanketed the town. Her gaze traveled from the impressively carved mantel, which was flanked by two ornate curio cabinets filled with leather-bound books and knickknacks, to the side porch door.

She stepped into the room but stopped when she noticed the round table set in front of the porch doors didn't look quite right. Its paisley tablecloth was messy and partially off of the table's surface, with what looked like tarot cards scattered. And a chair was missing.

Where was Bernadette? If she was really psychic, wouldn't she know Kelly was waiting in the living room? Kelly didn't have time to hang around for the ghost whisperer.

Just before she turned to leave, something caught her eye and the hair on the back of her neck prickled.

Something was wrong. She craned her neck to look past the deep red velvet armchair draped with a throw blanket and saw a peek of a chair spindle.

A shiver shot through her body. The chair couldn't have fallen over by itself.

She took another step forward and was able to see why it was on the floor. Bernadette was sprawled out on the beige carpet. She was lying on her side, and her hair covered her face. Kelly dashed across the threadbare carpet and pushed aside the toppled chair to get a closer look at Bernadette. Up close she didn't look like she'd fainted. There was blood seeping out of the back of her head.

No, it was far worse than a fainting spell.

She had to call for help. She fumbled to search her cavernous tote bag to find her cell phone. *Why isn't it in the cell phone pocket?*

The 911 operator would ask if Bernadette was alive, if she was breathing. God, Kelly hoped so, but she needed to be sure. Since the psychic's chest wasn't visible, Kelly didn't know if she was breathing. Even without the hands-on experience from a first aid class, she knew she had to check for a pulse.

Squatting next to the body, she hesitantly stretched out her fingers and reached forward. She shuddered. Her fingers curled up into a tight ball. She couldn't. She didn't want to touch her.

Time was running out if she was alive. Kelly inhaled a deep breath and stretched her fingers and made contact with Bernadette's skin on the side of her neck. No pulse. Her stomach flip-flopped as a wave of nausea hit.

Bernadette was dead.

A scream shattered the stillness, making Kelly jump, her backside landing on the floor. Why on earth did she challenge the powers-that-be with asking what else could go wrong?

She looked over her shoulder, and her eyes bulged.

Bernadette?

Confused, Kelly looked back at the body on the floor. Who was dead then? She looked back to Bernadette.

"Oh my God! Maxine!" Bernadette paled as she bolted from the doorway, giving Kelly barely enough time to scramble to her feet and grab her before she reached Maxine's body.

"Max!"

"She's dead." Kelly held on tightly to Bernadette, preventing her from getting too close to her cousin. By the look of the back of Maxine's head, it didn't appear she died from an accident. It clearly was murder, and the police would want the crime scene to remain as undisturbed as possible. From binge-watching crime shows, she knew they'd already contaminated the scene. "There's nothing you can do for her now. We have to call the police."

Bernadette dissolved into despair and sobs, her head landing on Kelly's shoulder and her body going limp. Kelly had to call 911 and get Bernadette somewhere safe.

Safe.

She glanced back to Maxine. Her skin was still warm when Kelly checked her pulse. Maxine couldn't have been dead long. Coldness lodged in her gut. Was the murderer still nearby? In the house somewhere?

Bernadette heaved a mournful sob, drawing Kelly's attention back to her.

Or, was the murderer in Kelly's arms?

Chapter 4

"What the hell happened?"

Startled again, Kelly looked to the direction of the voice. A man stood in the doorway. Her heart raced with fear, and adrenaline pumped through her body. Was he the murderer?

"Who are you?" she demanded of the stranger.

"Evan Fletcher." The balding man's eyes lingered on Maxine's body. He then looked at Kelly and took a step forward. "I have an appointment."

"Stop! Call 9-1-1. There's been a murder." Kelly struggled to keep Bernadette upright. Her limp body was becoming too heavy to hold. She shuffled Bernadette over to the tufted sofa and set her down. She glanced back at Evan Fletcher. He hadn't moved or pulled out a cell phone. "If you don't have a phone, I have one. It's just my hands are full, as you can see."

"No, no, I have a phone." He hastily pulled out a cell phone from his blazer's breast pocket. "Who's been murdered?"

Bernadette wailed as her head dropped to her knees.

"Maxine Lemoyne." With Evan Fletcher calling for help, Kelly shifted her attention back to Bernadette. "Where were you? I called out, but you didn't answer." The only reply she received was a deep, sorrowful sob. Kelly patted Bernadette's head. She doubted Bernadette would be answering questions anytime soon.

"The police are on their way," Evan Fletcher said. "Is there anything I can do?"

"I don't think so." Kelly stood, keeping her eyes focused on Evan, rather than looking at poor Maxine.

He was a pudgy man in a cheap suit. Kelly's expertise was in women's fashion, but she had worked alongside several male fashion buyers at Bishop's and gotten firsthand experience on well-dressed men. Evan Fletcher wasn't one of them. His suit was off the discount-store rack, his shirt was rumpled, and his oxfords were scoffed. Was he spending all his money on psychic readings?

"Who are you?" Evan asked.

"Kelly Quinn."

"You're a client?"

"No. Friend." Her answer surprised Kelly because she wasn't Bernadette's friend. They were barely acquaintances. Looking back to the psychic, Kelly saw the reason why she had said they were friends. Still sobbing hard, Bernadette needed someone. For the moment, Kelly was happy to be there for the grieving woman. Seeing the pain Bernadette was in gave Kelly pause to consider her as the murderer. She didn't believe anyone could be such a good actor. The raw emotion that seeped out of Bernadette had to be real.

"This is crazy. I've never been at a murder scene before. Have you?" Evan asked.

"No." Kelly wasn't up for polite chitchat. What was keeping the police? Would Gabe be the responding officer? She hoped so. Seeing a friendly face would be a relief. "Did you see anyone outside when you arrived?"

Evan shook his head. "No."

"How long have you been here?" Kelly hadn't seen another car outside when she arrived. But that didn't mean he couldn't have parked somewhere else and walked to the house.

"What are you? A cop?"

"No. I own a consignment boutique."

"You think I did this?" His voice was heavy with offense.

"I don't know. Did you?" Kelly swallowed hard because there was a chance she was in the company of a killer, who she appeared to be annoying with her questions.

Before he could answer, Kelly felt a tug on her arm. She turned to face Bernadette, who'd lifted her head, her face wet from crying and streaks of mascara trailed down her cheeks. "Is Maxine really dead?" Her voice was quiet and shaky.

"Yes. I'm sorry."

"I need to go to her. To make sure she crossed over."

"We should wait for the police to arrive before we move." Kelly didn't have a clue what the appropriate etiquette at a murder scene was, but she believed letting a distraught cousin approach the deceased was a bad idea.

"You think you can talk to her now?" Evan asked.

Bernadette nodded in the affirmative.

Evan let out a low whistle. "Impressive."

Kelly wasn't sure if Evan was being complimentary or sarcastic. If he didn't believe, why did he have an appointment for a reading? Maybe to murder Maxine?

She heard approaching sirens. *Finally.* "The police are here. We'll ask them if you can go to Maxine. Okay?"

Bernadette nodded again. Her hold on Kelly tightened. "Please don't leave me." Her sadness was deep, and the tears flowed again.

Kelly gave a reassuring pat to Bernadette's hand.

"Lucky Cove Police!" Gabe's voice drifted into the living room, and he appeared by Evan's side. "What happened?"

"I found her." Kelly pointed to Maxine, still trying to avoid looking at her. "She's dead." Why she chose to state the obvious was beyond her.

She, along with Bernadette and Evan, was removed from the room immediately. Gabe attempted to separate Bernadette from Kelly, but she had a meltdown and the lead detective allowed the two of them to stay together. While they waited to be questioned, Gabe cautioned Kelly against talking to Bernadette about the murder. Given the fact Bernadette had curled up on the sofa in the study, stared out the stained glass window, and didn't utter a word, not discussing the murder didn't seem to be a problem.

"Thank you, Miss Quinn." Detective Nora Wolman closed her notepad and turned to the ornately carved writing desk. On the blotter was the detective's forensics kit. She'd taken fingerprints and a DNA sample from both Kelly and Bernadette. Kelly assumed she did the same with Evan. "If I have any further questions, I'll be in contact."

"Can I go?" Kelly had been consoling Bernadette since discovering Maxine's body, so the full impact hadn't hit her completely until her fingerprints were taken.

Her body began to shake, and flashes of Maxine's body slammed her one after another. Bernadette's scream reverberated in her head, and an echo of Evan's demand of who she was repeated; each time his voice got deeper and deeper. She prayed the detective would release her. She just wanted to go home.

"Yes." Detective Wolman turned to Bernadette. "You're going to the hospital to be checked out, and we'll contact your family."

Bernadette didn't respond. She just continued staring out the window. Her answers to the detective's questions earlier were vague, and Kelly noticed the detective seemed frustrated by the lack of information. Though, Kelly supposed Bernadette was in shock from seeing her cousin's lifeless body in the living room.

"It seemed odd Evan Fletcher appeared right after Maxine was murdered." Why wasn't Kelly heading for the door so she could leave like the detective said she could? Why was she asking questions?

"How do you know she was just killed?" The detective turned to face Kelly. She shoved her hands into her pants pockets.

As a detective, she'd traded one uniform for another. Kelly had seen it often when she lived in the city. Professional women, especially those in male-dominated fields, were still leery of dressing more femininely. Dark colors, knee-length skirts and sad, sensible shoes. The detective was one of those women. She left her patrol uniform for drab pantsuits. Kelly would love to have styled her.

"Is there something you haven't told me?" The detective arched an eyebrow, waiting for an answer.

Kelly snapped out of her styling daydream. "Well, rigor hadn't set in, her skin was still warm, and the blood was still seeping out of the wound on her head." The skittering chills came back, and Kelly hugged herself to warm up. "I watched a lot of crime shows."

"Watched?"

"These days I barely have time to sleep."

A glimmer of recognition touched the detective's hazel eyes. "You're Martha Quinn's granddaughter. I'm sorry about your grandma. She was a sweet lady. My mom consigned at the shop."

Kelly gave a weak smile. She wasn't comfortable receiving condolences and wondered how long she'd be receiving them. "Thank you. What do you think of my theory?"

"I appreciate you sharing it. I can't comment on the investigation. You're free to go." Detective Wolman gestured toward the door before turning to the desk to gather up her things.

"He was very defensive when I asked if he saw anyone else around the house and how long he'd been here."

The detective looked over her shoulder. Her expression was unreadable because it was neutral. If she didn't play poker, she should because she'd clean up. "What exactly did he say?"

Kelly didn't have to work hard to recall their conversation; after all, they'd been waiting with a corpse for the police to arrive. "He said he hadn't seen anyone else when he got here. When I asked him how long he'd been here, he didn't answer the question. Instead, he asked if I thought he killed Maxine." Evan Fletcher's nonanswers reminded Kelly of an ex-boyfriend who evaded questions by answering them with questions. She soon tired of the game and left him and his questions.

"Anything else?"

Kelly shook her head. "He seems shady. Suspicious. You know?"

"Thank you for the information. As I said, you're free to go."

"Gotcha. I'll be going." Kelly stood from the armchair she'd settled onto after she was fingerprinted and walked to the door. She passed a wall of tall, narrow sparsely filled bookcases and each was topped with a pointed arch. The design mimicked lancet windows, which were commonly found in Gothic architecture. She recognized the design, thanks to an interior decorating elective she took in fashion school.

"Your tote bag," Detective Wolman said.

"Right." Kelly turned and dashed back to the chair and picked up her tote bag. As she slung the bag over her shoulder, she began walking to the door again. "Evan Fletcher said he had an appointment. Who was it with? Bernadette or her cousin?"

"What difference does it make?"

Kelly shrugged. "I guess none." Distracted by a niggling in her brain and Bernadette's new round of sobs, she wasn't paying attention to where she was stepping and tripped over a power cord beside the desk. Luckily there wasn't anything attached to it. "Oops."

"Officer Donovan will escort you out of the house."

Before Kelly pulled open the door, she looked back at Bernadette. Her body was folded over, and she looked so small and helpless. She hated leaving Bernadette.

"I'll make sure her family comes to take care of her," the detective said as if reading Kelly's thoughts.

Great. Another psychic. Kelly nodded and left the house.

* * * *

Staring at the ceiling wasn't making Kelly any drowsier. Rather, she was more awake than she had been when she crawled into bed an hour ago. How was that possible? She'd been on her feet all day, rearranging merchandise, ringing up sales, and finding a dead body. A simple visit that was all it was supposed to be.

Finding the body had freaked her out more than anything else had. Even when she discovered an ex-boyfriend trying on her clothes. Yeah, talk about a night she'd never forget. He looked like a deer caught in the headlights and somehow was surprised when she told him to leave and take the dress with him. He'd stretched out the maxi dress, and she couldn't possibly wear it again, ever. She didn't care what Kevin wore to make himself feel good, but it was a Max Mara dress she didn't get on sale. That was too much to forgive.

Drumming her fingers on her abdomen, she guessed she and Irene Singer had something in common. They each had had a dress they never, ever wanted to see again.

Traveling down memory lane wasn't helping Kelly fall asleep, and she was exhausted. So why wouldn't her mind shut off? Because her day had been horrendous. Business had started off well then declined once word spread Bernadette had had a vision of murder when she tried on a dress. Next up was getting tossed out of Irene Singer's house and, to round out the day, she walked into a real-life murder scene.

Fear pricked her skin when she thought of a near miss with the killer. If she had arrived just a few moments earlier, she could have come face-to-face with the killer.

A pouncing on her bed startled Kelly. She screamed and bolted upright. Her heart skipped many, many beats before her vision caught up with her panic.

Howard. Granny's rescue cat.

Kelly's hand rested over her heart, and she fell back into her tower of pillows while Howard settled by her feet and proceeded to wash his face. It took a couple of minutes for her heart rate to return to normal. Boy, her heart was getting a heck of a workout.

Howard stopped washing his face and stared at her. They were still in the getting-to-know-each-other phase of their relationship. The first few days she stayed in the apartment he made himself scarce. To coax him out, she began leaving cat treats for him. She'd never had a pet before and had no idea if she was offending him with her bribery.

He made a move forward. Progress, she hoped.

"Are you going to sleep here tonight?"

He didn't reply. Typical male.

"How was your day?"

Given what she knew about cats, which was little, she guessed he'd slept most of the day. Her cell phone rang, interrupting her one-sided conversation with her new roommate. She snatched the phone from the nightstand and glanced at the caller ID. Julie. Thank goodness. Her closest friend from Bishop's.

"I found a dead body," she blurted out on speakerphone before Julie could say anything.

"What?! Are you okay?"

"No, no, I'm not." The floodgates opened. She'd managed to hold herself together for longer than she expected. First, at the Rydell house, where she had to be strong for Bernadette. Then, back at the shop when she had to tell Liv and Pepper what happened. She needed to be calm and strong. After all, Pepper was her employee and Liv was a gentle soul who burst into tears at the news. But now, alone in her bedroom with her cat and her closest friend from Bishop's on the phone, she lost her composure. "It was horrible. She was laying there in a pool of blood... Her own blood."

"Who? Wait, was she murdered?"

"Yes. Maxine Lemoyne." Kelly went on to recount the events in the shop and what happened at Bernadette's house.

"I don't believe it. Wow. They say the city is dangerous. You never find a murder victim here." Julie had a valid point.

Not once had Kelly ever come upon a crime or been a victim of one in the years she lived in the city, but back home for a couple of months and she stumbled onto a crime scene and was questioned by the police.

Howard stood and walked toward Kelly. He climbed on her stomach and sat, staring at her.

"Ouch!" she exclaimed.

"Are you okay?" Julie asked.

"Yes." Kelly shifted.

One of the cat's back legs was pressing against her ribcage.

"Howard decided to sit on me. You have bony elbows," she told him.

"You're keeping the cat? Wait, never mind the cat. I called because I have a lead on some inventory for the boutique."

Kelly's shoulders slumped. "If today was any indication, I won't be needing any inventory."

"The gossip will pass. You'll see. Actually, it's creating buzz, and buzz is good for business."

"Unless the buzz is about me selling haunted clothing in my boutique."

"Well, you know you can always target a new market for your merchandise. You know, people who like haunted clothes."

"Not helpful." Kelly ran her fingers through her hair and exhaled a breath. "I thought I could do this, but I can't. I've made a terrible mistake. I'm not ready to own a shop or a home. I'm too young. I'm too inexperienced. I don't know anything about running a store."

"Whoa. Slow down. Take a deep breath. Close your eyes and take a deep breath. Go ahead, do it."

Kelly closed her eyes. She thought it was silly, but Julie always seemed to know things. Like how to talk Kelly off the ledge. She took in a breath, filling her lungs with slightly musty air. A couple of years ago her granny began having difficulty climbing the stairs to the second floor, so she had rented a cottage a few streets away. She hired a cleaning lady to come in monthly to clean the apartment, but it'd been a long time since the windows had been opened. Kelly exhaled slowly and opened her eyes. Howard jumped off of her and curled up tightly at the foot of the bed.

"Feel better?" Julie asked.

"Yeah, I'm feeling better." Kelly snuggled into her down pillows she brought with her from her city apartment. Even though her new residence was larger, she was forced to downsize because she couldn't afford to hire movers. She was left with bringing only what she could fit into Pepper's SUV. Luckily her two fluffy pillows fit, along with everything in her closet. Priorities, you know.

"My cousin Beth works at a boutique near Lucky Cove, and it's closing. The owner is looking to liquidate, and they have merchandise leftover from their closing sale. It's not consignment, but she's looking for a fast sale, so she'll give you a good price."

Kelly chewed on her lower lip. Buying a lot of merchandise from a closing boutique would give her some breathing room to acquire consigned merchandise, but the price would have to be really good.

"That would be a lifesaver."

"I'll text you the deets. Beth is expecting to hear from you. I better get going. I have an early morning."

An early morning, which was code for arriving at Bishop's an hour earlier than the buyer Julie reported to. Kelly missed those mornings at Bishop's. She missed passing through the employee entrance, chatting with security, and taking the elevator up to the top floor, where the offices were located. She missed her cubicle.

She powered off her phone and set it on the nightstand. She extended her arm to reach for the lamp but decided not to switch it off. Normally she didn't spook easily, but after Bernadette's vision and finding Maxine dead, she was beyond spooked because there was a murderer somewhere in Lucky Cove.

Chapter 5

Within minutes after her alarm went off, Kelly was on her computer with the graphics program opened, and she had a cup of coffee to fuel her creative juices. After her meltdown the night before and Julie's pep talk, she woke up with the idea to create a flyer to hand out to every customer who came into the boutique. The flyer would remind customers she was looking for merchandise and they could make some extra money.

An hour later she had a colorful and fun flyer asking the ladies to go through their closets and look for items to consign. Satisfied with the final product, she printed one copy, but there was no way she was going through all the ink on her printer. Doug's was the only place in town open early with a copier.

She dashed across Main Street to Doug's Variety Store, which was a hodgepodge of all sorts of things you could ever need. Part diner, part newsstand, part mini-mart, and, thankfully for Kelly, part office supply store that included a color copier.

The multipurpose store filled the needs of year-round residents and tourists. Though, all Kelly cared about was the copier. She waved to familiar faces as she made her way to the back of the store and prayed no one would ask about the previous day's events. She suspected Bernadette's vision and the murder were the hot topics over many breakfasts.

The copier was tucked into a corner and, while the locals caught up over a cup of coffee, some late-season tourists dashed in for newspapers and lattes. Doug's started selling fancy coffee drinks years ago and charged fancy prices for them too. Just as the final few copies printed off, she heard an all-too-familiar voice.

"Kelly!" Summer squealed as she rushed toward Kelly and air-kissed her on both cheeks.

Uncle Ralph's third wife loved dramatic greetings, while Kelly preferred a simple wave, preferably a wave goodbye where Summer was concerned.

"I didn't expect to see you here. Guess I'll have to get used to seeing you around town since you're back to stay." Summer laughed, tossing her head back, and her long chestnut-colored hair bounced.

"Guess you will." And Kelly had to get used to avoiding Summer on a regular basis. A beeping caught her attention. Her flyers were finished. Something was finally going right.

"Since you're a full-time resident again, you'll have to come for classes. Have you done Pilates before? I'll give you the family discount. After ten classes, you'll notice the difference." Her deep green eyes scanned Kelly from head to toe. She wagged a finger. "Don't slouch dear. It adds pounds."

If Kelly hadn't been insecure about her body before then, she was now. She and her uncle's wife stood eye to eye only because Kelly was wearing four-inch heels. She glanced at Summer's footwear. The former model turned Pilates guru wore leather sneakers. Summer had a dancer's body, long and lithe with an elegant neck and perfect posture. Unfortunately, Kelly didn't have the leisure of doing Pilates sessions all day long like Summer did at her studio.

Kelly removed the original flyer from the machine and gathered up the stack of flyers. But not fast enough.

"What do you have there?" Summer snatched one of the flyers from the stack.

They really needed to have a conversation about boundaries.

"Isn't this cute? Homemade flyers for your shop." Her condescending smile had Kelly counting to ten mentally. Then she upped it to twenty.

"Boutique," Kelly corrected.

"Right. *Boutique*." Summer flashed a smug smile when she made the correction.

Kelly added another ten to her mental count.

"Well, it was good seeing you." Kelly was okay with Summer keeping the flyer as long as she could get away.

Summer returned the flyer to the top of the stack. "I heard what happened yesterday in your *boutique*."

"You heard we had record shoppers?" And then the number plummeted to almost zero by the end of the day.

Summer shook her head and wagged her manicured finger again. "About Bernadette Rydell seeing a vision of murder when she tried on a dress. You know a thrift store attracts riffraff," Summer whispered. Little did she know, several of her clients consigned at the boutique, which wasn't a thrift shop. So that meant Kelly's riffraff was also Summer's riffraff. "This is the reason why your uncle wanted you to sell the business."

No, Uncle Ralph wanted Kelly to sell because it would have been less work for him in the long run. Granny made him the executor of the estate to spite him. Granny might have been old, but she knew the score. Her bouncing baby boy grew up to become a greedy real estate developer, and she had no doubt, if she agreed to sell, he'd have found a way to make money on the deal on the sly.

"You know, I don't want to keep you. I'm sure you have to get to the studio. Pilates doesn't wait for any woman, right?" What the heck was she saying? Clearly, she needed more than just one cup of coffee.

"Right." Summer's head bobbed up and down. "You have to come to dinner soon. A family dinner. Ooh, ooh, ooh. Thanksgiving! You have to come to Thanksgiving dinner. It'll be Juniper's first Thanksgiving. You must come."

Kelly managed not to roll her eyes. It was a huge accomplishment worthy of a new purse as a reward if she could afford it. She'd rather wear mom jeans and sensible shoes than go to a family dinner with Summer and her uncle. Though, visiting with their adorable bundle of joy would be a bright spot in any day. Juniper had just turned six months old, and she was the most precious creature Kelly had ever laid her eyes on. "Wow. Thanksgiving. You're making dinner?"

Summer waved away the apparently silly notion. "Heavens no. It's being catered."

"Thank you for the invitation. These days are really busy for me." *You know, with the riffraff,* but that went unsaid.

"Triple mocha with skim!" Doug called out.

Summer's head swung around, and she raised her hand. "My coffee is ready!"

"Don't let me keep you. Enjoy your coffee."

"I will, but we must talk about what happened at Bernadette's house yesterday. How unpleasant for you to have found a dead woman. But, dear, why on earth were you at her house? It's been a while since you've lived here and you may not realize how important our family is here in Lucky Cove. You're a part of the family, which means there's an expectation of appropriate behavior."

"A woman was killed."

"I know, but your association with those type of people doesn't put *your* family in a good light. Please keep what I've said in mind."

"Triple mocha with skim!!" Doug called out again.

"I have to go. Don't wait too long to sign up for classes. We can always change our bodies, but it gets harder the older we get and when we're neglectful. Bye." Summer scooted off to the counter to pick up her drink.

Kelly adjusted the strap of her crossbody purse over her shoulder and started toward the door. Her cell phone rang, and a chorus from Billy Joel's "Uptown Girl" sounded from the inside pocket. She pulled the phone out and saw a text from Liv, who was already at the shop with Pepper. The message read:

911, need you here now

* * * *

It was déjà vu when Kelly entered the boutique. She inhaled a fortifying breath as she approached the sales counter, where Irene Singer stood with a hand propped on her hip and a scowl on her face. Pepper busied herself with some paperwork and barely made eye contact.

"I've come for my dress. The one Bernadette tried on yesterday." Irene's dark eyes weren't teary like they were when Kelly left her house yesterday; rather they were hardened and cold.

Kelly dropped the stack of flyers on the counter, followed by her purse. "You told me you never wanted to see the dress again."

Liv's words, *poking a bear with a short stick,* repeated in her head.

"I've changed my mind. The dress is still mine."

"This happens quite frequently." Pepper looked up from her paperwork.

"I'm sorry, but the dress was sold." Kelly shot a look to Pepper, who tilted her head, and her brows knitted in confusion.

"How can that be possible?" Irene dropped her hand from her hip and squared her shoulders. Kelly wondered how much more confrontational Irene was going to get. Which made her curious of Irene's sudden change of mind.

"When merchandise is displayed properly, it sells." Kelly was past skirting the truth. She was outright lying.

"Who purchased the dress?"

"I'm sorry, we don't share customer information." Kelly walked around the counter and joined Pepper. She glanced at the paperwork Pepper was filling out. It looked like a job application. Pepper must have noticed Kelly's interest, because she quickly gathered the papers together and shuffled them into a folder.

Irene pivoted to keep Kelly in view. "Surely you can make an exception." Irene's voice dragged Kelly's attention from the folder Pepper was now stuffing into her tote bag. "I'm sorry. I can't."

Irene huffed. "Fine. I expect my payment at the end of this week."

Kelly's stomach churned. She hated lying. She'd never lied, so why start now? "Of course."

Irene gave a curt nod before she spun around and marched to the door. The bell chimed as she exited the boutique.

"Why did you lie about the dress?" Pepper asked over Kelly's shoulder.

"Why are you filling out a job application?" Kelly stepped aside and turned fully to face Pepper. "I saw it, so you can't deny it."

Pepper's head dipped. "I think my time here has come to an end. You girls are doing a great job. You don't need an old lady hanging around."

"Old lady? What are you talking about?" Kelly was bound to make mistakes as she found her footing back home, but she never thought she'd hurt Pepper. She never thought she'd made her feel like an old lady whose contributions weren't valuable. She never thought her decisions impacted others. She had much to learn. "I need you."

Pepper shook her head.

Kelly stepped forward and rested her hands on Pepper's shoulders. "Hey, I need you. You have to believe me."

"We're not seeing eye to eye about the shop...boutique...see!"

Kelly smiled. "You'll get used to saying boutique. If I didn't have you, I'd be completely lost. Granny loved you and trusted you. I feel the same way about you. I need for you to trust me."

"I love you too."

"Well, I know that. I'm very lovable." Kelly laughed. "Now, tear up the application and get to work. And do I smell apple cinnamon muffins?"

"Yes, you do." Liv appeared, carrying a pastry box from the back of the boutique. "Freshly made this morning. She's gone, right?"

"Yes, she is, you chicken." Kelly flipped open the box and snatched a muffin.

"I'm not going to apologize. The woman is scary sometimes. Did you give her the dress?" Liv a set the box on the counter.

Pepper picked up a muffin. "No, she didn't. She told Irene the dress was sold."

Liv's forehead crinkled with confusion. "Sold? Was it?"

Taking a bite of the muffin, Kelly shook her head. She swallowed her bite. "No. I still have it."

"Why didn't you give it back to her?" Liv asked.

Kelly shrugged. "I'm not sure. It's hard to explain. I have a gut feeling something isn't quite right." Kelly stepped out from behind the counter with her half-eaten muffin and a small stack of the flyers. "I just need some time to figure things out."

She grabbed her purse off of the counter and headed to the staff room. It seemed all of a sudden Irene wanted the dress back after Maxine was murdered.

Were the vision and Maxine's murder connected?

Chapter 6

"Miss," a delicate voice called out from the home accents department, housed in a bland, square addition to the house, as Kelly passed by.

Kelly veered into the room dominated by random home accents and small furnishings, though one large bookcase did block the only window in the room. She definitely needed that piece of furniture moved out to allow for some sunlight in the room. She approached the petite, elderly woman bundled up in a full-length gray wool coat with a checkered scarf tucked in the coat's neckline and a red knit cap topping her white hair. She stood beside a chair Kelly had marked down by fifty percent, and Kelly said a little prayer it would sell.

The day after Kelly returned from the lawyer's office where she officially accepted her inheritance, she'd done a walk-through of the boutique to see exactly what she was up against. She struggled to detach herself emotionally from the store and look at the merchandise objectively. Otherwise, the chance she could turn the store around and earn a decent living would be slim, if not impossible. Granny had crammed the room with so much merchandise it was no wonder why none of it was moving. Customers were overloaded by the sheer volume of merchandise. There were six coffee tables alone, covered with dusty knickknacks. It was as if Granny couldn't turn down a consignment. Kelly crossed her fingers that a new customer would take one of these burdens off her hands.

"Hello, I'm Kelly. Is there something I can help you with?"

The elderly woman nodded. "Yes. I'm Dorothy Mueller, and I'd like to buy this chair." She patted the top of the tired, old ornate chair with intricate carvings and a wide seat.

Kelly had been able to see past the chair's garishness. Once, it must have been a stunning piece of furniture.

In the right setting, of course, like Bernadette's house.

"Really?" Kelly hoped she didn't sound too surprised, or else she might be haggling over the price. Back in the city, she loved to scour flea markets where negotiating prices was an art form. Experience taught her looks could be deceiving. Sure, Dorothy Mueller looked like a sweet old lady who baked apple pies and knitted the hat she wore, but she could be a stealth ninja price haggler if given the slightest opportunity. "I think you're making a fine choice."

"It's quite an interesting piece. Don't you agree?" The small woman smiled expectantly at Kelly.

"It is an interesting piece of furniture. You have a spot already picked out in your home?"

"Yes, I do. In my entry hall. It's quite sturdy. It'll be perfect to sit on and take off my boots."

"Dorothy, did you find something you'd like to buy?" Pepper came up behind Kelly.

"She's buying the chair." Kelly pointed, and surprise registered on Pepper's face but was quickly replaced by a smile.

"I'm going to check out the rack of cardigans. One caught my eye as I passed by." Dorothy started to walk away but stopped. "Is it possible to have the chair delivered?"

"Absolutely. I'll bring it by later this afternoon for you, okay?" Kelly asked.

"Yes." Dorothy turned and walked to the front of the boutique.

"At least we have one less piece of furniture to donate." Kelly removed the price tag from the chair.

"Martha invested quite a bit of money when she added on this addition for the home accents." Pepper busied herself with tidying up the displays.

Kelly knew exactly how much her granny had invested in the addition. The loan was still open and was now her responsibility to pay back.

"This space will bring in more per square foot with clothing than vases and paintings." Kelly stared at a pair of whimsical frog salt and pepper shakers. Where on earth did her granny find those things?

Before she opened for the three-day sale, Kelly worked long hours, with the help of Pepper and Liv, to prep the home accents section for the event. They cleaned, polished, and staged, to the best of their ability. The result? One chair, a dozen pillows, and three vases sold. Not exactly stellar sales.

"Well, you do know more about retail sales and square footage than I do." Pepper patted Kelly's arm as she passed by and continued to the front of the store.

Kelly took a long look around the room and envisioned the space freshened up by a coat of paint, a few mirrors, and well-merchandised clothing racks. If she could weather the haunted dress fiasco, the boutique just might thrive.

Enough with the daydreaming. She had work to do. She took off to the staff room and settled at the desk. She turned on her laptop and opened her email. She scanned the list and saw one she'd been waiting for.

Her heart raced with anticipation as she hovered the cursor over Heather's email and clicked. Heather was the senior fashion editor for Budget Chic. After Kelly was fired and publicly humiliated by Serena Dawson, she quickly became fashionista non grata in the fashion industry from magazines to suppliers. Serena's reach was far, and no one dared to cross her. Hiring someone Serena personally fired would be the kiss of fashion death.

Kelly went from an up-and-coming fashion buyer to being treated like last year's It Bag, and no one wanted to be seen with her.

Budget Chic was solely a website operating out of Los Angeles, and she guessed they weren't worried about the all-powerful and mighty Serena Dawson.

Kelly had pitched an article on using coupon codes to score discounted fashions online. She titled the article "How to Be a Couponista." Liv wasted no time in pointing out that couponista wasn't a real word, but Kelly argued it was catchy and who knew, maybe it would land her a regular column on the budget-conscious website.

She clicked on the email and prayed Heather accepted the pitch. She scanned the greeting. Who cared about salutations? Were they buying the article or not?

We're happy to publish...

Yes!

Kelly did a little triumphant jump and let out a scream. Granted, the pay wasn't huge, but it was something, and maybe it was a good sign of things to come. For a few moments she indulged in thinking the boutique would be a success and she'd become a sought-after fashion writer.

A ping from her computer dragged her back to reality. Turning an old and tired consignment shop was going to be an enormous job, while she'd be competing with thousands of other wannabe fashion writers. Reality was a buzz kill.

She closed Heather's email after she wrote a quick reply thanking her and confirming she'd turn in the article on the date assigned. Then she opened the new email.

Karma apparently needed to balance things out for her. Email number two was from a contractor she'd spoken to. He'd attached the estimate for the minor roof repair—emphasis on minor. She clicked the attachment and nearly fell off her chair as she screamed, which was nothing like the one earlier. It was one of horror, of shock, of disbelief a price could have so many digits and didn't come with a designer purse.

How on earth was she supposed to come up with that much money to repair the roof? She didn't think it would have been such a big thing, but as she read through the estimate, she learned she was wrong. Roofing was complex and expensive, even for something minor.

She closed the email because she couldn't reply, not until she had a clear head and an idea of how she'd get the money to pay for it. She propped her elbows on the desk and rubbed her temples. A tension headache was looming, threatening to explode at any moment.

A knock at the swinging door was followed by Liv popping her head into the staff room. "Kell, got a sec?" Worry was etched all over Liv's heart-shaped face.

What was wrong now?

"Actually, I do." Kelly leaned back.

Liv pushed the door open, and Detective Wolman entered the room. The detective looked over her shoulder and thanked Liv then dismissed her.

"Miss Quinn, I have a few more questions, if you don't mind." The detective moved farther into the room and took a look around. She looked like she was cataloguing every item in the room. Was that what detectives did? Scanned their surroundings and kept a record for future reference? It made sense at a crime scene, but Kelly's office? Unless she was looking for evidence.

Kelly bolted upright and then stood. "You have more questions? I thought you were quite thorough yesterday."

Wolman dragged her gaze from the kitchen area to Kelly. She studied Kelly for a moment before speaking. "Thank you. Unfortunately, we don't always have all of the information available to us at the crime scene, so we follow up. You understand?"

Kelly nodded. The detective made sense.

Wait. What information?

Wolman walked toward Kelly's desk and scanned the surface before picking up the one and only framed photograph on the desk.

"My parents and my sister," Kelly offered.

"Christmas show. Did you enjoy it?" Wolman lifted her gaze to meet Kelly's. Her deep-set eyes were warm.

"Of course. It was magical. My sister and I wanted to be Rockettes. We practiced their famous kick all winter."

"My girls did the same thing last year when we took them to see the show." Wolman replaced the photograph in the exact spot from where she took it. "It looks like you're settling in nicely to your new shop."

"Boutique," Kelly corrected out of instinct and immediately regretted it. She wanted to stay on the good side of the detective.

"Boutique? A little upgrade?"

"Sort of." Kelly stepped out from behind her desk. "At some point I'd like to remodel this space into a proper office."

"Sounds like you have a lot of plans." Wolman moved to the table where Kelly and Pepper usually ate their lunch and sat. She leaned back against the chair and crossed her legs. Her pants leg hiked up, revealing navy-blue ankle boots with a sturdy, block heel and a hint of pattern tights. That's where the detective had a little fun with fashion.

"I do. How can I help you today, Detective?" Kelly moved along to the front of the desk and leaned back against it. She willed her heart to stop beating so fast. The detective probably just needed to tie up a few loose ends.

"When you told me yesterday that Bernadette had a vision here, in your *boutique*, you failed to mention your business slowed down significantly and, from what I can see today, it's not much better. Your boutique is pretty much empty." The warmth that filled Wolman's eyes a few moments ago vanished and, in its place, was a hardness. The detective was there for more than just to tie up a few loose ends.

Kelly cleared her throat. "It'll pass. Retail is a very fluid business. We just sold a chair and a cardigan. And I made up flyers." Kelly twisted around and grabbed one off of her desk to show the detective.

The detective barely glanced at the flyer. "Why did you go to Miss Rydell's house yesterday?"

Kelly set the flyer back down on the desk. "She called here looking for me, and then Liv called to let me know. She said Bernadette was upset and needed to talk to me. Bernadette didn't share why she was upset."

"You just went over there?"

"Yes, she asked me to."

"Where were you when you got the call from Miss Moretti?"

Kelly sighed. "I've already told you. I was at Irene Singer's house."

"Why?"

"I asked her about a dress she consigned."

"Do you always do that with your consignees?"

"No. But in this case, I felt it was necessary." Why on earth did Kelly add the last part? If she'd learned anything from her binge-watching crime shows, she should have learned to simply answer the question and not offer any more information.

"Why was it necessary?"

Kelly pushed herself away from her desk and walked to the table. She crossed her arms over her chest and then wondered what type of body language she was conveying to the detective. No doubt Nora Wolman was scrutinizing every nuance of Kelly's reaction and speech pattern and how she moved her body. She uncrossed her arms. She had nothing to hide or be defensive about. "I really don't see how that relates to Maxine's murder."

"I'm the detective. Let me be the judge of what relates and what doesn't."

"Fine. Bernadette's vision was of a man being murdered. She said the dress was connected to the murder."

The detective's lips started to form a smile but stopped short. "You went to see Mrs. Singer to ask her if she murdered her husband wearing the dress in question?"

"Something like that. Detective Wolman, I didn't kill Maxine. I didn't have anything against her."

Wolman stood. "But you had something against Miss Rydell?"

"No, I never said I had anything against Bernadette."

"But do you?"

"No!"

"The two women were similar-looking. Miss Rydell is costing you business. I've heard some of the talk. You could've mistaken Miss Lemoyne for her cousin when you snuck in."

"I didn't sneak in. I was asked to come over, and the door was unlocked. I didn't kill Maxine." Kelly stepped back. Her tension headache had exploded across her forehead. Even her eyeballs hurt. "Do I need a lawyer?"

"It's always good to have one handy." Wolman turned and walked out of the staff room. Her exit was immediately followed by Liv's entrance.

"What happened?" Liv sat on the chair Wolman had just occupied. "Are you okay?"

Kelly dropped to the other chair and rested her head in her hands. "I think I'm a suspect in Maxine's murder."

Chapter 7

Kelly's fitness tracker vibrated, prompting her to get up and move. She'd been perched on a stool behind the sales counter for over an hour as she finished logging in all of the store inventory into her laptop. While her fitness tracker thought she needed to walk, she craved a glass of wine and a hot bubble bath. She guessed the walk up to her apartment to the wine bottle and then to the tub would placate the fitness tracker. Right?

She pushed the laptop away from her and rubbed her temples with her fingers. To say it had been a long day would be a huge understatement. A restless night's sleep compounded by a run-in with Summer, lackluster sales, and a visit from Detective Wolman made for a really bad day that almost rivaled her last day at Bishop's. Almost.

She looked out the store front window. When had it gotten dark? She glanced at her fitness tracker. It was almost five and time to close the boutique.

She'd let Pepper leave a couple of hours earlier to head home and start baking for the library's bake sale. The boutique hadn't been filled with customers, and Kelly was confident she could handle the rest of the day by herself. And sure enough, she had.

Only three customers came in after Dorothy Mueller purchased the chair and cardigan. The upside to the quiet day at the boutique meant she was able to catch up on all of her paperwork and she was able to email a few representatives of inventory management software without being interrupted. Though, if business didn't pick up, she wouldn't need a new inventory software, just more sale signs.

She slid off of the stool and stretched her arms out and rolled her head gently around in circles, releasing the tension in her shoulders.

The stretch felt good. Maybe she should consider Summer's offer of Pilates sessions. Years ago she took a Pilates class with a coworker, and the gentle workout stretched out her body and, for the first time after a workout, she didn't have any soreness the next day.

But, the Pilates classes in Lucky Cove came with Summer. That would be a whole different kind of pain.

Shaking off the idea of signing up for classes at Summer's studio, she headed to the front door to flip the open sign to closed. Just as she reached the front of the store, a woman pushed the door open.

"I know you're probably about to close, but I've been running around all day, and I just got back to Lucky Cove." The frazzled woman tucked a lock of wayward dark hair behind her ear.

"I have a few minutes before I have to close. Please come in." Kelly stepped aside to let the customer in.

"Thanks. I've been meaning to come here for days, but, you know, things get all crazy." The woman unbuttoned her plum-colored suede barn jacket to reveal an ivory cable-knit sweater. "I'm Regina Green." She extended a hand.

Kelly shook Regina Green's hand and officially welcomed her to the boutique.

"I'm not here to buy anything." Regina looked around the shop. "Rather, I've gone on quite an organizing binge, and I have a bunch of clothing to consign. My sister has a consignment shop near her home in Greenwich, Connecticut, and the shop comes out to her house to give an estimate and take the clothing. I assume you offer the same type of service."

Kelly knew the type of consignment store Regina was talking about. They were the high-end consignment shops, selling designer labels such as Chanel, Hermes, Chloe, and Prada. They offered white-gloved service for their wealthy consignees, which included in-home estimates and pickup. Kelly wanted to up the fashion in the boutique, and she'd give anything to get her hands on a Chanel bag or a Prada anything, so offering an in-home estimate might not be a bad idea.

She eyed Regina's black purse. It was a structured Kate Spade top-handle bag. Kelly was curious what Regina had in her closet.

"I do now." Kelly turned and walked to the sales counter. "Let me get your information."

"Marvelous. It's all in-season clothing." Regina followed Kelly and then rested her purse on the counter. "And I promise none of it is haunted." She gave a big smile.

Kelly, caught off guard by the comment, was speechless. Regina seemed to find the whole situation amusing. At least someone did. "Good to know."

"Honey, I'm joking. I don't believe any of that nonsense about the murder dress."

"Murder dress?" Kelly pushed down the lump in her throat.

"That's what everyone's calling it." Regina leaned forward. "Tell me, is the dress hanging on any of those racks?" She laughed.

Kelly joined in and laughed but, deep down, she was dying. It was far worse than she'd thought. Her boutique was now home to *the murder dress*. "No, no, it's not. When would you like for me to come to your house?" Kelly had opened her date book.

"How about Monday morning?"

"I can come over before the boutique opens."

"Marvelous." Regina gave Kelly her address, and they set a time for the appointment. "I have a bunch of St. John and Ralph Lauren and Ann Taylor."

Kelly nodded. Regina had a nice variety of price points to consign, and she appeared to be a size 6/8, which was a bonus. Kelly wanted to have a mix of sizes for her customers. If she ever got any customers.

"We're all set for Monday." Regina buttoned her jacket. "I haven't consigned here before. But I did know your grandmother, and she was a very nice lady. I'm glad you've decided to keep the shop."

"I am too." Kelly followed Regina to the door. "Have a nice weekend, and see you on Monday." She waved goodbye to Regina and shut the door, flipping over the sign to closed and locking the door.

She peered out to Main Street for a moment. The now-quiet two-lane street was gently lit by tall lampposts. Mid-October brought back the normalcy to Lucky Cove. Gone were most of the tourists, yet a few hearty ones stayed through to the end of the month. Late fall and winter could be harsh with frigid nor'easters, and power outages were a common occurrence. Which reminded Kelly, she needed to check the generator to make sure it was functional for the season.

The opening of the bakery's front door across the street caught her attention. She scanned the shops on both sides of the bakery, and they all had harvest bounty decorations. Was her boutique the only business on Main Street that wasn't decorated for the season?

She'd been busy settling the estate and diving into the preparation for the three-day sale. She'd completely forgotten about dressing up the outside of the building. Maybe a wreath on the front door and a couple of bales of hay would suffice until the Christmas decorations went up. Granny had holiday decorations, and she needed to find them.

She stepped back from the door and walked through the boutique, straightening racks and refolding some sweaters before she did a check on the dressing rooms. They also needed a little facelift, and she'd tackle that project after Halloween. At the last dressing room, she pushed the curtain to the side, and the hairs on the back of her neck rose at the sight of one of her flyers tacked to the wall with the words *"Murder Dress. Does it fit you, Kelly?"* scrawled in red marker across the sheet of paper.

She lunged forward and snatched the flyer off of the wall. She stared at the messy writing. Was it supposed to be scary? Or, was it supposed to be funny? Either way, it wasn't cool.

A hand grabbed Kelly's shoulder, and a surge of panic shot through her body. Screaming, she swung around, ready to fight or flee.

"Geez, you scared the daylights out of me," Liv cried, her hand on her chest.

"Scared you? What were you thinking sneaking up behind me?"

"I wasn't sneaking. Didn't you hear me call out from the staff room? You left the door unlocked. I came over to see if you want to grab something to eat? Mom is closing the bakery, which means I'm free."

"Well, I'm recovering from a heart attack." Kelly walked past her friend.

"Dramatic much?" Liv followed. "Hold up. What do you have there?"

Kelly held up the flyer. "I found this tacked to the wall in the dressing room."

"Kell, how awful. Do you think it's some kind of threat?"

Kelly shrugged. "I have no idea." She crumpled the flyer into a ball as she marched to the sales counter, and then tossed it into the trash can.

"Wait, do you think you should? Maybe you should call Gabe and report it."

Kelly propped a hand on her hip. "What do you expect him to do?"

"Write a report."

"For a flyer tacked up in one of my dressing rooms? Liv, it's a not a major crime."

"But what if it really is a threat? Maxine was murdered, and the person responsible for that is out there." Liv pointed toward the street, and her eyes bulged with concern as her hand dropped to her side. "The murderer could have come into the shop today and left the flyer for you."

* * * *

"You barely ate anything." Liv followed Kelly out of Gino's Pizzeria, carrying a pizza box of their leftovers, four slices of a vegetable pizza. "I don't have much of an appetite." Kelly pulled her cashmere scarf tighter around her neck and reached into her tote bag for her suede gloves. They'd arrived at Gino's an hour earlier and, because it was the end of the season, they didn't have to wait for a table.

"You were doing fine until Camille came over asking about the murder." Liv reached Kelly's side under the restaurant's striped awning.

Kelly shrugged. She thought she could enjoy a meal and celebrate her assignment for Budget Chic, but she was wrong. Their waitress wanted to know all about the murder dress, to which Kelly assured her there wasn't such a thing. Camille darted over to the table and asked about Maxine's murder, and when Kelly told her that she wasn't at liberty to discuss the ongoing investigation, Camille frowned before sulking away. Gino himself approached them and asked about all the hoopla Kelly had gotten herself involved with since moving permanently back to Lucky Cove. Hoopla. The word sounded so much more fun than the chaos Kelly was living.

"I'm sorry I'm a downer. I know you wanted to celebrate my sale." Kelly shoved her gloved hands into her wool peacoat's pockets. The evening temperatures had started to dip lower and lower, and soon she'd be pulling out her cozy down coat. "It's just been a crazy few days."

"I understand. Sure you don't want to take the leftover pizza home?"

Kelly shook her head. "No. It would go to waste."

"Okay. I'm going to head home. See you tomorrow!" Liv turned and walked north on Main Street, toward her apartment over the floral shop. Up to a year ago, she'd shared the apartment with her sister Ana who moved out when she married. Before that, Liv's oldest sister lived there until she married. Liv joked that maybe Kelly should move in with her and let the apartment do its love connection thing.

Kelly's phone buzzed, and she pulled her hand out of her pocket to reach into her tote bag. She checked the message. "Lulu Loves Long Island? Who on earth is she?" She tapped on the link, and the website opened up. She scanned the homepage, and her stomach clenched. "Good grief."

Looking for something fashionably spooky to wear? Look no further than the Lucky Cove Consignment Shop. Yesterday local psychic Bernadette Rydell conjured up a vision of...wait for it...a man being murdered, while she was trying on a black lace dress! Now, if you ask me, it seems like the dress is haunted. Hmm...Halloween is just days away. A psychic. A vision of a murder. A black lace dress. Sounds like the perfect combination for Halloween. I wonder what other magical clothing the shop has?

More like a perfect storm for losing her business. Her grandmother's business.

"You've got to be kidding me," Kelly muttered.

"What's wrong?"

Gabe's unexpected voice startled Kelly, and she nearly dropped her phone. "Why does everyone keep sneaking up on me?"

Gabe raised his hands. "Whoa. You okay?"

"What do you think?" She held out her phone to Gabe for him to read the post, and he whistled. Not a "hey, babe, you're lookin' good" kind of whistle. More like an "oh, crap, that's a low thing to do" kind of whistle. "Just what I don't need. Do you know anything about the website Lulu Loves Long Island?"

"I think it's about events happening on the island. My mom reads it all the time."

"She does?" Kelly pulled back her arm and looked at the website one more time. How many more people read the website? "This isn't good for the boutique." She was on the verge of breaking down into tears and giving up. She'd lost so much in just a few months, and now she could lose the shop. "It's not good for me. What am I going to do?"

Gabe stepped forward and placed his hands on her shoulders and squeezed. "Take a breath."

Kelly pressed her lips together. She hated being told what to do, especially when the other person was right. Spinning out of control would be of no help. She needed to keep a clear head in order to figure out a way out of the mess Bernadette created for her.

She looked at Gabe. A nearby lamppost cast a glow, softening his firm jaw, and his crooked smile broke through her self-imposed feeling of doom. She inhaled a deep breath and expelled it, hoping it took all of the bad stuff with it.

"Feel better?"

"A little," she admitted reluctantly.

"Are you going in or leaving?" He nodded to the front door of the restaurant.

"Leaving. I just had dinner with Liv. Though, I didn't have much of an appetite. All anyone wanted to talk about was Bernadette's vision or Maxine's murder."

"You're surprised? Be prepared for tomorrow because word really broke this morning about Maxine."

Well, wasn't he the bearer of good news. "Detective Wolman came by today. She pretty much said I killed Maxine by mistake."

"She did?" He sounded surprised, which Kelly expected. She didn't know much about how a police department worked but, from the crime shows she watched, the detectives didn't keep patrol officers in the loop during investigations.

"Does she really think I killed Maxine?"

"Kell, I'm not at liberty to discuss an ongoing investigation."

Ouch. He used her exact words to Camille on her. She sighed. "That's what you tell reporters and nosy people. I'm your friend."

"Doesn't matter. Besides, you're a suspect."

Kelly's eyes widened, and she pointed her finger at Gabe. "I knew it! I didn't kill Maxine. How could you even think I could kill someone?"

"I don't. But I'm not the detective on the case. She's just doing her job, and that includes investigating everyone involved with Maxine and Bernadette."

"Maybe she needs a little assistance." How hard could it be to ask a few questions? She knew practically everyone in Lucky Cove. She didn't doubt people would be willing to talk to her.

"Oh, no. Stay out of the investigation. It's official police business. Let Wolman do her job. I gotta go, I'm meeting someone for dinner."

"Date?"

"Dinner," he corrected as he began walking to the restaurant's front door. "Remember what I said. Stay out of our investigation."

Kelly cocked her head sideways and considered Gabe's advice as he disappeared into the restaurant. She shifted to face the other side of Main Street, and her boutique came into view.

She never thought in a million years she'd be the owner of a shop. Her career plan was to work her way up the retail buying food chain and sit front row at fashion shows in New York and Paris. Selling used clothing wasn't even a consideration. Yet, there she was.

Chapter 8

Kelly planned to sleep in. After all, it was Sunday, and that was what she always did. Sleep late, meet a couple of girlfriends for brunch, visit flea markets, or scope out new boutiques and stop for takeout on the way back to her apartment, where she hunkered down until Monday morning rolled around. Yes, it was the perfect way to spend a Sunday.

But Howard had a different plan.

He pounced on Kelly bright and early and nearly gave her a heart attack. When she finally calmed down, her roommate was sitting at the end of her bed licking a paw.

Victory was his.

Wide awake and doubtful she'd be able to fall back to sleep, Kelly threw off her covers and began her day. Maybe a new Sunday morning routine wasn't a bad idea since she had to open the boutique at noon.

She stretched and then folded herself over and let her arms dangle freely. Tension and stress had built up, and she needed to find a way to let go of all of it. Yoga came to mind, but yoga classes weren't in her budget, and she didn't feel like searching the internet for free workouts. No, this makeshift stretch was the closest she was going to get to unleashing her inner yogi.

She closed her eyes and willed her mind to empty. No work. No threatening flyers. No murders. Just peace. Just tranquility. Just a meow?

She opened her eyes. Howard had traveled to the edge of the bed and was meowing at her.

"What are you, hungry?"

He responded with a louder meow as he leaned forward and butted her with his head.

"Okay, okay. I'm at your service." She straightened up, slipped into her cozy slippers, and pulled on a flannel robe then padded through the apartment. In the kitchen, she prepared a bowl of food for Howard and a pot of coffee for herself. Pumpkin spice was her selection.

There were a few rituals Kelly indulged in once the hint of fall was in the air. Nothing big or fancy. First, there was the annual reading of all the September fashion magazines. When the massive issues hit the newsstands, she snatched them up and hauled them home to read every issue like it was a novel. Then there was the first cup of pumpkin spice coffee of the season. Sure, people said Labor Day was too early for the hot beverage, but she told them she didn't need that kind of negativity in her life and sipped unapologetically. Third, the first wearing of tall boots. She pulled them on over leggings and did a little happy dance. Fall was the fashion season she lived for and her most favorite to buy for—personally and professionally.

She pressed the brew button on her coffeemaker and waited impatiently for the aroma of pumpkin spice to fill the tiny yet functional kitchen. Even with its small square footage, it was more spacious than the kitchenette she'd had back in the city. She pulled a mug down from an upper cabinet and set Howard's bowl down for him. He wasted no time diving into his food.

When he wasn't terrorizing her by his unpredictable "attacks" while she slept, it was kind of nice to have a pet. And maybe, if he stopped being a jerk, they could really get along.

The coffeepot beeped, and she poured a hot, steaming cup of coffee. After adding a dash of milk, she savored the first sip, fortified to face whatever the day had to throw at her. And, seriously, could it get any worse than it had been? After a refreshing shower, she turned to her closet and chose a pair of black ponte knit slim pants and paired them with a raisin-colored V-neck cashmere tunic and tall riding boots. She pulled her blond hair back into a casual ponytail, leaving a few tendrils loose to frame her face, and added a pair of gold stud earrings. One last look in the mirror and she trotted downstairs to the shop.

She set her travel mug on the counter and flipped over the closed sign to open. A little earlier than noon, but since she was all ready to start work, why not? After she unlocked the door, she returned to the sales counter. She pulled out a notebook and took a drink of her coffee. She wanted to use the quiet time to brainstorm events to draw customers into the boutique. A few ideas popped into her head right away.

A Holiday Edit event. The curated event would be like a fashion magazine feature come to life for her guests. She jotted down a few notes about hosting a one-day event to showcase holiday attire and accessories. She should schedule the event for the Saturday after Thanksgiving, to tie in with Small Business Saturday. Which reminded her, she needed to contact Lucky Cove's Chamber of Commerce.

Another thought was to hold private shopping parties a few times a month. The hostess could invite her nearest and dearest and receive ten percent store credit based on the total amount of sales for her party. Kelly jotted the idea down. The boutique would provide some wine, cheese, and music for the ladies to shop for a couple of hours. Who didn't love a party? She could also have a Resort Edit at the beginning of January for mid-winter vacations.

She lifted her travel mug and took a sip just as the bell over the front door jingled, and she looked up. She choked on her sip of coffee when she saw who had entered her boutique.

"Hi, Kelly." Ariel halted her wheelchair once she crossed the threshold and the door closed. "Long time."

Kelly set the travel mug down with a thump and continued to cough. "Are you okay?"

Kelly nodded because she wasn't able to speak. She hadn't expected Ariel Barnes to show up in the boutique. She also couldn't remember the last time she'd seen Ariel. It had to have been right before she packed up and her dad drove her into the city for her first semester at fashion school.

"Yeah, yeah…a long time." Kelly stepped out from behind the counter and walked to her sister's best friend. "It's good to see you." It wasn't completely a lie. A part of her knew there'd be no avoiding Ariel since she was back in Lucky Cove permanently. But another part of her dreaded coming face-to-face with the biggest mistake of her life.

"I'm sorry about your grandmother. She was a great lady. She always baked the best apple pie." Ariel's face lit up with a big smile. She hadn't changed at all. She still had that girl-next-door fresh face and boundless cheerleader energy.

"She did bake the best pie." Kelly's earliest memories of her granny were in the kitchen. Granny baked with practiced ease and always had something hot coming out of the oven when Kelly visited.

"Unfortunately I was away when she died and I couldn't make it to her funeral."

"It was sudden," Kelly said.

They'd talked just days before Granny died. Looking back, she wished she'd said more meaningful things rather than prattled on about job interviews, her endless string of loser boyfriends, and Serena Dawson, the most fashionable witch on Seventh Avenue. She would have told her granny how much she appreciated everything she'd done for her and told her she loved her more than just once during the call.

"As soon as I came home I went to the cemetery and laid flowers."

"Thank you. How thoughtful of you. Daisies?"

Ariel nodded. "Her favorite."

"She always said they were the simplest flower."

Ariel laughed. "She did." Ariel's laughter faded. "I miss her... I miss you."

Kelly wasn't prepared for Ariel's visit or for her saying she missed Kelly. Her lower lip quivered. "It's complicated."

"It doesn't have to be." Ariel pressed the power button on her wheelchair and moved closer to Kelly. She looked to Kelly with big, brown doe eyes fringed with sleek bangs. "Look, I wanted to welcome you back home. I'm also curious to see what you're doing to the shop. Are you really changing the name?"

The boutique was neutral territory, and Kelly could handle that conversation. "Yes, I am."

Ariel arched an eyebrow. "Along with the new name, you're adding haunted clothing to your inventory." She flashed a wicked smile.

"Funny. Real funny." Kelly snorted a laugh. Embarrassed, she clamped her hand over her mouth. But she just ended up laughing harder, and Ariel joined in.

"We're not selling haunted clothes, I assure you," Kelly eventually said once the laughter died down.

"Not according to Lulu from—"

"Lulu Loves Long Island. I know. I read her post last night," Kelly grumbled.

"It's all everyone at Doug's is talking about this morning. Lucky Cove is abuzz with the murder dress and Maxine's murder. Did you really find her body?"

Kelly nodded. "I did."

Ariel moved over to the counter. Kelly settled on the stool, and she told Ariel what she felt she could say about finding Maxine's body. She wasn't sure how much information Detective Wolman would want her to share, so she left out most of the details and only gave Ariel a summary of finding the body.

"Wow. Talk about crazy. Did you know Maxine came here a few months ago from Chicago, where she was under investigation for fraud?"

"How do you know?"

"I'm working on a story about psychic scams."

Kelly tilted her head sideways. "I thought you worked at the library."

"I do. I'm a library assistant. It's part-time. I love the work, but I'm also a freelance writer. Have been for years."

"I had no idea. Good for you."

Ariel's head bobbed up and down. "I got into it a couple of years after the accident."

Kelly's body tensed. The *accident*. In her mind, the fateful summer night flashed and she saw the faces of classmates, heard snippets of conversations, and felt Davey's tug on her hand when she tried to go find Ariel.

"I'm working on an article for *Senior Spotlight* magazine," Ariel continued. "It's not a big magazine, but the article is important and it pays well. Anyway, in my research for the article, I came across Maxine Lemoyne."

Kelly snapped out of her fog and caught up to what Ariel was saying. "Why did her name pop up?"

"The article is about financial schemes. Maxine defrauded a whole bunch of people in Chicago, where she lived before coming east. It's actually disgusting how she took advantage of them. Especially the elderly. In my research, I found they were bilked out of thousands of dollars, practically their whole life savings."

"Unbelievable." Kelly suspected most people who claimed to be psychics weren't legit, but she'd never thought about how destructive their scams could be.

"Right after the accident, I got taken by a psychic. I wanted to hear that everything was going to be okay." Ariel rolled her eyes. "The con artist posing as a psychic told me he could speak to my dead grandmother and she had a message for me that I could walk again."

Kelly's shoulders sagged from the weight of guilt. "I'm so sorry."

"I was vulnerable and willing to believe anything. I should have known better. Hey…" Ariel wheeled closer to Kelly and reached out her hand and patted Kelly's knee. "None of what happened was your fault. I think it was something I had to go through. And I'm a stronger person because of it. Now I focus on writing articles to help protect people."

Ariel always found the bright side, and Kelly admired her ability to do so. Maybe one day she'd find the bright side of causing the accident that put Ariel in the wheelchair.

"A couple of weeks ago I went to Bernadette for a reading." Ariel moved back a little bit.

"You did? Why?"

"It was a part of my research. I have to say, the woman is good. If I hadn't known about Maxine, I would've fallen for Bernadette's act."

"You don't think she has any psychic abilities?"

"Absolutely not. However, she's very skilled at reading people and telling them what they want to hear." Ariel glanced at her watch. "I better get going. Mom and Dad are hosting Sunday supper, and I don't want to be late. Mom's making her pot roast, and I'd promised to help."

Kelly stood. She was sad Ariel had to leave. Catching up with her was fun and not as awkward as she had anticipated. "I'm glad you stopped by."

"I am too." Ariel backed up her wheelchair. "You should come by my house and I'll show you my notes on Maxine and her scam. They might be some help to you."

"Help?"

"I heard you're a suspect. You might want to do some investigating on your own. Detective Wolman has a tendency to get tunnel vision. Bye!" She navigated her wheelchair out of the boutique just moments before Summer breezed in with a handful of brochures and a plastic caddy.

"Was that Ariel Barnes I saw leaving here?" Summer approached the counter. Her stride was perfectly executed in four-inch rhinestone-studded ankle boots. Once a model, always a model. "Isn't she the girl—"

"Yes." Kelly cut Summer off. She didn't want to discuss Ariel or what happened. "Nice skirt."

Summer glanced at her tweed miniskirt. "Thank you."

"What are you doing here?" *Among the riffraff,* Kelly thought but decided not to say.

Summer arrived at the counter, and her free hand reached out to the mini-pumpkin display Pepper had set up on the counter. "Cute little pumpkins." With one sweeping motion, she pushed them aside and plopped down her display caddy and stuffed her brochures inside it.

"What are you doing?" Kelly and her step-aunt definitely had to have a conversation about boundaries. Soon.

"I had brochures *professionally* printed for my Pilates studio. They'll probably just sit here and collect dust, but you never know. Your business may pick up."

"Thanks for your vote of confidence," Kelly said dryly.

"That's what family is for, honey." She glanced at her blinged-out watch. How she managed to lift her forearm was a mystery to Kelly. Between the gold and the diamonds, it had to weigh a ton. "I've gotta run. Ralphie is waiting for me. Bye." She wiggled her fingers in a wave as she spun around and dashed out of the boutique.

Footsteps coming from the direction of the staff room caught Kelly's attention. Pepper had finally arrived. She'd called earlier to let Kelly know she was running late. She had to drop off the loaves of bread and cookies she'd made for the library's bake sale. Kelly told her not to rush, because she didn't expect to have a flood of customers first thing. And she was right.

"What on earth was she doing here?" Pepper joined Kelly at the counter. "What happened to my pumpkins?" She reached forward to the chubby little pumpkins and then noticed the brochure caddy. "What on earth are these?" She plucked out a brochure. Her lips set into a grim line. "Did you tell her she could leave these here?"

"No. She just came in and plopped them there." Kelly took the tri-fold brochure from Pepper and opened it. While Summer was a thorn in her side, she had to admit the studio was gorgeous. No expense was spared by Uncle Ralph to give his wife the perfect fitness studio. She looked around her boutique. No matter how much she cleaned and arranged merchandise, she'd never have the perfect boutique she envisioned in her mind without an infusion of capital.

"Talk about nerve." Pepper wasted no time in removing the caddy from the counter and rearranging her pumpkins. "Sorry I was late, but it took a little longer to finish my baking. There's a loaf of apple cinnamon bread in the staff room."

Kelly sighed. Her willpower was weak when it came to baked goods. If she didn't get a rein on her snacking, she'd have to start embracing elastic waistbands.

"I know I should be strong, but I can't resist your apple bread. I saw Gabe last night outside of Gino's."

"He told me. You have some crazy idea of investigating Maxine's murder."

"Not exactly. But I can't just sit around and do nothing while Detective Wolman builds a case against me. Did you know Maxine was under investigation back in Chicago for fraud?"

"Where did you hear that?"

"Long story. I'll tell you later." She'd have to give Pepper a detailed account of her visit with Ariel after, because Kelly wanted to finish brainstorming store event ideas. They'd talk over a cup of tea and a slice of apple cinnamon bread. "Gabe told me you read Lulu's blog."

Pepper's face brightened. "Yes, I do." Then she frowned. "Do you know what she posted yesterday?"

"Yes. Who is this woman?"

"She's anonymous. Lulu is like a pen name. I can't believe you haven't heard of her before. She's very popular."

"How popular?"

"Well, the post she wrote yesterday got hundreds of comments and pretty much the same number of social media shares."

"Oh boy." A wave of nausea hit Kelly's stomach. "I need more coffee." She began to step out from behind the counter when her cell phone buzzed. She pulled the phone out of her back pocket and found a message from Bernadette.

Kelly, please come over as soon as you can.

"Good grief." Kelly stared at the message. "What now?" Kelly showed Pepper her phone's screen, and Pepper shook her head.

"Remember what happened the last time you went there?" Pepper warned.

How could Kelly forget? Two days ago when she went to the Rydell house, she found a dead body and became a murder suspect. What could possibly top that?

Chapter 9

Before leaving the boutique, Kelly called Bernadette to find out what was going on, but all she got were sobs and mumbled words. Against her better judgment, Kelly got into her car and headed out. On the drive over to Bernadette's house, Kelly made a few decisions in hopes of not repeating history. First, she wasn't going to enter the house unless Bernadette opened the door and welcomed her in. The last time she entered the house on her own resulted…well, it wasn't good. Second, she was going to stay out of the living room because the room would give her the creeps. She shuddered just thinking about finding Maxine's body. Third, she wasn't going to get any more involved with Bernadette than she already was. All she wanted was some answers.

She parked her car in the driveway and grabbed her tote bag. As she closed the car door, a gust of wind hit her hard and stirred up a swirl of fallen leaves. Crunching noises off in the distance had her turning, and she spotted a squirrel bounding through a thick layer of leaves with a nut in its mouth. He was getting ready for winter. It'd been a long time since she'd spent an entire winter in Lucky Cove. The season could be long and brutal, especially on the tip of the island, where it was open to the Long Island Sound and the Atlantic Ocean. Maybe she should start collecting nuts.

She tugged her gray marled sweater coat tighter around her body to stave off the brisk air as she stared at the house and summoned up her courage to approach the front porch. Finding the courage was taking longer than she expected. When did she become such a scaredy-cat? Best guess was the day she found a dead body in the house in front of her. She gave herself a quick mental shake. She was being ridiculous. She'd ridden the subway late at night, walked down some questionable streets, and even eaten from street carts a few times. Those were all scarier than being there at Bernadette's house.

She pushed off and made her way to the porch. After she climbed the steps and was standing on the battered floorboards, sheltered from the harsh wind, she felt warmer but not safer.

The front door swung open, catching Kelly off guard. Bernadette appeared, and she flung herself at Kelly, wrapping her arms around for a tight hug.

"I'm glad you've come over." Bernadette's voice was shaky, and her hold on Kelly got tighter. "I don't know what to do," she wailed.

Barely able to breathe, Kelly pried Bernadette's arms off of her and freed herself from the most suffocating hug she'd ever been in. "How about we go inside? It's a little chilly out here." She guided Bernadette back into the house.

Kelly closed the door and turned to face Bernadette, who seemed swallowed up by the entry hall. Her tall, lanky body looked frail in a loose black jersey-knit maxi dress. Her curious eyes were somber, and her shiny blond hair had lost its luster and was tamed by a beaded barrette.

Bernadette did her best to pull herself together after dabbing her eyes with a tissue. "I've tried to talk to Maxine, but I can't. I don't know why I can't reach her. I need to make sure she crossed over safely."

"Crossed over? What exactly happens?" Now if Kelly's cousin Frankie was there with her, he'd understand Bernadette's lingo. Frankie was into everything paranormal, from the Salem witch trials to *Twilight*. She could have used his expertise with her ghost whisperer.

"There are many mile markers on the path to the afterlife."

"What? You're telling me there are different stages of deadness?"

Bernadette looked annoyed at Kelly's unfamiliarity with how the ghost world worked. "When a person dies, they don't necessarily cross over immediately to the other side. Sometimes they can't see the light or choose not to cross over."

"They become ghosts?"

"Spirits," Bernadette corrected.

Thanks for the correct terminology. "You think Maxine is still here? In this house?"

Bernadette nodded. "I don't know why she won't talk to me. I've tried reaching out to her. Something's not right!" She crumpled.

Kelly rushed to Bernadette and led her to the kitchen. She tried to set the mournful psychic at the table, but Bernadette grabbed her hand and dragged her into the study.

"I can't find it," Bernadette said as she and Kelly arrived at the desk. She pointed to the leather side rail blotter. "It was here. It's always here."

"Take a breath," Kelly said in a soothing voice. "What was here?"

"The laptop. Maxine always kept it here." She jabbed at the blotter.

"You wanted me to come over because you can't find Maxine's laptop? I take my laptop with me all over the place. Up in my apartment, in the staff room, and even on the sales floor. The computer could be anywhere in the house," Kelly reasoned.

"No, it's not. I've looked everywhere. Well, except the living room. I can't go in there."

Kelly couldn't blame her for not being able to enter the room. She herself was barely able to enter the house a few minutes ago. She tried to recall what she'd seen, besides Maxine's body, two days ago in the living room. From the intriguing fireplace mantel to the worn area rug beneath the sofa and armchairs to the corpse. She didn't remember seeing a laptop. Though, she was distracted at the time.

"See." Bernadette pointed to the plugged-in power cord and power adapter next to the desk.

Kelly remembered because she'd tripped over the cord.

"This is where Max worked. She was very particular. She said she liked the energy in this room." She gave a small smile, which quickly faded. "Her computer is missing, and she won't talk to me. I need to make sure she's okay."

"Why won't she talk to you?"

"She could be angry with me. She may think I killed her."

"That would be a good reason to be angry with you. Did you kill her?" Kelly braced herself for the answer.

"No! Of course not. She was my family. I'd never hurt her."

"Why did you want me to come over?" Kelly asked again.

"Because Max's not the only one who thinks I killed her. The detective does too. You should have heard the questions and wild accusations."

Kelly had a pretty good idea of what Detective Wolman had said. "She has a job to do, which means she has to ask hard questions." And now Kelly was defending the detective, but she was a little relieved not to be the only one on the detective's radar.

"She should be looking for the killer, not interrogating me."

"Bernadette, why did you ask me to come over?"

"I have to find the laptop, and I have to make sure the police look for my cousin's killer."

"You think her killer's information is on the laptop? You know, I've heard some things about your cousin."

"I'm sure you have. Some people don't like what we have to tell them, and they get angry. Max was a good person. She didn't deserve to die."

"You think her killer was someone who was a client, and all of her client information is on the laptop?"

"That's the only thing that makes sense," Bernadette said.

"Was Evan Fletcher here to see you or Maxine?"

"Me. Do you think he killed Max?"

Kelly shrugged. "I don't know. Has he been a client for long?"

"Not really. He just moved to town from Maryland."

"How did he find you?"

"My website. He often seeks the assistance of psychics."

"There's another theory." A theory from Detective Wolman, but still a viable option, Kelly had to admit.

"What's that?"

"You could have been the intended target. You and Maxine looked a lot alike. From behind, someone in a rage could have easily mistaken Maxine for you."

Bernadette gasped. "I... Now I understand why she's not talking to me. I caused her death. It was all my fault. Who? Why?"

Kelly was at a loss for how to console Bernadette. Luckily, before she could say something, a loud whistling sounded.

"The teakettle. You'll have a cup. I'll be right back." Bernadette spun and darted out of the room, leaving Kelly alone.

She dropped her tote bag on the desk and looked around the room. A large oak tree just outside the window blazed in red hues. A leafy green vine wrapped itself around the thick trunk of the tree. Only a small section of what Kelly assumed was the original fencing, and if not, an early replacement of the first fence. Historic fences tended to mirror the motifs of their home.

She turned her attention back to the current problem—Maxine's missing laptop. She drummed her fingers on the polished desk. Who would have taken Maxine's laptop? And why? Kelly walked around to the other side of the desk and pulled out the chair then sat. The obvious answer would be the killer. But what wasn't obvious was what the heck Kelly was doing in the Rydell house? Didn't Bernadette have someone closer in her life to turn to?

Kelly surveyed the desk. This was the space where Maxine recorded her scams. She shook her head in disgust. Her laptop probably held all the down and dirty details of her cons. Was it realistic to believe that Bernadette didn't know her cousin was a fraud?

Fraud or not, the woman was dead, and Detective Wolman had Kelly in her sights as a suspect. Clearing her name was the utmost important thing for Kelly to do. Based on what Ariel had said, Maxine had a few people angry enough that they contacted the authorities about her and, even though she kind of liked Bernadette, she was willing to bet there were some people equally unhappy with her.

Was the laptop the only thing missing? Back at the boutique, Kelly was transferring handwritten files to her computer, so maybe Maxine had some paper files of her own. She pulled open one drawer and found office supplies. No leads there.

She pulled opened another drawer and found a thick legal-sized file. Not sure how much longer Bernadette was going to be with the tea, she hastily flipped through the file. All legal documents with Maxine's name on them. She wondered if those files contained any names of people she supposedly defrauded. Before she thought too long about right and wrong, she stood and pulled her tote bag to her and shoved the file into the bag. She quickly closed the desk drawer, and just in time, because Bernadette appeared in the doorway with a tray of tea.

"It's not your fault," Bernadette said.

Kelly's heart was beating hard against her chest. She almost got caught stealing. She never stole. What was going on with her? Why not just ask Bernadette if she could look through the file? Because she could say no, reasoned the little devil on her shoulder.

"What's not my fault?"

Bernadette shook her head. "I don't know. Your granny wants you to know the accident wasn't your fault." She entered the room and set the tray on the desk.

Kelly swallowed hard. "The accident?"

"Something happened a while ago. You blame yourself. You shouldn't."

Everybody in Lucky Cove knew what happened the night of the party and that Kelly blamed herself. Liv was right. There wasn't anything Bernadette could tell her she couldn't have learned from gossip.

Bernadette held Kelly's gaze. "It's not complicated. Just be a friend."

Whoa! How did Bernadette know Kelly told Ariel that their relationship was complicated?

Bernadette poured Kelly the tea and handed her a cup. "Will you help me?"

* * * *

Kelly downed her first glass of wine as she filled Howard's bowl with kibble. She'd gone straight to the wine rack as soon as she'd walked in the door then juggled the bottle opener while tugging off her boots. As Howard chowed down, she sank onto the sofa with her second glass of wine and tried to will the tension out of her body.

The shop had been busy with curiosity seekers, but not actual paying customers. A few browsers who lacked filters came right out and asked to see *the murder dress*. One woman even offered a hundred dollars to buy the dress. Maybe Kelly's friend Julie was right about marketing to a different clientele. She might have to consider it because, when she closed out the cash register, it was pitiful. For a five-hour day, there were few sales and nowhere near Kelly's projections for the weekend.

She tamped down the anxiety of the failed three-day sale event and tried to fortify her resolve with a reminder that running a business wasn't a sprint, it was a marathon. She was in it for the long haul. Maybe a few mornings of affirmations and a T-shirt with "You've Got This" written across it would be a good place to start. Another place to not start, but to finish up, would be clearing all the home accents out of the addition. She had the option to return the items to their original owners, but she'd like to make some money. Then an idea sparked. If the mountain wouldn't come to... She grabbed her cell phone and texted Liv.

Does your brother still have his box truck?

While she waited for Liv to reply, Kelly took a long drink of her wine. She probably should pace herself, but the past few days had been rough, and there was no sugarcoating it: she was scared. Scared she was going to be arrested and convicted of killing Maxine. Scared the defaced flyer tacked to the fitting room was truly a threat. Scared she'd lose her granny's beloved shop. Her next drink was more of a gulp.

She checked her phone again. No reply from Liv.

Gabe had told her Detective Wolman would be investigating everyone involved with Bernadette and Maxine. That could be a lot of people, depending on how many clients they had in Lucky Cove and how social they were. A good place for Kelly to start her investigating could be the file she'd removed from Bernadette's house. With her glass in hand, she swiped up her cell phone from the sofa and walked over to the table where she'd tossed her tote bag when she got home earlier. She sat and pulled out the file. After another drink of wine, she flipped through the thick stack of papers and swore it was in a foreign language. All the legalese quickly sobered her up. Her brain hurt as she tried to read it, and she was reminded of high school algebra. Seriously, she'd yet to find a use for that bit of knowledge.

From what she could gather, which wasn't much, Maxine had been served court papers by a man named DJ Brown. She came across what looked like a list of dates and, from the paragraphs above the list, she figured those dates were his appointments with Maxine. Wait. There was another name mentioned. Ruth Brown. Wife maybe? She read a little bit more. No, Ruth wasn't his wife. She was his mother.

Mother and son conned by the same psychic? Now talk about sad.

Her cell phone buzzed. She reached for the phone and found Liv's reply. Her brother still had his truck. Great. She could pack up most of the home furnishing items and take them to the indoor flea market that was open once a month. She could actually make some cash if she could secure a booth. Nothing in the consignment agreement stated the items needed to be sold on the shop's premises.

She typed a thank-you reply and sent it.

She reached for the legal file again but remembered she had an article due for *Budget Chic*. Just in case she had to close up shop, she needed to start building her portfolio. She pushed the legal file away. She walked back to the sofa and found Howard curled up in a ball on the center cushion.

"Please, don't get up. I'll just sit over here." She dropped onto a cushion and set her glass on the end table before reaching for the laptop, which was set on the coffee table. She gathered a crochet afghan from the back of the sofa and draped it over her legs. Like the window over the sink downstairs in the staff room, the apartment was drafty. Now that heat wasn't included with her rent, she resisted the temptation to crank up the thermostat. Cuddling in a warm afghan was a more budget-friendly way to stay warm. The multicolored afghan was the last one her granny made, and being wrapped in it felt like a hug from Granny.

She set her computer on her lap and opened a file to review the in-progress article. She nodded. Not bad. She still had a few more websites to check out before she submitted the article.

Websites.

Against her better judgment, she opened the internet and brought up the Lulu Loves Long Island website.

Gloss. Sleek. The header image was a collage of images from all around Long Island. Kelly could see why Lulu loved the island. Across the top of the homepage was a tab for the blog, and Kelly clicked on it. She found the post about the boutique and *murder dress*. Seeing it again and knowing how it affected the day's business had Kelly finishing off her wine.

She clicked off of the blog and continued to search the website and found another section dedicated to local news and a link to Lucky Cove. Curious, she clicked on the link and read through the headlines. Lulu was a busy gal, compiling all this information for her readers.

Local businessman dies in car accident in Maine.

That must have been about Eddie Singer. She should be working on her article, and yet she was clicking on the link. Up came a couple of paragraphs about the self-storage facility owner.

Eddie was fifty-six at the time of his death. Apparently speed and bad weather played a part in the fatal accident. In his pickup truck, he was transporting an extra canister of gasoline for a fishing boat, and the explosion was intense.

Kelly shivered at the thought of dying in a blaze of fire. Then she recalled Maxine's death. She concluded there wasn't any good way to go.

Chapter 10

"I'm glad you were able to come over and take all this clothing to your shop. You have no idea of how much time you're saving me." Regina Green led Kelly into the living room of her beachy cool two-story colonial.

Light and airy with large windows, the cavernous space was filled with a comfortable seating area designated by a sprawling multicolored area rug. Atop the rug was a massive white-slipcovered sofa anchored by two deep-cushioned black wicker armchairs. A collection of oversized artwork hung on a whitewashed shiplap wall. Where did the woman shop? Gigantic Furniture "R" Us? Pine end tables and a sideboard grounded the room. Kelly could definitely spend some serious leisure time in Regina's living room.

"No problem. I'm happy to be here and to see what you have." Kelly had made an effort to push away all the stuff she'd been dealing with over the past few days so her first in-home estimate would be successful. She needed a clear mind as she appraised the clothing and tallied up an estimate of what the clothes were worth. It was hard, but she managed. She even applied a pair of false eyelashes to lift her spirits and hopefully disguise her tired eyes.

"How about a cup of coffee. You look a little tired."

Kelly sighed. The false lashes weren't working. Before she could decline—she'd already had two large cups of pumpkin spice coffee before leaving home—Regina thrust a mug decorated with fall leaves in her hand.

"It's not flavored. I prefer a robust blend to all those fancy flavors." Regina returned to the coffee table and filled her mug from the white coffeepot. She looked less harried than the other day when she rushed into the boutique. Her dark hair was sleek rather than tousled, and her makeup was smudge free. She wore a simple yet elegant twinset, Kelly guessed a cashmere blend, and black trousers with black suede pumps. Her jewelry, only a wedding band, necklace, and earrings, was understated but expensive.

"It's good," Kelly said after a sip. "I'm excited to see what you have here." She set the mug on the coffee table and walked to the rolling garment rack Regina had loaded with clothes. The thrill of the hunt sent adrenaline pumping through Kelly. She scanned the entire rack, and something didn't quite seem right. She slid a glance to Regina, who was perched on the arm of the sofa and smiled brightly.

Kelly began sliding the hangers on the rack to get a look at the clothing and the labels. Regina said the other day she had St. John, Ralph Lauren, and Ann Taylor. She pushed a woven blouse aside and then another and then another. They all had the label of Susannah Gray. The name was familiar. A dozen stretch knit pants in a rainbow of colors, also from Susannah Gray. Then she remembered. Gray was a popular designer for the Shop at Home channel. Her heart sank. She'd been led to believe there would be designer pieces for consignment. Disappointed, she continued to go through the hangers and saw pieces from J.Crew and Talbots. All the clothing looked to be in good condition, and she was certain she could sell them. An added bonus was Regina's size, a healthy size eight. It was important for Kelly to offer a variety of sizes for customers. Regardless of size or budget, every woman should have fabulous clothes.

"Do you have any other clothing you'd like to consign?"

Regina laughed. "You're looking at a loaded rack of clothing. Isn't that enough?"

Kelly wasn't sure how to bring up the designers Regina had dangled in front of her the other day. Bait and switch. Regina had dangled the designer names to get Kelly to come out to her house and haul off all those clothes for her. Wow. Regina Green played Kelly like a well-tuned violin.

A look of feigned surprise came over Regina's face. "I think I know what's going on. You misunderstood me the other day. I didn't mean I had any St. John or Ralph Lauren to sell."

There wasn't any misunderstanding, but Kelly didn't want to argue because if the woman did actually have those designers in her closet, and Kelly wasn't convinced yet she did, then maybe when she decided to get rid of them she'd consign with the boutique.

"What you have here is great, and I'm confident it will all sell." And that was important—sales.

"Has the post on Lulu's website had an effect on your business?"

Kelly shrugged. So much for not thinking about all the stuff she'd been dealing with. "It did encourage curiosity seekers." She walked back to her tote bag and took out her cell phone. She tapped on the calculator app, punched in some numbers and came up with an amount she believed she could sell all the clothes for and then calculated the percentage Regina would receive. She showed her consignee the final number and emphasized it was only an estimate. Regina smiled. Great. She seemed pleased.

"Every little bit helps, right? Now, how about we finish our coffee before you run off with all my clothes?" Regina moved over to a cushion on the sofa and sat.

"Sounds good to me. I have a little time before I need to open the boutique." Kelly picked up her mug from the coffee table and sank into one of the wicker armchairs.

"I heard up until recently you worked as a fashion buyer for Bishop's in the city."

"Actually, I was an assistant fashion buyer." The specifics of Kelly's downfall at the store weren't public knowledge back home, which she was eternally grateful for.

From day one, she'd been on Serena Dawson's bad side and never quite got away from it. On her last day of employment at Bishop's, she was sent to get Serena's coffee, which was more of a task for an office assistant than an assistant buyer, but Kelly went. Somehow, she returned with the wrong coffee order; then a designer's assistant gave her the wrong pencil skirt sample and an appointment that wasn't confirmed had Serena arriving at a showroom with no one there to greet her. Serena returned to the office furious, but her Botoxed face didn't show the emotion, which was why Kelly was caught off guard when Serena appeared at her desk and publicly fired her. She shivered at the memory.

"And now you're back here in Lucky Cove. Though, it doesn't seem to have been an easy transition. First, Bernadette's vision right there in your shop. And then you found her cousin dead. Murdered! I still can't believe there was a murder right here in town. But I guess it can happen anywhere to anyone." Regina took another drink of her coffee.

"I admit it hasn't been easy, but I guess it could be worse." Why? Why did she challenge the almighty gods again?

Regina nodded in agreement. "It seems so many bad things are happening. Just a few months ago Irene lost her husband." She tsked-tsked before refilling her coffee cup. She gestured to refill Kelly's cup, but Kelly declined.

"Irene Singer? I heard her husband died in a car accident up in Maine."

"He did. One minute she was telling him to have a good trip and the next she was a widow. Maybe, in some way, it was a blessing for Irene." Regina lifted her mug to her lips and took a sip.

"What do you mean?" Kelly never really thought about dying as a blessing unless it ended a prolonged, painful illness. Under those circumstances she could understand someone finding relief in death.

Regina leaned forward. "I hate to gossip, but what happened to Irene should be a lesson to all you younger gals."

Kelly's interest was piqued. "What's the lesson?"

"Irene's husband liked to gamble. Eddie was always betting on something. I wouldn't be surprised if his fishing trip was really a poker game."

Curiosity won out. Kelly had to ask. "How bad was his gambling?"

"Let's just say if he didn't die in the car accident, I'm sure Irene would have killed him. Irene was always a frugal person. She'll fight you down to the last penny."

Kelly was familiar with that personality attribute of Irene. "Why didn't she divorce him?"

Regina leaned back. "The fact Eddie kept losing money infuriated Irene. It had gotten worse the past year. They didn't divorce because, for all of Irene's frugality and hardness, she was hopelessly in love with the man. High school sweethearts. But, love only goes so far."

"Do you really think Irene would have killed Eddie?"

Regina shrugged. "Who knows what someone is capable of? I'd like to think she couldn't do such a thing, but I witnessed a huge blowout between them just before the car accident. From what I overheard he'd lost a lot of money to someone."

Kelly finished her coffee in silence as her mind churned over what Regina had just said. It sounded like Irene had a motive for murder. However, if Eddie did indeed owe someone money, Irene might not have been the only person with a motive.

As Kelly was packing up the back of Pepper's SUV, which she had graciously loaned to Kelly until she purchased her own vehicle, she got another 911 text from the boutique. A part of her wanted to know what new level of craziness was happening while another part of her wanted to get behind the wheel and drive far, far away from Lucky Cove.

* * * *

Kelly pushed open the boutique's front door and was stricken by the eerie silence. There wasn't a soul in the store. Where was everyone? Where was Pepper?

"Thank goodness you're back!" Pepper appeared from the home accents section of the boutique with panic etched on her face. "You have to make it stop."

"Make what stop? We don't have any customers again?"

"There are people here, and they're all back there!" Pepper pointed to the addition. "I've tried to break it up, but no one is paying attention to me."

"Break what up?" Kelly started walking toward the addition.

"The séance."

Kelly skidded to a halt. "The what?!"

"Valeria Leigh came in and, before I could intercept her, she sat down at the pine table and took out her crystal ball."

"Her what?"

"Then everyone started to gather around her, and some of them even joined her at the table."

"Good grief." Kelly spun around and marched into the addition. This nonsense was going to stop. She was going to make Bernadette publicly recant her stupid vision then insist Lulu write a post letting everybody and their mother know the boutique wasn't haunted; but first, she was going to kick Valeria Leigh out of her boutique.

New store policy—no more freak shows.

A lyrical voice drifted from the addition. Was someone singing? She entered the dark room. Great. Someone had turned off the lights, which was probably some type of code violation in a commercial building. She flipped the light switch, and a chorus of groans replaced the singing.

Good, she'd gotten their attention.

"Please return the room to darkness," a woman seated at the table requested.

Kelly guessed she was Valeria Leigh, the medium.

"I don't think so. I'm Kelly Quinn, and this is my boutique. What is going on here?" Kelly stepped farther into the room and approached the woman.

"I'm Valeria Leigh, and I'm holding a séance. I'm reaching out to the departed. I'm sensing a lot of spirits in need of assistance." She let go of the hands she was holding.

This had to be a Halloween prank. Kelly was certain of it.

"Not anymore. I'm running a business here, not reaching out to the dearly departed. If any of you would like to make a purchase, I'm happy to assist. Otherwise, I must ask you to leave." She looked around the table and saw a very familiar face. "Frankie? What on earth are you doing here?" "Hey, cuz." Frankie gave a little wave.

"Seriously? You're involved with this nonsense?"

"This isn't nonsense. Through séances, I connect with the spirits of those who have departed this earth and assist them with unfinished business." Kelly leveled a stern look on the medium. "You can depart now, Miss Leigh."

"Why, I never—"

"I'm sure." Kelly tugged at the chair Valeria Leigh sat in. Asking politely wasn't working, so now it was time to get a little more forceful. "If you don't leave, I will call the police and have them remove you and perhaps charge you with trespassing."

Valeria Leigh huffed as she stood. Her long burgundy dress swooshed in her rapid movement to the small chest of drawers where her purse was set. She grabbed hold of the bag and returned to the table. Her silver hair was swept up into a stiff bouffant hairdo, and badly applied false eyelashes lined her dark eyes. What decade was the woman from? And where did she learn to apply fake lashes?

"I take no offense to your ignorance regarding this matter. But be assured there are spirits here. In fact, I've connected with one." She pointed to a simple oak ladder-back chair. "There's a deceased man attached to the chair."

Kelly looked over her shoulder. "Could he be the same man Bernadette saw in her vision?" she thought out loud.

"Since it was her vision, I couldn't tell you. But if the dress and chair came from the same person, then it's reasonable to assume he's the same man who was murdered."

Reasonable? What was Kelly thinking asking the question in the first place? "The chair isn't haunted, and you haven't connected with any spirits."

Valeria Leigh huffed again before she picked up her embroidered bag and put her crystal ball in it. "You'll be begging me to come back when the spirits haunting your shop rise up."

"Yeah, yeah, yeah." Kelly gestured for the medium to leave the room, and when she did, the bystanders began to shuffle out of the room one by one, griping at the sudden turn of events. Included in the group was Frankie, but she grabbed him by the sleeve of his turtleneck sweater. "You. Stay."

"Oh boy," he murmured.

"Pepper, make sure they all leave," Kelly instructed. Then she turned her attention back to her cousin.

"What were you thinking? Do you have any idea of how destructive this mumbo-jumbo has been to my business?" She propped both hands on her hips and waited for an answer.

Frankie lowered his head. "Sorry, Kell."

"What? I didn't hear you. What did you say?"

Frankie looked up. "You're not going to make this easy, are you?"

"Nope."

"I'm sorry. I came over to check on you, and then Valeria swept in and I got caught up. You know how much I love this paranormal stuff. She started singing... It was so cool!"

Kelly shook her head. "This isn't a joke. I may lose my boutique if I can't turn this around. You! You being here, participating in it... I can't even explain." She swiveled and marched out of the room with Frankie on her heels. She needed to cool off because she was so angry she frightened herself.

"Kell, come on. I'm sorry. I didn't mean to hurt you." Frankie stopped at the sales counter, where Pepper was standing with a scowl on her face. "Tell her, Pepper. Tell her I didn't come here to hurt her."

Pepper crossed her arms over her chest and shook her head. Kelly suppressed a smile. Pepper wasn't going to make it easy for Frankie, either.

"We're family. I'd never do anything to intentionally endanger your business. I just got carried away. You know what that's like, right, cuz?" Frankie whined a little bit and gave his best puppy dog eyes, which he knew would melt Kelly's resolve to stay angry with him because it always worked.

"You really came in to check on me?" She joined Pepper behind the counter. She noticed the boutique had cleared out. Not one of those people had any interest in buying anything.

"Yes. I got back home late last night from Atlantic City. I talked to Liv yesterday on the drive back, and she filled me in on what's been going on."

"It's been insane. I really have to put an end to this parade of ghost whisperers strolling in and conjuring up spirits." Kelly rested her elbows on the counter and set her chin in her palms. "Something's been nagging at me. Nothing like this has happened before. So why now?"

Frankie shrugged. "It's almost Halloween."

"There have been other Halloweens and Friday the Thirteenths. Why now?" She racked her brain, trying to pinpoint a reason for the spike in

paranormal activity coming into the consignment shop. "Wait a minute."
Kelly straightened up and pointed to Frankie. "Your father!"

"Ralph?" Pepper asked.

Frankie looked surprised by the suggestion. "Dad? You think Dad
has something to do with this?"

"Yes, I do. He's never wanted to see me succeed with this shop. Being
executor means he has to do a whole lot of work for pretty much nothing
in return. If I close and sell, he'd be off the hook."

Frankie shook his head. The physical similarity between him and his
father was strong. They both shared the same sandy-blond hair, though
Frankie's hair had a slight wave to it. They both had narrow noses and
squared chins. "Sure, he wants you out, mostly because he's angry Granny
didn't leave him this building, but hiring a psychic and a medium to ruin
your business doesn't sound like something he'd do."

"Why not?" Pepper asked.

Frankie cocked his head to the side. "Because this type of plan requires
creativity, and Dad isn't creative."

"Excuse me," a voice called out.

Kelly looked over her shoulder in the direction of the soft voice and
found Dorothy Mueller standing with her hands clasped together. She
didn't look good.

Kelly darted out from behind the counter and rushed to the older
woman. "Are you okay, Dorothy?"

"I'm a little frazzled. So much excitement. Do you really think
ghosts are attached to your stuff here?" Dorothy looked at Kelly with
wide, clear eyes.

"No, no, I don't. I'm sorry Valeria Leigh upset you." Kelly cupped
Dorothy's elbow and guided her to a chair beside the sales counter, but
Dorothy hesitated before sitting. "It's not haunted, I promise. Would you
like a glass of water?"

"I'd rather go home, but I don't feel like driving. Would you be a
sweetheart and take me home?"

"Of course I will. Let me get my jacket and bag." Kelly stepped
away from Dorothy.

"I wanted to see what else you had for sale, you know, to go along
with the chair I bought. I didn't think there would be a witch holding a
séance," Dorothy said.

Neither did I. Kelly shot a look at Frankie. He was her family and
should've stopped the medium. She then looked at Pepper. She supposed

her employee was doing the best she could under the circumstances. At least she summoned Kelly back to the boutique right away.

"Please hurry, dear. Judge Carmen is on in half an hour, and I never miss an episode." Dorothy smiled.

Chapter 11

Kelly pulled her vehicle onto the gravel driveway of Dorothy Mueller's house with just minutes to spare. She checked the dashboard clock. Judge Carmen's show would be on in eight minutes.

The charming little cottage with weathered shingles and bare window flower boxes looked to be the perfect home for Dorothy. Kelly could imagine bright, pretty flowers spilling over the tops of the boxes in the warmer months and Dorothy watering them each morning. Not a gardener herself, she had no idea which types of flowers would do well in a container. That reminded her, she still needed to get some autumn decorations for the boutique.

"We've had quite a bit of excitement, haven't we?" Dorothy dug in her purse for her house key.

Kelly nodded at the understatement of the year. "We certainly did."

"Ms. Leigh was quite fascinating. I hope none of your merchandise is haunted. Do you think your grandmother's spirit is still in the store? After all, she did die there."

The reminder of her granny's death hit Kelly hard, right in the chest. The memory of Pepper's phone call to let her know she'd lost her grandmother replayed in her mind. Martha Blake had collapsed just after opening her shop and was found by Pepper, but it was too late. She was gone. Now every time Kelly passed the spot where Pepper discovered Martha, her stomach constricted and her heart broke all over again.

"Oh, dear, I didn't mean to upset you."

Kelly wiped away a fallen tear and forced a smile. "I'm okay."

"Listen to me prattle on. All this talk about ghosts and murder. I still can't believe that psychic's cousin was murdered. What is happening to our Lucky Cove?" Dorothy rested a hand on Kelly's forearm. "Would you like to come inside for a cup of tea? I think a nice cup of herbal tea would do us both a world of good. I have a honey lavender brew."

Brew? Perhaps not the best choice of words considering all the paranormal talk. "Thank you, but I need to get back to the boutique. Will you be okay getting inside?"

"Of course. I'm not so old I need assistance walking." Dorothy opened the passenger door and stepped out.

"No, no...that's not what I meant," Kelly called after Dorothy.

"I appreciate the ride, dear." Dorothy closed the car door and carefully made her way to the front porch of her house. After unlocking the door, she disappeared inside. Kelly had done her good deed for the day by delivering the elderly woman home.

Staring at the house and replaying the comment that Granny's spirit could be hanging around the boutique reminded Kelly she needed to clear out the rental cottage. The owner had been gracious enough to allow Kelly some time to take out her granny's possessions since it was at the end of the season, but she felt the clock ticking on the homeowner's generosity.

Just as Kelly shifted her vehicle into reverse, she caught a glimpse of a familiar face walking up the path to the front door of the house next door. Evan Fletcher.

Sometimes living in a small town had its advantages. She was still suspicious of his refusal to answer what she considered simple questions. It felt like he was hiding something. Since the opportunity presented itself, Kelly wasn't about to waste it. She swept her arm over the front seat and grabbed one of her sales flyers. She stepped out of her car and trotted across the lawn, her feet plowing through a thick layer of fallen leaves.

Evan turned his head. He must have heard the leaves crunching as she made her way to his property.

"Hello! I'm Kelly Quinn, and I own Curated by Kelly. It's a resale boutique, and I'm looking for inventory." She thrust the flyer into Evan's hand. "Perhaps the lady of the house has some clothing she'd like to sell."

The man had traded his cheap suit for a more casual yet rumpled look. His dark green baggy chinos puddled at his scuffed loafers, while his untucked striped shirt needed a good pressing. He glanced at the flyer and then back at Kelly. Recognition gleamed in his eyes. "You were at Bernadette's house. You found Maxine dead."

Kelly did her best fake recognition look, even clutching her chest with her hand. "Evan Fletcher. Right. Small town life. Geez." She hoped she wasn't overacting, something she was accused of doing in her middle school play when she played Matilda in *Alice in Wonderland.*

"Does everybody know everyone here?" he asked.

"Pretty much. You're not from around here, are you?"

"No, I'm from Maryland."

"What brings you up to New York? Business? Pleasure?"

"You could say that."

Great. More vagueness. The man couldn't seem to answer a question directly.

"Have you heard anything from the police about the murder?" Kelly asked.

"It appears they're keeping a tight lip. I guess it's understandable."

"Detective Wolman interviewed me again. Has she contacted you again?"

He shook his head. "No. Do you mind me asking what she followed up with you about?"

"Just reviewed what I saw when I arrived." Not exactly the truth, but she wasn't going to admit to a stranger the detective had discovered Kelly had a possible motive for murder. "She just wanted to review my statement. Like how long after I found Maxine's body you appeared for your appointment."

"Right. It was a shock coming onto the scene. Yet, you managed to keep it together."

"I didn't have much of a choice with Bernadette falling apart. When I arrived, there was no one else around the house and I didn't hear anyone in the house. How about you? Did you see anyone? Outside? Inside?"

Evan glanced at the flyer. "Do you own a clothing shop or are you a detective?"

Kelly smiled. "I own a clothing boutique. You know, Bernadette told me Maxine's laptop is missing. To get to the living room you have to pass the study where the computer was. Did you see the computer?"

Evan stiffened and shoved the flyer back into Kelly's hand. "There's no lady of the house here. Goodbye, Miss Quinn." He turned and walked to the front door of his cottage and disappeared after he slammed the door shut.

* * * *

The bell over the front door jingled, and Kelly poked her head out of the doorway from what used to be the dining room. Now it was a sales space she hoped to makeover with additional changing rooms and added shelving for sweaters and other tops that could be displayed folded. She wanted to give her customers the feel of a hip boutique, not a dowdy consignment shop. She even considered installing a chandelier for added ambiance. Maybe she could find one at the indoor flea market.

A group of four teenage girls bopped in, giggling, and they dispersed throughout the main sales area checking out the clothing on the racks. All four wore some type of Vera Bradley bag—tote bag, backpack, or crossbody. Vera bags were popular among younger girls, but seeing it in real life gave Kelly the idea to create a window display next August in time for back-to-school shopping. She made a mental note to actively acquire Vera bags.

Next August? She only hoped she'd be able to stay in business until then.

She walked out to greet the girls, who didn't seem fazed by all the haunted merchandise talk going around town. Three of the girls pulled earbuds out of their ears and returned her greeting, while the fourth one glanced up from her phone; she was busy texting.

"Is there anything you're looking for specifically?"

"We want to dress up for Halloween. Do you have any vintage clothes?" a petite blonde asked, who wore a Vera Bradley backpack slung over a shoulder.

"There are a few pieces scattered throughout the store. But I really don't specialize in vintage."

All four girls frowned with disappointment.

"Though, there are some pieces you can make work. Do any of you have any other clothing you'll be wearing already?"

Two girls nodded.

"Great, something to work with. Let me help you find some things and see what you think." Kelly moved to one circular rack and began sliding the hangers. This was what she loved doing—putting looks together.

The girls started chatting with her about what they liked, what they didn't, and, before long, they were trying on garments and giving an impromptu mini-fashion show Kelly styled.

By the time the girls left the boutique, they'd purchased a few items for Halloween and a few items each for themselves. They admitted they were surprised to find clothes in a consignment shop they would actually wear, and it was all because Kelly styled the looks for them. A parting suggestion from the petite blonde was to sell prom dresses because they were expensive.

Kelly hadn't thought about catering to a younger demographic, but it was a genius idea. She quickly made notes in her notebook so she wouldn't forget them. Pepper joined Kelly at the sales counter.

"Good news?" Pepper asked, herself now smiling.

"Sales!" Kelly's grin stretched ear to ear. "I made a few sales. Four teenagers came in looking for garments for Halloween and not only found some things useful for that but also a few items for themselves. We actually made some money!"

"How wonderful!" Pepper threw her arms around Kelly and hugged her. "This is exciting. Maybe our luck is turning around." She let go of Kelly. "I also have some ideas for marketing next year because those kids came in."

The front door swung open, and Bernadette ran in with her arms flailing. Kelly was caught off guard and braced herself for another dire vision.

"Kelly! Thank goodness you're here." Bernadette continued to the sales counter and dropped her purse on the countertop with a thud. "I was just at the police department. Detective Wolman wanted to interview me again. There's no doubt in my mind anymore. I'm a suspect."

"And you're here why?" Pepper asked.

Kelly glanced at Pepper. The older woman's lips had set in a thin line, and she glared at Bernadette. Clearly, Kelly wasn't the only person fed up with the circus atmosphere.

Bernadette looked taken aback for a moment, but then it passed and her attention shifted back to Kelly. "I don't know what to do. I've never been suspected of any crime, much less killing my own cousin. It's absurd. What should I do? You have to help me. I think I need a lawyer."

Pepper pulled on Kelly's arm and dragged her out of Bernadette's earshot. "I admit, I've been difficult lately because of all of the changes you're making, and I know I've hurt you. But, you have to know I only want the best for you. Your grandmother loved you so much, and I've always thought of you as a daughter, so I want you to know I don't trust her." She glanced over to Bernadette and then back to Kelly. "Something's not right with her."

Torn between Pepper's concern and Bernadette's need for help, Kelly was at a loss for what the right thing to do was. She looked at Bernadette. She'd just lost her cousin, and now she was a murder suspect. Then she looked back to Pepper. Worry filled her blue eyes. The worry for Kelly's well-being.

"I appreciate what you've just said, but I can't stand by and do nothing. She needs help. I hope you can understand."

"You aren't responsible for her."

"I know. I know."

"You say that, but I don't feel you believe it. Look. Look at your boutique. Do you see any customers?" Pepper did a Vanna White motion with her hand to drive home her point. The sweeping view showed no one in the boutique, other than the three of them. "She's responsible for this. For the lack of customers, aside from the teenyboppers who came in earlier. You don't owe her a thing. It's the other way around."

Kelly nodded. What Pepper said was true. She couldn't argue with it. She returned to Bernadette, who looked forlorn, and she caved. Yeah, Kelly Quinn was a sucker. How could she not help someone who obviously needed help?

Wait a minute. Detective Wolman said Kelly could have mistaken Maxine for Bernadette and killed the wrong woman. Okay, the thought sent chills down her spine because she never thought anyone would think she'd commit such a heinous crime, but that was beside the point now. If she could have mistaken Maxine for Bernadette, then maybe someone else could and did.

Bernadette could have been the intended target.

"What's wrong, Kelly?" Bernadette asked.

"She has something to say. Don't you?" Pepper prompted Kelly.

"What? Right. I do know a lawyer. Though, I'm not sure she'll take your case. Actually, I don't think she handles criminal cases, but maybe she can refer someone."

A small smile touched Bernadette's lips. "I'd appreciate any help." She stepped forward and rested a hand on Kelly's arm and squeezed. "Thank you." She released Kelly's arm. "I have to go. I have funeral arrangements to make."

In a flash, Bernadette was gone from the shop and Kelly was yet again on the receiving end of the "Pepper glare." Oh boy.

"I thought we agreed you'd stay out of her problems."

"I didn't agree. Besides, she could be in danger."

"How so?"

"Detective Wolman suggested I mistook Maxine for Bernadette and killed her by mistake."

"Absurd. You didn't kill anyone."

Kelly appreciated Pepper's confidence in her innocence. "Yes, but the killer could have mistaken Maxine for Bernadette. And he or she may decide to finish the job."

Pepper gave Kelly a concerned look. "I hope you're not still planning on poking around Maxine's murder. It's too dangerous."

"Why do you think I would?"

"Other than what you said to Gabe the other night? You and Liv played Nancy Drew all the time. One of you hid something, a clue or piece of evidence of some crime, around town, and the other one had to try and find it."

Kelly thought back to her childhood, and Pepper was right. She'd forgotten all about her Nancy Drew phase. "As I recall, I was quite good at it."

"Well, it was a game back then. Nobody was really murdered." The boutique's door opened and drew Pepper's attention from her lecture. "We'll continue this later." She stepped out from behind the counter and approached the customer.

If Kelly had any sense, she'd be quaking in her suede booties because Pepper's voice had been stern and she meant business. She was also right. Poking her nose into an ongoing investigation wouldn't be the smartest thing for Kelly to do. First, she could be arrested for interfering with the police investigation. From what she'd seen on social media, no one ever took a good mug shot. Even with false lashes. Second, tracking a killer was dangerous and she could end up, well, dead. Third, she had a business to salvage, and it didn't leave her much time to chase down a murderer.

Speaking of business, she needed to get back to work. While Pepper assisted the customer who'd walked into the boutique, Kelly turned her attention to pulling garments and putting up a new display in the boutique's window.

The rest of the day flew by, thanks to a handful of customers who seemed to throw caution to the wind and shop in the supposedly haunted boutique. Kelly put the final touches on the new window display and made a note to pick up some autumn decorations for the boutique. She locked up after Pepper left and then headed out the back door. Ariel had called after lunch and invited her to dinner. She also said they could review her notes on Maxine's scam back in Chicago.

She had just pulled the door closed behind her and locked it when she heard her name. She looked over her shoulder. Her uncle Ralph was walking toward her. His short legs carried his stumpy body across the parking lot. His arms swung as his suit jacket flapped in the cold breeze.

"Glad...I...caught you." The short walk from his Cadillac had left him winded. "We need to talk about the roof. I heard you've been calling around for estimates. I have a roof guy, and he's ready to start next week." Ralph dug into his jacket breast pocket, pulled out a business card, and shoved it in Kelly's hand.

She glanced at the card. Fast Bernie's Roof and Siding. And then she glanced at the roof of her building and back to her uncle. "Cancel the appointment. I'll find my own contractor."

Ralph shook his balding head. "What do you know about roofs?"

"Not much, but I know I don't want some guy named Fast Bernie fixing my roof." She gestured for her uncle to take the card back, but he refused. Fine. If he was going to play that game, she would be happy to join him. She ripped the card in half. "I don't need you to interfere in my business."

"Interfere? You've got it all wrong, kid. I'm just trying to help."

"And don't call me kid."

"You don't have any experience owning a business, or a building for that matter. There are plenty of people who'll try and take advantage of you."

Yeah, she was looking at one of them. She didn't doubt for one second Fast Bernie would kick back some money to Ralph if she let him repair her roof. Dear Uncle Ralph didn't do anything if it didn't in some way give him a payoff.

"Thanks for the warning." She shoved the torn card into her tote bag at the same time she remembered her theory from earlier. "Do you know Bernadette Rydell?"

"That psychic nutcase? Hey, whatever pays the bills, right? As long as her check clears, I don't care what she does."

"Check clears? The house she rents is one of yours?"

Ralph owned dozens of properties in and around Lucky Cove, so she wasn't surprised to find out he owned the Gothic Victorian house. Though, it seemed more than just a coincidence he was Bernadette's landlord. Maybe her idea he'd put Bernadette up to causing the disruption in the boutique wasn't such a far-fetched idea after all.

"What's with all the questions? Listen, Bernie is a good guy. He'll do right by you."

"I doubt it. I have to go." She brushed by her uncle and hurried to her borrowed SUV. Once behind the wheel, she glanced at the rearview mirror and spotted Ralph throwing a punch in the air and stomping back to his car. He definitely wasn't happy with her, and she wondered how far he'd go to drive her out of business.

Chapter 12

Kelly followed Ariel into the spacious eat-in kitchen, and her stomach growled as the heavenly aroma of lasagna wafted in the air. "Dinner smells delicious."

She dropped her tote bag on the table and slipped out of her suede barn jacket. She left her scarf wrapped around her neck because she was still chilled. Late October was turning out to be an early preview of December weather. She rubbed her hands together for warmth.

"You're just in time." Ariel navigated her wheelchair over to the wall oven and grabbed two potholders from the counter. She opened the oven door and slid out the casserole dish.

Kelly dashed over to the oven and felt the comforting rush of heat from the oven wash over her as she took the lasagna from Ariel and carried it to the table and set the dish on a trivet. Her gaze fixed on the bubbling dish of cheesy comfort. "Oh. My. Goodness. It looks delicious."

"Thank you." Ariel moved to the island and grabbed the bowl of salad greens. "The lasagna should set for a few minutes."

At the table, she placed the salad greens next to the lasagna. "Why don't I show you what I have so far on Maxine? Then the lasagna will be ready to eat." She wheeled past Kelly and led her down the wide hallway to an office.

Ariel's home was an average-sized ranch house that had been custom fitted for her needs with wide doorways and hallways and ramps at both the back and front doors. Kelly heard Ariel's parents had paid for the renovations to the home so their daughter could lead an independent life. A twinge of guilt flickered inside Kelly. She took so many things for granted, like climbing the staircase to her apartment, while Ariel had to do extensive renovations to her home to live there.

"I have bunches of notes and interviews from people who have been scammed by psychics. For the article I'm writing, I had to focus on the over sixty-five set. Luckily, at least for me, Maxine had several elderly victims."

"I can't believe she took advantage of all those people, especially the elderly. How could she lie to those poor people and take their money?"

Ariel shrugged. "More than half of her elderly victims were far from poor, but when Maxine finished with them, they were exactly that. But she wasn't just giving them phony readings."

"What do you mean?"

Ariel wheeled over to her desk and gestured for Kelly to sit on the leather ottoman next to it. "She used the readings to convince her clients to invest in Ponzi schemes."

"Are you serious?" Kelly was all too familiar with that type of fraud. One of the biggest Ponzi schemers came from New York City and, for months, captured the headlines of major newspapers. "She convinced them a deceased loved one wanted them to invest their money, and her partner acted as the financial advisor?"

"Pretty much." Ariel opened a file and spread out the papers on her desk. "She worked with her brother, Marco. He does have some background in finance so he sounded legit. What happened was, Maxine referred her clients to him and he set them up with an investment and made sure it paid a healthy return. Which resulted in the client wanting to invest more because he or she felt confident they'd made a sound decision. After all, he was getting money back. Who wouldn't want to continue with a winning investment?"

"Let me guess. Maxine reinforced the client's decision by telling them the deceased loved one was pleased and wanted the client to continue to invest?" Ariel's nod indicated Kelly was spot on. "How awful. Why aren't people more suspicious of a *sure thing?*" Kelly used air quotes for "sure thing." In the city, there was always someone looking to take advantage of a tourist, a new Big Apple transplant, or someone who chose to believe the best in people.

"You would think their bullcrap radar would pick up the scam, but Maxine and her brother preyed on a vulnerable population. Believe me, when you have no hope, you'll believe anything that promises a glimmer of it."

Pain swelled in Kelly's chest as she swallowed the lump lodged in her throat. The events of the late-summer night party flashed in Kelly's mind. "If I could take back what happened that night I would."

"Me too, but it's not possible. We both made the decision to go to the party, and we both decided on how the evening would end. Your decision was in no way the cause of me ending up paralyzed."

"How can you say that? If I hadn't snuck away with Davey, you wouldn't have gotten in the car with Tamara."

"Getting into Tamara's car was on me. I shouldn't have. I knew she'd been drinking a lot. I had other options, and I chose the wrong one. You have to stop beating yourself up about how my life turned out."

Kelly dipped her head. "I don't think I can."

"Hey, yes, you can. I know you went through a lot after the accident." Kelly shook her head and lifted her chin. "Nothing compared to what you went through."

"The rift between you and Caroline is still there."

"True. She's still angry with me for abandoning you that night. At least my parents found a way to stop blaming me. But, you know, what I've gone through pales in comparison to your paralysis. I'm not looking to wallow in pity. I'd just like a chance to be friends with my sister again."

"You're back here in Lucky Cove, so maybe you both can work on repairing your relationship."

Kelly's heart swelled with hope. She'd love nothing more than to be able to send a text to her sister about something not very important or maybe even go for lunch together. The fact that she was sitting in Ariel's house with all the baggage between them did give her a little hope.

"Are you sure you're doing okay?" Kelly asked.

"I'm alive and I have a full life. Not one day goes by I'm not grateful I'm still here."

"What about those days when you had no hope?"

Ariel shrugged. "There were definitely bleak days following the accident. I didn't think anyone understood how I felt, and it seemed like no one knew how to handle me. My own parents didn't know how to talk to me. Everyone was afraid I was too fragile and would break, and the more they treated me like that, the more I became like that. That's when I latched on to the telephone psychic."

"Telephone? Really?" Dial-a-psychic? Who fell for a 900 psychic these days? "Sorry, I don't mean to be all judgey."

"I know. I know. Lame, right? But I was desperate to talk to someone who didn't talk to me like I was some crippled girl."

Kelly arched an eyebrow at Ariel's description of herself.

"I know no one says that word anymore, but that's how I felt. Physically and emotionally. Let's face it, if my own family couldn't communicate with me like they used to, how on earth was a guy ever going to be able to? Seriously, they suck at communication to begin with."

Kelly and Ariel shared a deep laugh, and it felt good, just like old times. For the first time in a very long time, the weight of Ariel's accident eased from her shoulders.

"The psychic told me what I wanted to hear, and that's why I called her again and again. I spent a ridiculous amount of money, but, luckily, I finally realized the calls were nothing but a scam. At the time, I was seeing a therapist twice a week, and he helped me realize what was going on with the psychic. But there are people out there who don't have someone to intervene on their behalf."

Kelly dipped her head and looked through the papers from Ariel's file. They were all accounts of victims of psychic fraud. A handful were clients of Maxine and her brother. "You've compiled quite a bit here."

"It's taken some time. I think when I'm done with the article for *Senior Spotlight,* I will rework the material for another article. I think I have a few angles I could exploit."

Kelly looked back at Ariel. "You're hardcore."

Ariel nodded. "Damn straight. My parents helped me retrofit this house for my needs, but I'm the one who pays the bills around here."

"We gals gotta be independent." Kelly returned her attention to the papers, and one newspaper clipping caught her eye.

"What is it?" Ariel asked.

"This man." Kelly held up the piece of paper.

"DJ Brown. He lost fifty thousand dollars to Maxine. It cost him his marriage. His wife was convinced Maxine wasn't just doing readings with DJ, if you get my drift."

"But he said his name was Evan Fletcher."

"When?"

"At Bernadette's house. After I found Maxine's body, he showed up."

"Wait! Is he here in Lucky Cove? Where? I need to interview him."

"I doubt he'll give you an interview because now he has a motive for murder." And he'd slammed the door on Kelly earlier when she attempted to talk to him about Maxine's murder. "Can I get a copy of this?"

"You're not going to scoop me, are you?"

"No. I promise. It's for my own investigation."

"Good. You're being proactive. I'll make a copy after we eat. The lasagna should be set now, and I'm starving." "So am I." Kelly followed Ariel back to the kitchen and, over heaping servings of lasagna and salad and a generous glass of wine, they caught up on life, laughed at their memories of high school, and made a promise to each other to not dwell on the past. As Kelly slipped into her jacket and shoved the copy of the article Ariel had made for her into her tote bag, she hoped she could live up to the promise she'd made. Letting go of all of the guilt she'd carried for years wasn't an easy thing to do, but she would give it her best shot. Just like tracking down Maxine's killer.

Thanks to the large mug of coffee she drank to counteract the wine she enjoyed while she ate dinner, Kelly was wide awake and had nowhere but home to go to. Lucky Cove, especially during the off-season, didn't have a hopping nightlife. She could work on another article for *Budget Chic,* or she could do something she'd been dreading for weeks—clear out her granny's belongings at the cottage she had rented.

The small, one-bedroom cottage was just a couple blocks from the boutique, and she could pop in to take a look at how big of a job waited for her. The one good thing was the cottage came furnished, so she didn't have to worry about moving out furniture, just personal belongings, but she wasn't sure how much at home Granny had made herself in the cottage.

With the decision made to check out the cottage, she drove past the boutique and turned on Pine Street, and halfway down the quiet street she found the cottage. Lights from the houses were dimmed through drawn curtains. The residents of Pine Street were tucked in for the night. Kelly should follow suit, but since she was caffeinated, sleep wouldn't come easy.

She pulled her SUV into the driveway and then made her way to the front door of the blue cottage. She unlocked the door and closed it behind her. She fumbled for a light switch and found one. After flipping on the light in the tiny entry space, she stepped forward into the living room. She detected a slight musty odor of the closed-up house. Sadness swept through Kelly. Granny had begun her last day like any other. Just like Kelly had. Never in a million years did she think she'd get a phone call with such terrible news.

She stepped farther into the living room. The sofa and armchairs were slipcovered, and oak accent furniture filled the rest of the space. She searched for another light switch but didn't find one. She eased her way over to a lamp on an end table and switched it on. The soft light brought her eyes into focus. The room was tidy and clean. While her granny had difficulty climbing stairs, she didn't have difficulty in using a vacuum.

Kelly didn't see much in the room that belonged to Granny except a collection of family photos on the fireplace mantel. She crossed the room and picked up one of the framed photographs. A smile touched her lips. Granny posed with her and Caroline at a family wedding. Back then life was simple. Her fingers touched the glass. Why was life as an adult so complicated?

She stared at Caroline's face. She looked to be about ten years old in the photograph. When they were kids, they fought like sisters did, but they always made up. She wondered, since she was able to rebuild her relationship with Ariel, would it be possible to do the same with Caroline?

A sound dragged Kelly from her thoughts. Her ears perked up and she heard the sound again. The cottage was small, just a few hundred square feet, the kitchen wasn't far away, and it sounded as if someone was trying to open the back door. She set the photograph back on the mantel. Who would be trying to get in through the back door? Why not use the front door?

She looked around the room for a weapon because her instinct kicked in to protect herself. Unfortunately, the room was light on weapons. The only thing close to a weapon was the chunky shabby-chic candlestick holder on the mantel. She grabbed it and eased her tote bag from her shoulder to the floor.

As she crept along the wall, her heartbeat kicked up and her palms began to sweat. She made her way to the entry of the kitchen. All was quiet until the sound of shattering glass broke the silence. She pressed her back into the wall so hard she was certain she was leaving an imprint.

Whoever was outside was now about to enter the house.

She sucked in a deep breath, hoping to steady her frayed nerves, as she braced herself for a confrontation, because heavy footsteps were approaching from the kitchen. Her heart thumped against her chest as she lifted the candlestick holder over her head with both hands. The footsteps stopped. An uncomfortable quietness settled in the house until the footsteps started again, but now they seemed to be going in a different direction. Was the intruder retreating? Leaving the house? Had something scared him or her off?

Kelly pulled herself away from the wall and made her way to one of the living room windows. She swept back a lace curtain, and a beam of light blinded her and she screamed bloody murder.

The light bounced across the garden bed, and then a pounding at the front door shocked Kelly out of her screaming fit. What was going on? Who was peeping into the window with a flashlight? Who was at the front door?

"Lucky Cove Police! Open up!"

Gabe?

Kelly rushed to the door and opened it. "What are you doing here? You nearly scared me to death."

"What are you doing here?"

"Did you see him? Or her? Someone broke in through the back door. I heard the glass shatter and I heard footsteps. Then he or she left. That's when I looked out the window and you blinded me."

"Stay right here."

Gabe raced through the house and into the kitchen. A moment later he returned to the living room. "Yeah, there was a break-in."

"Thank you, Captain Obvious."

"I'm not a captain... Oh, not funny, Kell."

She smirked. Yeah, it was good to be home. And it was nice to have a moment of lightness as she calmed down. "Why were you looking into the window?"

"I saw the light on, and no one is supposed to be here."

"Didn't you see your mother's car in the driveway? Never mind." Kelly went to retrieve her tote bag. "I guess whoever broke in thought the house was empty and easy pickings."

"Probably. You didn't answer my question. Why are you here?"

"I was on my way home, and I thought I'd stop by to check out how much stuff I needed to move out of here. I think I'll come by when there's daylight. What are we going to do about the back door?"

Gabe arched an eyebrow. "We?"

"You're the police."

"I'm not a handyman."

"Neither am I. Besides, this isn't even my house." Kelly supposed she'd have to call the homeowner and inform her of the break-in. Great. One more unpleasant thing on her to-do list.

Gabe shook his head. "I'll board it. You should head home. You'll have to stop by the police department tomorrow to sign the report."

Kelly sighed. "Can't you bring it to me? I don't want to run into Detective Wolman."

"No can do. Policy."

Kelly slung the tote bag over her shoulder. "The house has been empty for weeks, so why hasn't someone tried to break in before? Why wait until I show up in the middle of the night?"

"What are you saying? Do you think someone followed you here and broke in because of you?"

"Yes, I do."

"I know I'm going to regret asking, but why do you think someone followed you here and broke in?"

"It's just a feeling I have. And after finding the threatening flyer tacked in one of the changing rooms—"

"Whoa. What threatening flyer?"

"Didn't I tell you?" Kelly thought she'd told him. She recalled the conversation with Liv about reporting the incident to the police, and she remembered she didn't think the police would be interested. "Oh, no, I didn't tell you. Someone wrote in red marker on one of the flyers I made for the boutique 'Murder Dress. Does it fit you, Kelly?' I found the flyer tacked onto a wall." The words were etched in her brain. She'd never forget them or the surge of fear she felt when she found the flyer.

"Why didn't you tell me this earlier?" Gabe demanded.

"There wasn't anything you could've done about it, but now I think someone is trying to scare me."

"Why?"

"Because I've been dragged into Maxine's murder."

"You think the killer is after you?" He gave Kelly a dubious look.

Kelly sighed. "I'm serious. And since it's your sworn duty to protect the citizens of Lucky Cove, I think you should start doing your job."

"Then let me start by following you home to make sure you arrive safely and the bogeyman doesn't get to you."

"Ha ha." Kelly started walking to the front door with Gabe behind her. "Oh, I think Uncle Ralph was behind Bernadette's performance at my boutique."

"Do I dare ask? What makes you think that?"

"He owns the cottage she rents. They have a connection, and he never wanted me to keep the building."

"Not much of a case you've built against him."

Cold air greeted Kelly as she stepped outside, and when Gabe was by her side, she pulled the door closed and made sure it was locked. "It's a theory. And I feel it in my bones that he's behind all the craziness going on. You heard about the séance, right?"

Gabe nodded. "Everybody has. Come on. Let's get you home. I'll come back and board up the back door. You'll need to contact the landlord tomorrow and let them know what happened."

Kelly climbed into her vehicle and cranked up the heat after she started the ignition. She waited until Gabe was in his police cruiser. She used the time to replay the events in the cottage. The shattering of the glass, the click of the knob turning, and the heavy footsteps. Was it a random intruder as Gabe suggested, or was it Maxine's killer coming for Kelly?

Gabe started to pull his vehicle from the driveway, and Kelly shifted her car into reverse, backed out of the driveway, and headed to the stop sign with Gabe behind her. Her nerves settled down, but she couldn't stop thinking about what could have happened if her friend hadn't shown up. Would Kelly have come face-to-face with a murderer?

* * * *

Another yawned escaped Kelly's lips as she waited for her triple-shot, extra-tall, caffeinated drink in Doug's Variety Store. When she climbed out of bed after barely sleeping a wink, she knew her home-brewed pumpkin spice coffee wouldn't cut it. After showering and dressing, she reached for her go-to animal-print leggings and black cashmere sweater, filled Howard's bowl, and dashed across the street.

Even off-season, Doug's was filled with customers desperate for their caffeine fix. Because he did so much business with coffee orders, he set up a small coffee-to-go section, and the line was long when Kelly arrived.

"Hey, Kell." Gabe approached her from the main order section of the store and had a cup of coffee in one hand and a half-eaten old-fashioned donut in the other. "How are you doing this morning?"

"Okay, I suppose, for someone who was targeted by a murderer last night."

"You're being a bit dramatic."

"I know. I'm tired. I didn't sleep well. Listen, I found out something you should know. Evan Fletcher is lying about his name. His real name is DJ Brown."

"How do you know that?"

Of course he'd want to know how she came across the information. She didn't want to drag Ariel into the investigation unless she absolutely had to. "That's not important. When I saw him yesterday, he refused to talk to me about the murder."

"Wait. You talked to him yesterday?"

"Yes. Before I knew he was using an alias. I asked if he saw anyone else around Bernadette's house or perhaps knew what happened to the laptop in the study."

"What laptop?"

"The missing one. Bernadette said Maxine had a laptop, and I did notice the day of the murder there was a power cord plugged in but no computer."

"You talked to Bernadette since the murder?"

"Gabe, I talk to a lot of people."

"You shouldn't be talking to people who are associated with this murder investigation. We don't know who the killer is yet. You could be putting yourself in danger."

Like last night? "Thanks for your concern, but I'm a big girl."

"We're the police. Let us do our job."

"Three shots, extra tall!" Doug called out from the counter. Kelly's coffee was ready.

"Fine. I'll let you do your job, Officer Donovan. Enjoy your *donut.*" She spun around and hurried to the counter to get her lifesaving beverage. She took a grateful sip as Gabe passed by her, mumbling. Maybe the donut crack was too much. She smiled. Nah. Even exhausted she was still on top of her game.

Around eleven, Frankie texted Kelly to come over to his restaurant for lunch. He was preparing a special meal for her. Even though she was still a little annoyed with her cousin, she couldn't pass up his cooking. When noon rolled around, she was out the door and on her way over to Frankie's Seafood Shack.

She tucked her legs under the picnic table after dropping her tote bag on the bench next to her. Eating outdoors on a cold, autumn day was something she, Caroline, and Frankie used to do when they were kids. Kelly's mom made a lunch of grilled cheese sandwiches and tomato soup and brought the tray out to the picnic table. Kelly bundled up in a hat, a big, thick crocheted scarf from Granny, and a heavy coat. The three of them ate the meal, laughing and joking, and then ended the meal with big cups of hot cocoa. Today, Kelly didn't have to bundle up. The weather wasn't as cold as it had been, and a leather jacket draped over her shoulders seemed to stave off the chill of the afternoon.

She unfolded the paper napkin and draped it over her lap as Frankie set a plate of scallops in front of her on the picnic table. Her mouth watered. The lunch was definitely an upgrade from the grilled cheese sandwiches. Pan-sautéed in butter and fresh herbs, the scallops were cooked perfectly because, even though her cousin was a pain in the butt, he was an excellent chef.

"Your favorite." Frankie scooted around to the other side of the table and slung his legs over the bench and sat. He also had a plate of scallops and a beer.

She eyed him, still leery of his motivation for their impromptu lunch. She then turned her attention back to her food. Whatever the reason, she was going to enjoy her gourmet meal. She picked up her fork and pierced one of the scallops. She bit into the delicacy and savored the mild sweetness and silkiness.

"You like?"

Kelly glanced at Frankie and found him looking expectantly at her. Seriously, he had to ask her? He was a trained chef who studied a year in Paris and worked his way up the culinary ladder to become the head chef at one of the most exclusive restaurants in New York City before turning his back on it all and opening Frankie's Seafood Shack. What was there not to like?

She swallowed her bite. "This is fabulous. But you know that. I could eat this every day and not get bored."

Frankie laughed. Tiny lines creased around his medium-brown eyes. "I know. Your jam is scallops while Caroline can't get enough of shrimp."

"You've seen her recently?" Kelly took a sip of the artisan beer Frankie poured for her. His restaurant was known for its commitment to using local ingredients and locally produced beverages.

"Sure. We had dinner last week. When was the last time you two saw each other?" Frankie broke his sourdough roll in half and soaked up the juice on his plate then popped the bread in his mouth.

Envy stabbed at her heart. Frankie and Caroline were close. They had dinners together, they texted each other, and they probably were spending Thanksgiving together.

Kelly blew out a regretful sigh. "Granny's funeral."

Frankie stopped chewing and gave his cousin a sorrowful look.

"I know. I know. I tried reaching out, but she's incapable of understanding my side of the story." Kelly set her fork down because, all of a sudden, she'd lost her appetite. "I'm going to try again. Soon."

Frankie finished chewing his bread and swallowed. "How soon?"

"The next few days. I need her help."

"With what?"

A crunching noise drew her attention away from her cousin for a minute. They weren't the only ones eating alfresco. She spotted a squirrel sitting on top of a heap of leaves eating a nut. "A lawyer recommendation."

Now she'd completely lost her appetite. "I think I'm a suspect in Maxine Lemoyne's murder."

Frankie let out a laugh. "That's ridiculous. You couldn't kill anyone."

"Tell that to Detective Wolman. I think she's building a case against me."

"Why on earth would you murder Maxine Lemoyne?"

"Because her cousin's performance in my boutique the other day has cost me business and Wolman thinks I killed Maxine by mistake because I meant to kill Bernadette. The detective thinks that's a good enough motive."

Frankie laughed again. "I'm sorry, but you're so not the killer type."

"Is that so? Well, I wanted to murder you yesterday when I found you seated at the table with the medium. You think this is all funny, but it's costing me business, and it may cost me my freedom if I'm charged with murder. This is serious, Frankie."

"I apologized, didn't I? You know I couldn't resist a séance with Valeria Leigh. She's a legend around here."

"Pffft." Kelly pushed her plate away. "So much for family loyalty."

"You know how much I dig paranormal stuff." Frankie took another gulp of his beer before he polished off his scallops.

"Do people still say 'dig'?"

"Yeah, man."

"Jerk." Kelly laughed, and her cousin joined in. Family. She couldn't live with them and she couldn't live without them. Especially the screwball cousin seated across from her.

"You used to love Halloween. All the spooky, scary movies and crazy things we did. What happened?"

"I grew up."

"I did too, but I still love all that stuff. You should loosen up a bit, cuz."

"Loosen up? I've inherited a business on the brink of financial disaster, I own an old house with drafts and a bad roof, and I'm a murder suspect. Why did Bernadette have to try on that stupid dress Irene Singer consigned?"

"Eddie's wife?"

"You know Irene? Did you know her husband? Is it true Eddie was a gambler?"

"Yeah, I heard he was getting in deep with his bookie."

"Bookie? In Lucky Cove?"

Frankie shook his head as he drained the last of his beer. "Just outside of town. The guy's a real peach. He operates out of the Thirsty Turtle."

"That dive is still open?" The bar was a place Kelly never went even though her friends tried several times to drag her there in high school because the bar staff didn't card its clientele. Nothing but trouble happened there, so Kelly kept her distance from the establishment. "Why am I not surprised a bookie works out of the bar? It's almost cliché."

"Leo Manning is a cliché. Want a refill?" Frankie pointed to Kelly's glass. She shook her head. One beer was enough for her since she had to drive back to the boutique.

Frankie stood and dashed into the restaurant and returned a moment later with a full glass for himself. "One of Leo's ex-girlfriends waitressed here one summer." Frankie sat and took a sip of his beer. "Nice girl with fake boobs and no work ethic. She was the kind of girl who is used to others taking care of her."

Frankie's description sounded vaguely familiar to someone they both knew, but she didn't say Summer's name. Frankie's relationship with his stepmother was amiable, but he preferred not to discuss her if he didn't have to.

"She said Leo took good care of her until he found another girl to take care of," Frankie continued.

"Huh. Eddie owed him a lot of money?" Kelly recalled the conversation with Regina. She'd said pretty much what Frankie had said. It appeared Eddie was up to his eyeballs in debt.

Frankie shrugged. "Don't know. Don't care. The guy's dead. Wait. You're not thinking of going to see Leo? No. Bad idea. He's not a nice guy. I've heard he's hurt people."

"Relax. Don't worry so much. I'm just asking questions. I hate to eat and run, but I have to get back to the boutique." She stood and grabbed her tote bag. "Lunch was delicious."

Frank rose quickly to his feet and walked around the table. "Are we good?" He held open his arms for a hug.

"Of course we are." She stepped into Frankie's hug. "You cooked me my favorite meal."

Frankie let out a breath. "It worked."

Kelly pulled back and slapped him on the chest. "Yes, it did. Just don't attend any more séances in my boutique."

"Promise."

"You better." She turned to head back to her vehicle. Glad she and Frankie had cleared the air, Kelly now could focus on what was important—clearing her name and saving the boutique.

Chapter 13

Kelly had every intention of returning to the boutique when she drove away from Frankie's restaurant and every intention of keeping her long-standing tradition of staying away from the Thirsty Turtle. So why on earth was she parked in the gravel driveway of the bar?

The niggling thought that the Singers were somehow involved in the mess of Maxine's murder poked at her. What if Bernadette's vision was real and Irene did kill her husband and, fearing discovery, Irene intended to kill Bernadette but made a mistake and killed Maxine? Yeah, there were a lot of "ifs," but her theory was plausible.

As plausible as her theory was, there was no evidence to support it, and finding any at the seedy bar was unlikely. She looked around the parking lot. A handful of rusty cars and battered pickup trucks were parked haphazardly. Lunchtime looked like it drew a crowd. She gathered up her nerve and pulled the keys out of the ignition and made her way to the front door of the bar.

The Thirsty Turtle was a box of a building painted three colors—red, white, and blue. Very patriotic. Chipped and dirty, the paint had seen better days. A sign with the bar's name hung over one of the two front windows, and a glass door in need of a washing was the entrance to the dimly lit establishment.

Kelly stepped over the blackened threshold, and her nose was assaulted by a strong whiff of cigarette smoke and beer and a hint of sea air. Her eyes watered as she adjusted to the uncomfortable odor. The place needed fresh air, maybe a window should be opened. Surveying the bar, it didn't look like anyone else had a problem with the stale air.

About five men, all sporting scruffy beards and beer bellies, were seated at the bar chowing down on hamburgers and fries and guzzling beer, while a few tables had other diners eating the same meal. Huh. Not much of a menu.

No one seemed to notice her. Maybe she looked like she belonged. Somehow, she'd had the foresight to dress appropriately for her trip to the bar. Yeah, animal-print leggings and a leather jacket were dive bar chic.

"You lost, hon?" a crusty old bald bartender asked as he wiped down the bar with a towel.

Okay, she didn't look like she belonged in the dive bar. No doubt, the black cashmere sweater was too much. It was too late to turn and leave. Besides, she'd passed by worse on her way from the subway to her apartment in the city. She could handle a bartender in the suburbs of Long Island and the lunchtime crowd, who turned their gazes in her direction.

With all eyes on her, she squared her shoulders and sauntered to the bar. "No. I'm not lost. I'm looking for someone." She tossed back her head, her hair skimming over her shoulders, and stood confidently.

The crusty old bartender smiled, revealing a few missing teeth. The rolled-up sleeves of his white shirt revealed a snake tattoo along his forearm. "Who might that be?"

"Leo. Leo Manning."

The crusty old bartender chuckled as he threw down the towel. "What's a nice girl like you doing looking for Leo?"

"Is he here?"

"No. Wanna leave him a message? Let me get my notepad and pen." He paused then grinned and snapped his stubby fingers. "Sorry. I ain't got any of that."

A low rumble of laughter drifted in the air. Apparently, the lunch crowd found the crusty old bartender amusing. Somehow his humor was lost on Kelly.

"Thanks anyway." She would have felt more disappointment if she hadn't realized the likelihood of the bookie being at the bar at the moment she showed up was unreasonable. Maybe it was for the best. What did she really think Leo would tell her about Eddie Singer? She turned and started to walk away from the bar. She couldn't get out of that place quick enough.

"Hey, wait, honey."

Honey. She hated being called honey, especially by men like the bartender. She looked over her shoulder. "What?"

"If you're looking for work, I need a waitress. With your *girls,* you could earn some good tips. You'd just need to show more of them." He grinned again, and Kelly shuddered. She needed a shower.

"No thanks." She continued to the door. If something didn't turn around at the boutique, she might have to consider the offer. She pushed the door open and stepped outside.

A gust of cold air blasted Kelly, and she wished she'd opted for a heavier coat. The first part of the day had been unseasonably warm, and she hadn't expected to make a detour on the way back to the boutique from lunch. As she reached her vehicle, she aimed the key fob and unlocked the driver's side door. As she got closer to the SUV, she noticed a flat tire. Just what she didn't need, and of all the places to get stranded.

Before she could think about who she was going to call for assistance—hopefully Pepper had a roadside service plan—her cell phone rang. She pulled the phone out of her jacket pocket and saw Ariel's name. She swiped the phone on.

"You won't believe what just happened."

"Same here," Ariel said. "Well, nothing really happened. I heard from a source that Marco Lemoyne was last seen in Philadelphia a week ago. My guess is he's working his way to New York. He may even be in Lucky Cove."

"Source? You have a source?"

Ariel giggled. "You betcha. I'm headed out to try and interview DJ Brown aka Evan Fletcher."

"I doubt he'll talk to you." Kelly walked around the front of her vehicle and saw another flat tire. "What the...?" One flat tire was understandable. Two flat tires was sabotage. Her pulse quickened, and she straightened up to look around, but she didn't see anyone. Though, how dumb would the vandal be if he stood out in the open admiring his work?

"Kelly, what's going on?"

"I'll call you back. I have to call for roadside service." She disconnected the call and scrolled through her contacts to get Pepper's number. She tapped on Pepper's name and waited for the call to be put through. "Come on, come on, answer the phone."

"You've reached the phone of Pepper Donovan. Leave a message."

"Ugh. Fine. Pepper call me ASAP. I have two flat tires." Kelly disconnected the call and decided to go through the glove compartment. Maybe the insurance card had a service phone number. After she yanked open the passenger side door, she heard someone approach. She looked over her shoulder. A woman about her age was walking toward her with a cup in one hand and waving the other.

"You got some trouble?" the woman asked.

Kelly pulled herself out of the car. "I do. Flat tires."

"I saw you out the window and suspected something was wrong. It's getting cold so I brought you coffee." She handed the mug to Kelly. "I'm Breena, and I waitress in there." She nodded in the direction of the bar. "Nice to meet you. I'm Kelly Quinn." Kelly took a drink of the coffee. "Not bad. Nice robust flavor."

"Thanks. I brewed it myself. It's about the only thing in there that tastes good and is full strength. Cody waters down all the drinks."

Somehow, Kelly wasn't shocked by the information. "I appreciate this. It's getting colder."

"Tell me about it." Breena started to button her denim jacket but struggled with the one at her ample bustline. "Do you have someone to call? Two tires? Oh, man. You must have ticked someone off."

Breena was on the same thought train as Kelly. Now she just had to figure out who wanted to enact sabotage and why. While Breena shook her head, staring at the flat tires, Kelly's mind was working to place the waitress. She was very familiar. Then it hit her.

"Sabrina? Sabrina Collins?" Kelly had finally placed the petite, busty woman. "We were in the same French class."

Breena fixed her stare on Kelly, and then her face lit up. "Oui." She giggled. "Kelly! Great to see you again. Oh, sorry about the circumstances." She hugged Kelly, jostling the coffee. "I go by Breena now. B-R-E-E-N-A. That was my stage name."

"Stage name?"

Breena's head bobbed up and down, and her wavy brunette hair bounced. "I headed for Broadway after high school. Remember? I was in drama club. I got some roles and a few commercials, but I eventually decided to come back home."

"To waitress here?" Kelly immediately regretted the slight judgment in her question. "I'm sorry. I didn't mean anything. Hey, I got fired from my dream job a few months ago and moved back here to take over my grandmother's consignment shop."

"No worries. I'm working here until I graduate college. Why are you here?"

"I'm looking for Leo Manning. Do you know him?"

Breena gave Kelly a dark look. "Sweetie, you don't want to meet Leo unless you want to place a bet or want to date him. He's not very nice."

"Have you ever dated him?"

Breena held up her hands. "Nooo. And I won't. I told you, he's not very nice. Besides, I'm juggling working here, school, and my daughter. It's tough."

"You have a daughter?"

"Hey! Get your pretty little butt back in here! You're on the clock!" the crusty old bartender yelled from the open front door and then retreated back into the building.

Breena winced. "I better get inside. Look, you should stay away from Leo. But if you really need to see him, he comes in here weekly to do business." She used air quotes when she said "business."

"Did you by chance know an Eddie Singer?"

Breena started back to the bar. "Leo had a regular named Eddie. The guy was in deep to Leo. He was desperate. He stopped coming around." Before she entered the bar, she turned back and called out, "I'll stop by the shop sometime." Then she disappeared inside.

Kelly's phone buzzed, and the caller ID said it was Pepper. Thank goodness. "Hey, I need help." She filled Pepper in on the recent events and did her best to avoid explaining why she was at the Thirsty Turtle.

* * * *

"I'm almost back at the boutique," Kelly said after she heaved out a deep breath. The closer she got to the boutique, the more anxious she became because she was going to be greeted by the Pepper glare.

"I can't believe you actually went there." Liv's voice was filled with disbelief even after a ten-minute conversation.

Kelly had called Liv right after the roadside assistance guy left the bar's parking lot. When he arrived, he was curious what a nice girl like Kelly was doing at the Thirsty Turtle. She considered telling him the truth—she was looking for a bookie—but it required too much of an explanation and it was none of his business. So, she opted for a noncommittal shrug and shifted his attention back to the reason he was there—the two flat tires. He took the hint and got to work and, in under an hour, Kelly was driving out of the parking lot of the dive bar and heading home.

Home to the Pepper glare. On second thought, maybe she should have tried her explanation for being at the bar on roadside assistance guy for practice.

"My mind is blown Sabrina works there."

"She goes by Breena these days," Kelly corrected.

"Whatever she goes by, the Thirsty Turtle isn't a nice place to work. But I guess she has to do what she has to do."

"Not all of us have a family business to rely on."

"Yeah, I know. Still, it never had a good reputation. What made you think Leo would even talk to you if he was there? And if he did talk to you, what makes you think he'd say anything about Eddie Singer?"

"What's with the third degree?" The light changed, and Kelly pressed her foot on the gas pedal and steered her vehicle through the intersection. Her boutique came into view. Home sweet home. The first thing she wanted to do was to take a shower and wash the stench of the Thirsty Turtle off of her, but she was certain Pepper would want to have a talk. Kelly also had to figure out a way to pay Pepper back for the new tires.

Liv laughed. "Just prepping you for Pepper. You know she's going to be all over you."

"I guess she has every right to be." Kelly wasn't sure if the flat tires were directed at her personally or if it was just a random act of vandalism. Whatever the reason, paying for the new tires was going to put a serious dent in her dwindling savings account. If she'd gone right back to the boutique, the tires probably wouldn't have been damaged. Sleuthing was turning out to be an expensive proposition.

The minivan ahead of her stopped, and its left blinker went on. It was going to make a left turn across Main Street, just like Kelly needed to do. Behind the row of shops on either side of the main thoroughfare were communal parking lots with a few reserved spots for shop owners and employees. Kelly drummed her fingers on the steering wheel while she waited. There was a long line of oncoming traffic approaching. It was going to be awhile before either she or the minivan moved.

"Don't you have more important things to do than track down Eddie Singer's former bookie?" Liv asked.

"I suppose I do, but I'm not convinced Detective Wolman won't try to pin the murder on me. I hear she gets tunnel vision."

Liv scoffed. "Who told you that?"

"Ariel."

"Ariel Barnes? When did you see her?"

"She came into the shop and we talked. Then I went to her house for dinner."

"What? How awesome! Is everything good between you two?"

Kelly shrugged. "I guess..." Kelly's gaze surveyed Main Street. The sun was setting and, in a few minutes, there'd be significant glare, so she was glad to be home now. She was still getting used to driving again. Her skills were a little rusty. In the city she either got a taxi, scheduled an Uber, or hopped on a subway. People were coming and going from shops, and one woman caught her attention coming out of the boutique. Bernadette? Good grief. What did she want now? "Oh boy."

"What's the matter?"

"Bernadette is leaving the boutique. I don't believe this. Not only do I have to deal with Pepper about the tires, but now also about Bernadette."

"Pepper doesn't like the psychic."

"I know." There was going to be a whole new level to the Pepper glare. Why couldn't the psychic stay away from the boutique? Was there really a spirit in there calling out for help to cross over? What was she thinking? The boutique wasn't haunted. This whole situation was making her crazy and angry. Her friend from Bishop's, Julie, would say she was crangry. Julie loved making up new words, and when she had one too many mojitos, she was practically talking a whole new language.

Bernadette tightened the wrap over her navy wool coat and looked around before continuing to the curb. She was going to jaywalk. The minivan in front of Kelly made the left turn, thanks to a break in the traffic. Seriously, what was with the late-afternoon traffic? It was like summer all over again. Kelly inched up to wait her turn as another stream of oncoming cars approached.

Bernadette stepped off the curb and out between two parked cars and waited until there were no oncoming cars. When the coast was clear, she stepped out from those cars and, just as she was past the rear bumper of a Mercedes sedan, a black van pulled out of a space.

The van sped up toward Bernadette.

Kelly's eyes widened in horror as Bernadette and the van were nanoseconds away from coming together, and not in a good way. She ignored the blaring horn behind her, prompting her to turn.

Why hadn't Bernadette seen or heard the speeding van.

Was she in a trance or something? Kelly shifted her vehicle into park and jumped out of the driver's side.

"Bernadette!" Kelly ran toward Bernadette as more horns blared. But all Kelly was focused on was the speeding van.

Bernadette's head swung to Kelly and then turned to the oncoming van, and she jumped back, landing on her side between two parked cars. Kelly's pace picked up, and the black van sped by her. She caught a glimpse of a male driver, but her attention was on whether or not Bernadette was hurt.

"Hey! You can't leave your car in the middle of the road, lady!" a man shouted.

Kelly scrambled to reach Bernadette and dropped down to her knees beside the psychic. Passersby stopped and started to converge around them. Her heart was pounding, and she was positive it would burst out. *Please, please, please be alive.*

"Bernadette?" Kelly reached her hand out.

Bernadette lifted herself up and sat on the pavement. "Did you see that van? It was like it was coming right for me."

Relief flooded Kelly. Bernadette was alive and looked unharmed from the incident. Kelly's gaze looked around the crowd now surrounding them. Did anyone else see the driver?

"I think you're right. I think he was trying to kill you."

Chapter 14

"My lord, what is going on in Lucky Cove?" Pepper had rushed out from the boutique and elbowed her way through the crowd that formed around Kelly and Bernadette. "Is she okay?" She peered over Kelly's shoulder.

Kelly nodded. "Did someone call 9-1-1?"

There was a round of "yeses" from the crowd.

Bernadette unfurled her body and straightened. "The van came out of nowhere! What was the driver thinking?"

"Did you see the driver?" Kelly asked.

"No! I barely saw the van in time. If you hadn't called out to me…" Tears streamed down Bernadette's face, smudging her mascara. She grabbed hold of Kelly's arm. "You saved my life!"

"Somebody gonna move this car?" a loud irritated voice called out.

"Geez. I totally forgot." Kelly's head swung up to Pepper. "Sorry. I left your car in the middle of the street." She wouldn't be a bit surprised if Pepper rescinded her kind offer to loan Kelly the vehicle.

Pepper exhaled loudly. "Is the key still in it?"

Kelly nodded, and Pepper hurried away to move the vehicle off of Main Street.

The *whoop whoop* siren of an approaching police car drew Kelly's head around just in time for the vehicle to come to a stop and Gabe to exit. The tension that stretched across her shoulders eased at the sight of her good friend. She waved him over and then realized she and Bernadette were hard to miss.

"What happened?" Gabe squatted next to Bernadette. "Are you hurt?"

Bernadette shook her head. "Just a little sore." She reached for her bag and slung it over her shoulder. She struggled to stand but eventually got to her feet.

"Did you recognize the van?" Kelly guided the psychic up off of the sidewalk.

"No, should I have?" Bernadette brushed off her maxi-length skirt.

"Kell, I can take it from here." Gabe stood and pulled out his notepad. "Can you describe the driver?"

"I already told Kelly I didn't see the driver." Bernadette then turned to Kelly at the same time Gabe gave Kelly an annoyed look.

Kelly seemed to be irritating a lot of people lately.

"Can we go into your boutique? I'm not comfortable out here with all these people around."

"Sure. If it's okay with Officer Donovan. I wouldn't want to step on his toes." Kelly cupped Bernadette's elbow and led her into the boutique, without waiting for Gabe to respond. "We can go into the staff room."

Gabe followed Kelly and Bernadette into the boutique, and when they arrived in the staff room, Kelly settled Bernadette at the table and turned around, coming within inches of Gabe's chest. Her gaze traveled upward, and he glared at her. He definitely wasn't happy with her.

"It's more comfortable in here, and your questioning will be easier."

"You think?"

Kelly nodded. "I'll make us some tea." She stepped away to the kitchenette, where she filled a teakettle and set on it on the stove. She pulled three mugs from an upper cabinet.

"Did either of you see the license plate?" Gabe asked.

Both women shook their heads.

Bernadette shrugged out of her coat. "It happened so fast. I walked to the curb and stepped out to cross the street. I know I wasn't in the crosswalk, but there weren't any cars coming." She stared off into space for a moment. "First Maxine's murder and now this." She turned back to face Kelly and Gabe. "I think my family is cursed."

"I don't know about that, but what happened appears to be an accident." Gabe wrote some notes on his pad.

Kelly doubted Gabe's assessment of the incident and opened her mouth to share her opinion when the kettle whistled. Tabling her thought, she prepared three cups of tea for them. She set two mugs on the table and then returned to the counter for her mug.

"Bernadette is correct, it happened so fast. I saw the driver was a male, but I can't tell you any more than that." She took a sip of her tea. "I swear it was deliberate."

"You think the driver intended to run Miss Rydell down?" Gabe looked up from his pad.

"I do! The van pulled out of the space just as Bernadette stepped out between the cars. It was as if the driver was waiting for her. And I think I know who did it."

"But you just said you didn't see the driver," Gabe reminded her.

"I didn't. I don't know his identity, but I believe he's the same person who killed Maxine." Kelly set her mug on the counter with a thump. "Who else would have been driving the van deliberately trying to run Bernadette down? I have a theory."

Gabe looked wary. "I'll bite. What's your theory?"

"I believe she was the target all along." Kelly pointed to Bernadette. Bernadette whimpered.

In an instant, Kelly regretted sounding so matter-of-fact about Maxine's murder, but there was a killer on the loose and she couldn't worry about feelings at the moment. "At the time of Maxine's murder, Bernadette was supposed to be giving a reading to Evan Fletcher. The killer mistook Maxine for Bernadette."

"That's definitely a theory, Kell. Look, let me do my job, and if the driver of the van was the person responsible for Miss Lemoyne's death, we'll find him."

"There's something you don't know about." Kelly pressed her lips together. She couldn't believe she was going to bring up the *murder dress,* but the police needed to know everything. "The day Bernadette collapsed here, she had a vision of a man being murdered while his murderer wore the black lace dress."

Gabe shifted, just a bit. "I'm aware of the incident. All of Lucky Cove is."

"What you don't know is the dress was consigned by Irene Singer." Kelly lunged forward. "Bernadette had a vision about a murder and then Maxine is murdered and then someone tries to run Bernadette down?"

Gabe just stared at Kelly and she huffed.

"Do I need to draw you a map? A map of murder? Oh, I forgot. There's also the threatening note left for me, and there was a guy who tried to break into Granny's rental cottage when I was there all alone. Seriously, think about it. All these events are connected."

"Man, this is above my pay grade." Gabe leaned back in his chair. "You said the driver was a man." Then Gabe looked to Bernadette. "You said the killer in your vision was a woman. I'm not seeing how those two events are connected."

Kelly sighed and threw her hands in the air. "Maybe Irene Singer has a lover."

"Irene Singer? You think she's involved?" Gabe asked.

Kelly propped her hands on her hips. "The black lace dress was consigned by Irene."

"Her husband died in a car accident up in Maine. How exactly did she murder him?"

Kelly sighed again. "I don't know yet." She crossed her arms over her chest and slinked down onto a chair.

"When you figure it out, let me know. I'm going to get some more statements. Miss Rydell, you'll need to come down to the police department to sign your statement. You too, Kelly. You also have that other statement to sign, remember?"

"Thank you, Officer Donovan." Bernadette took a drink of her tea.

Gabe excused himself and walked out of the staff room.

Kelly had to figure out a way to make him at least consider what she'd said, regardless of how unbelievable it sounded. "Be right back." She jumped up and chased after Gabe before he reached the front of the boutique and grabbed his arm. "Hey, I know how all this sounds. Believe me..."

"Kell, it sounds crazy. From the vision she had trying on the dress to you believing Irene Singer killed her husband."

"I admit I don't know how all of these events are connected, but I believe Bernadette is in danger."

"Then let us, the police, do our jobs. I'm sure Detective Wolman will follow up. I'll let you know when the report is ready to sign." Gabe turned and exited the boutique.

Pepper took his place in the hallway, and she didn't look happy. Her glare had taken on a whole new level of scariness. So much so that Kelly took a step back.

"How's business been today?" Kelly asked in a casual sort of way.

"Nice try. I swear if I could ground you, I would, but you're not my kid. With that being said, I care a great deal for you, like you were my own. I have no doubt you were at the Thirsty Turtle because you're trying to figure out who killed Maxine. And what's this I hear about a threatening note and someone coming after you last night at the cottage?"

"I can explain."

"I'm sure you can. And you will. But not now. We're going to close the shop early today. I'm going to drive Bernadette home. You're going

upstairs to your apartment to make something to eat and rest. And think."
Pepper's tone was firm, very maternal.

"Sounds like you're grounding me."

Pepper shrugged. "It does, doesn't it?"

"What am I supposed to think about?"

"If I have to tell you, then you might as well pack up your bags and
sell the business." Pepper swept past Kelly and entered the staff room.

Kelly leaned against the wall. Twenty-six years old and she was
being sent to her room to make her own dinner. And to self-reflect.
Was finding Maxine's killer worth losing the business her grandmother
entrusted to her?

Chapter 15

Kelly draped an infinity scarf over a torso dress form. As she adjusted the scarf, a yawn escaped her lips. She'd had a late night and a restless night's sleep, thanks to the events of the day before. After closing the boutique earlier than usual, she climbed the staircase to her apartment and was greeted by a cuddly Howard. At first, she was suspicious of the show of affection by the feline but, worn down by the day, she scooped him up and accepted his companionship. Maybe he sensed she was in need of a little love. Maybe he missed Granny and was finally willing to accept Kelly into his life. Or, maybe he was just hungry. Kelly smiled. Option three sounded more like the cat she inherited.

She came downstairs to the boutique thirty minutes before opening time so she could steam two of the tunic tops Regina Green consigned. After steaming, she dragged three torsos from the back storage room. She set them on a display table and covered two of them with tunics. The tops were in deep, rich jewel tones, perfect for Thanksgiving dinner or a Friendsgiving gathering. The infinity scarf, a watercolor of purple hues, came from another display table. Now combined with the eggplant-colored tunic, it was striking.

The middle torso was adorned with three necklaces. She mixed metals and sizes for a visual impact and added a wide belt at the base of the form. The third torso had a chunky necklace wrapped around the collar of the tunic. She stepped back and surveyed the display.

Pleased with the visual appeal, she tidied up the jewelry she'd displayed on the table. She'd gathered all of the bracelets and rings the store had on consignment and arranged them on the table for maximum impact.

One ring in particular, an oval leopard-print faux stone set in a six-prong golden base, called to her, but she was trying to make money and not spend it. Resisting anything leopard-print was a struggle. She caught a quick glimpse of her shoes—leopard-print loafers, enough said. She stacked a bunch of bangles in a rainbow of colors. She couldn't resist. She reached for a black-and-white-striped fashion bracelet and slipped it over her hand. It looked good. Though, it didn't go with the outfit she chose when she opened her closet after stepping out of the shower. She'd slipped on a midnight-navy velvet skirt and half tucked in a cotton collarless shirt. She took off the bracelet and set it back on the table.

"Kelly!"

Pepper's voice drew Kelly's attention from the display, and a moment later Pepper emerged from the staff room, carrying a travel mug, her Dooney and Bourke hobo purse hanging from her shoulder.

"Good morning."

"Not for long." Pepper scooted over to the sales counter and set her mug and hobo down. "Camille just texted me. Ralph is on his way over."

Kelly rolled her eyes. "What's with him? I told him I wasn't using his roofing guy."

Pepper walked across the sales floor and joined Kelly at the new display. "We all know he doesn't take no for an answer." She took a step closer to the display. "This is…interesting."

Kelly brightened. "You think so? The tops are from Regina Green."

Pepper folded her arms over her chest and then lifted one arm and tapped her cheek with a finger. "Very…different from Martha's displays."

Exactly what Kelly intended. Not only did the merchandise in the boutique need an upgrade, so did the visual merchandising. Luckily for Kelly, she took two classes on the topic while in fashion school and was involved in the window displays at Bishop's when she first started working in the buying office.

"It's the rule of three. It keeps the eyes moving around the display." Kelly adjusted a few more bracelets before she was satisfied with the overall display.

"If you say so."

"I finished my article for *Budget Chic* last night after I made a quick dinner of mac 'n' cheese."

Pepper nodded. "I'm glad you had a productive evening."

Kelly's head swiveled, and Pepper came into full view. "That's all you have to say? After yesterday when you sent me to my room?"

Pepper cracked a smile. "I did no such thing. You're a grown-up."

The bell over the front door jingled, and both women looked expectantly toward the door, only to be disappointed by the arrival of Ralph. It was a contest to see which one sighed the deepest as his heavy footsteps marched into the boutique.

"Quite a mess you have here." He came to an abrupt halt, his gaze fixated on the new pyramid display.

Pepper leaned into Kelly. "I now see what you mean by keeping the eyes moving. He looks confused."

Kelly stifled a laugh and shooed Pepper away. Pepper took the hint and walked back to the sales counter, where she sipped her coffee.

"What are you talking about, Uncle Ralph?"

"I heard all about the near hit-and-run yesterday outside the shop. And Nora told me that you told Gabe the psychic chick had a vision of murder and you suspect Irene Singer."

Well, wasn't he the busy bee?

"Since you heard all that, I'm not sure why you're here. I have nothing new to add." The fact he referred to Detective Wolman by her first name didn't escape Kelly. Ralph was deeply rooted in Lucky Cove, and there wasn't much he didn't know.

He sniffled and wiped his nose with the sleeve of his drab brown blazer. Classy. "The chief says Nora isn't happy you've inserted yourself into her case."

Kelly propped a hand on her hip. Nora and the chief of police. Her uncle was quite chummy with the local law enforcement.

"Is that so? Well, since she's looking at me as a suspect, I have every right to clear my name. Now, is there any other reason you're here? I do have a business to run."

Ralph took an exaggerated look around the empty shop. "Yes, yes, I can see how busy you are. How do you manage?" His smirk didn't last too long, a fit of coughing overtook him and his face turned beet red as he made disgusting gagging noises.

Kelly took a few steps back.

"Would you like a glass of water?" she offered halfheartedly. She'd prefer he leave and never step foot in the boutique again.

"No...I'm...good," he said between coughs. With the coughing fit over, he shoved his hands into his pants pockets. "Look, kid, we both know this place ain't for you. Your life isn't here in Lucky Cove anymore, it's back in the city. Let me pay you a fair price for this rundown building. Then you can get back to your life."

Fair price for who? Kelly had known Ralph her entire life, and there was no way he'd pay her a decent price for the building, because it would cut into any profit he'd receive when he sold the property.

"Thank you for your concern about my life, but I'm good. I'm staying."

"Stubborn. Just like your mother and grandmother." He took a step forward. His close proximity had her wrinkling her nose in disgust; his cologne was overpowering. His expression seemed determined. "I have friends in the city. I can get you a nice apartment. Even a break on the rent."

Ralph did know people in the real estate market in the city. Several of them bought weekend homes in Lucky Cove from him. The offer was tempting since she'd probably end up with a nicer place than the one she'd just moved out of, but the fact remained, the chances of her landing a job in fashion retail was zilch. A big fat zero because of Serena Dawson. She probably could get a job in public relations or editorial, but she loved buying, she loved retail.

"Thanks but no thanks. I'm happy here." Well, as happy as a gal could be who was saddled with a failing business and who was also a murder suspect. Happy was a relative term, she guessed.

"Even though you'll have to face the biggest mistake of your life every day now that you're back in town? Ariel works just down the street. And let's face it, it's not like you're close to your sister anymore."

Did he really just go there? Kelly's spine stiffened, and her hands balled into fists. She wanted to believe he couldn't be so insensitive, but he was taking a page out of his playbook. Go for the weakest link. Go for the jugular. She might have been his blood, his family, but that didn't matter to Ralph Blake. When he looked at her, all he saw were the dollar signs he wasn't getting his grubby hands on. Her stomach rolled. Disgust and anger and sadness washed over her, leaving her nauseous. And his cologne wasn't helping her stomach.

If she took him up on his offer, she'd be running away…again. Maybe everyone was right about her when she left for college and stayed in the city. Putting that distance between her and the past meant she didn't have to continually face the consequences of her actions. Maybe that was also a reason why Granny left her the shop. To own it meant she'd have to stay in Lucky Cove, and that would force her to face the past and deal with it.

"You can leave now." She breezed past him and stopped at a circular rack of blouses. She wanted to tell him off, to use words Pepper would disapprove of, but Ralph wasn't worth the effort. She'd only be sinking down to his level. As much as staying in town and dealing with the past scared the daylights out of her, she wasn't about to give Ralph the satisfaction of knowing she believed she couldn't cut it as a business owner or as an adult willing to own up to past mistakes.

Ralph swung around. His cheeks puffed out, and his eyes bulged. "You're making a big mistake, missy."

"Honoring Granny's wishes isn't a mistake." *So there!*

The bell over the front door chimed, and a woman entered the boutique. "Looks like customers are coming back." Kelly gave a cocky smile. "If you'll excuse me." She strutted over to the nicely dressed woman in a taupe-colored leather jacket. The woman's head was covered in a knit cap, and she held a sleek satchel in one hand. Kelly hoped the woman also had clothing to consign. "Welcome. Is there something in particular you're looking for?" She tossed a glance over her shoulder to Ralph.

The woman smiled. "Are you Kelly Quinn?"

Kelly nodded. "Yes, how can I help you today?"

"It's nice to meet you." The woman reached into her satchel and pulled out a folded document and handed it to Kelly. "You've been served. Have a nice day." The woman spun around and dashed out of the store before Kelly could utter a word.

"What?" Kelly began to follow the woman as she unfolded the document and scanned its contents. She stopped in her tracks. Her jaw dropped as she read. "I don't believe this."

"Where's your customer going?" Ralph approached his niece. "What do you have there? Legal documents?"

Kelly pressed the document to her chest. "None of your business! Weren't you leaving?"

Ralph grinned. "You just let me know when you're ready to do the sensible thing, and your uncle Ralphie will be happy to help you." He gave a curt nod and left the boutique.

Pepper wasted no time in rushing to Kelly's side. "I got the feeling that old blowhard would never leave. What have you got there?"

"I'm being sued."

"By who?"

"Dorothy Mueller."

"Whatever for? She's such a sweet old lady." Pepper snatched the document out of Kelly's hand. "Emotional distress? One hundred thousand dollars? Good lord!"

"She's claiming the chair she bought here is haunted. She can't be serious. This has to be some kind of Halloween prank. Some sick Halloween prank."

"This is getting completely out of hand, Kelly." Pepper drifted back to the sales counter and laid the document down. "Her lawyer is Mark Lambert. I don't know him."

"Huh?" Kelly looked around the shop before her gaze landed on Pepper. "I don't have one hundred thousand dollars. This could wipe me out. I could lose the business."

"You need a lawyer. How about Sam?" Pepper suggested.

"He handled the will. I don't know if he can handle this lawsuit. I can't afford to pay a lawyer."

"You can't afford not to have a lawyer. Don't worry, honey, Earl and I will help you. We're not going to let crazy old Dorothy Mueller take away your granny's business."

"Thanks." Kelly walked to the counter. "I can't put it off any longer. I have to go see Caroline." It wasn't how she wanted to repair her fractured relationship with her estranged sister, but she needed legal advice—civil and criminal. "Can you hold down the fort?"

Pepper reached over the counter and covered Kelly's hand with hers and squeezed. "You go do what you need to do. I've got this." Her encouraging smile fortified Kelly, and she was grateful.

* * * *

Kelly pushed open the door and entered the reception area of the law practice. Set off of the main road in East Hampton, Gilbert and Reese Attorneys at Law were housed in a tidy, white Cape Cod home with a capable-looking receptionist in the midst of ending a phone call. While the woman wrapped up the call, Kelly browsed the small waiting area.

A comfortable sofa with two armchairs anchoring the seating area, a coffee table covered with a variety of magazines, and several potted plants scattered throughout the space. It appeared Caroline had landed in a good practice. Something she'd always dreamed about and worked hard for.

"How may I help you?" the woman asked from behind her desk.

Kelly approached the desk. "I'm here to see Caroline Quinn."

"Do you have an appointment?" The dark-haired-with-gray-roots woman lifted the reading glasses from the chain dangling around her neck to check the calendar on her desk.

"No, I don't."

The receptionist frowned as she lowered her glasses. The whole trend of wearing reading glasses as a fashion accessory boosted sales of those glasses and boosted the egos of many "of a certain age" women because they clutched on to the belief they were rocking the "sexy librarian vibe." Unfortunately, not every woman could pull off the "sexy librarian look," and Kelly was staring at one of those women.

"I'm her sister, Kelly. It's important I speak with her." She'd considered calling but worried Caroline would put her through to voice mail. No, the conversation they needed to have was better in person.

"Her sister? Well, then let me tell her you're here. It'll be a moment." The receptionist stood and scampered into the back of the house, her stiletto heels tapping on the hardwood floor. A few moments later she reappeared and led Kelly to her sister's office.

"I wasn't expecting to see you." Caroline lifted her head from the laptop computer open on her desk.

"I wasn't expecting to be here." Kelly stepped farther into the office as the receptionist exited and pulled the door shut, leaving the sisters alone. "Thank you for seeing me."

"Luann said it's important. What's wrong now?" It was hard to tell if Caroline ever gave her resting bitch face some down time.

"I need a referral for an attorney. Maybe two or three, actually."

"Two or three? Wow, this is going to be good. Have a seat and tell me what's going on." Caroline pushed her chair back and reclined. She and Kelly were the same height and had the same eyes and hair color, though Caroline's blond hair was cropped short, giving her a more severe look. She rested her elbows on the arms of the chair and clasped her hands together. The tie detail on the sleeves of her green cashmere sweater hinted at the playful, girly side of Caroline she preferred to keep repressed. But, Kelly knew better than anybody fashion had a way of telling people who you were even if you didn't realize it. Caroline's style vibe was Ann Taylor with a touch of Lily Pulitzer. The golden tassel earrings she wore were all Lily.

"Well, it started with a psychic."

Caroline arched a perfectly sculpted eyebrow. "Sounds like the start of a bad joke."

"Trust me. It's no bad joke." Kelly gave her sister all the gory details in a condensed version of Bernadette's vision and Maxine's murder. "The police detective has said I have a motive for the murder. She also told Bernadette she has a motive. We're both suspects."

"You both need a criminal defense lawyer. I do know a few I can refer both of you to. Just be sure you don't use the same lawyer, for your own protection," Caroline said.

124 *Debra Sennefelder*

Their relationship was rocky, but Caroline's legal advice was solid. She'd graduated at the top of her class and had several offers when she left law school. Kelly was in good hands, at least from a legal standpoint.

"I understand," Kelly said.

"Where does a third lawyer come in?"

"I need one to defend me in a civil case." Kelly dug into her suede tote bag for the document she was served with earlier that morning and handed it to Caroline.

Caroline pored over the documents then lifted her gaze to Kelly. "You sold her a haunted chair?"

"I sold her a chair. It's not haunted."

"What makes her think it's haunted?"

"She was in the boutique when a medium, Valeria Leigh, showed up and held a séance and said that another chair in the shop was haunted."

"What on earth is going on at Granny's consignment shop?" Caroline tossed the document on her desk.

"Well, it's my consignment shop now, and I have no idea why every ghost whisperer on Long Island has decided to conjure up spirits there. And that stupid website, Lulu Loves Long Island, isn't helping me. Neither is Frankie. I found him at the séance."

Caroline cracked a rare smile. "He does love all the hocus pocus stuff. He lives for this time of the year."

"Tell me about it. Caroline, I can't afford to defend myself against Dorothy's insane lawsuit plus hire a criminal defense lawyer."

"I get it. Although I don't advise it, you could hold off retaining counsel in the matter of the police investigation. Have you given a statement?"

"I did."

"Okay. Have there been any follow-up interviews?"

"Just one. I have nothing to hide. I didn't kill Maxine."

"If the police want to question you again regarding this matter, don't say anything. Call me first. While I'm not a criminal defense lawyer, I know when a client should keep her mouth shut. Then I can get you a lawyer. As for this civil case, you really don't have the luxury of not hiring an attorney. Or, you can settle. Even then, I strongly suggest having counsel."

Any hope Kelly had of not having to spend more money vanished. Poof. Just like that. "I can't believe any jury would award her any money. It's such a crazy claim."

"I agree."

"But I still have to hire a lawyer?"

"You do. I make it a policy not to represent family. I'll call a friend of mine and see if he'll take the case. I'll ask him to try and discount his services."

Kelly breathed a deep sigh of relief. It was something, at least. "I'd appreciate it. I guess I should let you get back to work. Thank you." She stood and took back the legal document.

Caroline walked her to the door, and they stood there looking at each other. Emotion caught in Kelly's throat, remembering the last time they stood side by side. Granny's funeral. There was the obligatory hug and murmured words of sorrow, but there was a deep divide between them.

Caroline pressed her lips together as her head tilted slightly. "It's going to take some time."

Kelly knew her sister wasn't talking about any legal problems. "I know."

"I'm willing to try."

"That's all we can do, right? Thanks." Kelly pulled opened the door and left the law offices, confident she'd be well-represented and, with a small glimmer of hope, that somehow she and Caroline could rebuild their relationship.

Chapter 16

Kelly ramped up the windshield wipers' speed. She had heard the prediction for rain but had ignored it. Big mistake. The drops were coming down harder and faster. She'd left the boutique at the spur of the moment to visit Caroline and hadn't grabbed an umbrella; though, by the size of the tote she lugged around there, should've been one in there already. She flicked on the right turn signal and slowed to take the corner.

By some miracle, she still had the car keys. Pepper hadn't rescinded her generous offer to let Kelly drive her SUV. Though, Kelly was certain a conversation about the cost of the new tires was imminent, which meant she might be losing the keys soon if she couldn't pay for the new tires. Pepper had offered to help her pay for a lawyer, or two, but she couldn't accept money from her granny's best friend. She was an adult, after all.

An adult whose life had been thrown into utter chaos since her firing at Bishop's. When she returned home to her one-bedroom apartment with her entire career stuffed into a cardboard box, there wasn't anyone there to greet her. No one to pull her into a reassuring hug or make her a cup of tea. Though, she did pass by the building superintendent sweeping the sidewalk and got a curt nod from him. She'd managed to go through boyfriend after boyfriend, citing she liked her independence, but now, looking back, she wondered if she was too discerning. Too picky.

Wasn't hindsight a lovely tool? She could look back and see the errors of her ways.

At least now she had Howard to come home to.

Great. She'd gone from a fashionable single career woman to a cat lady in a matter of months.

In the distance, flashing strobe lights from a police car caught her attention and dragged her thoughts from her midtwenties life crisis to up ahead on the road. She slowed down. A police car was parked in front of Ariel's house. Panic stirred inside Kelly as her grip on the steering wheel tightened. What had happened now?

Up ahead of the police car she found a space and parked her vehicle. Not willing to risk her suede tote to the weather, she left the bag on the passenger seat and removed the car key from the ignition. She made her way around her vehicle and hurried to the front door of Ariel's house. As she approached, she caught a glimpse of the officer, and it wasn't Gabe. Not that she didn't want to see him, but she'd seen him at every crime scene she'd been at in Lucky Cove. It was time for someone new.

The officer stood inside the open front door talking with Ariel, who looked more stressed than the last time Kelly had seen her. Then again, there was good food and a bottle of wine involved the other night. Ariel's chocolate-brown corduroy jacket was unbuttoned, but her Burberry scarf was tied tightly around her neck. Her cell phone, which dinged with a notification, sat on her lap.

Ariel glanced down at her phone. "My dad is on his way."

"Hey, what's going on?" Kelly swooped in and gave Ariel a big hug. "You okay?"

"Yeah, I'm good considering someone broke into my house."

Kelly pulled herself up. "What? Were you home when it happened?" Visions of a home invasion froze Kelly in place.

"Fortunately, Miss Barnes wasn't home at the time of the incident," the officer said.

Kelly turned in his direction. About as young as Gabe, though his hair color was several shades darker than Gabe's beachy blond, he had the same kind eyes and solid build. The bonus dealing with the new officer was he didn't know who Kelly was or her long, recent list of run-ins with the law.

"You're Kelly Quinn, right?" he asked.

So much for being anonymous. "I am." She turned back to Ariel. "Was anything stolen?"

"My files from the desk. It looks like someone jimmied the back door and tossed my workspace." Ariel moved her wheelchair farther into the house. "It's getting a little chilly."

"Yes, yes, I'll finish this up and come back to see you before I leave." The officer spun around and closed the door after him.

"Want some tea? I have a new flavor. Salted caramel." Ariel turned her wheelchair around.

"Sounds delicious. Love some." Kelly followed Ariel to the kitchen. "Where were you when this happened?"

"Working at the library."

Kelly dropped into a chair at the table. "Have you spoken to DJ Brown yet?"

"I did. Yesterday afternoon, but he refused to give me an interview. He was very abrupt." Ariel filled the electric kettle, took two mugs off of the stainless-steel mug tree on the counter, and moved over to the table, where Kelly had settled. "What's wrong, Kelly? You have a weird look on your face."

"I don't want to scare you."

"Too late." Ariel wheeled to the refrigerator and grabbed a carton of milk.

"The intruder could have been Maxine's killer."

Ariel set the milk carton on the table. As Kelly expected, Ariel's face paled but, to her credit, she rebounded quickly. "Why would the killer want to steal my files? Everything I have is public knowledge. I don't have anything the police don't already know about Maxine's fraud scam." She unwrapped the scarf from her neck and set it on the table.

"The killer may not know that, and maybe he or she wanted to see how much information you do have."

"I guess you could be right. You know, it could also have been Bernadette. She might be trying to scare me off from writing the article. Then again, I don't know if she knows I'm writing it."

"You said you went for a reading."

"I did. But I didn't tell her I was a freelance writer."

"If she's psychic, then she knew."

"If she's psychic, she doesn't have anything to worry about." The kettle whistled, and Ariel moved to the counter and filled both mugs with hot water and dropped a tea bag in each. She served Kelly her tea and then set her mug down across from Kelly and took a sip of her tea after adding a dash of milk.

"I don't see Bernadette breaking and entering." Kelly added milk to her tea and took a sip. "Yum."

Ariel nodded. "Right?"

For a few minutes, they sat together in companionable silence and drank their tea. Kelly's thoughts were still on the possibility Maxine's killer broke in, and she worried about how vulnerable Ariel was living by herself.

"What are you going to do about the back door?" Kelly asked.

"Dad is going to take a look. He suggested I get a dog. A big dog."
Kelly laughed. "Doesn't sound like a bad idea, considering what's
been happening." When Ariel gave her a puzzled look, she filled Ariel in
on the incident at Granny's rental cottage, the flat tires, the threatening
note written on the flyer, and Bernadette's near-miss hit-and-run.

"Okay, now I'm officially scared. You really think all of this is
connected to Maxine's murder?"

"Actually, I think everything, including Maxine's murder, is connected
to the *murder dress*. Wow, I can't believe I just said that out loud."

"You told me the dress belonged to Irene Singer."

"It did."

"Her husband died up in Maine in a car accident. She was home when
she received the call from the police. She couldn't have killed him."

"Right. We've been thinking that all along. But she could have killed
another man. Who knows how long she had the dress." After Kelly took
another sip of her tea, she shook her head. "No. I guess I could start
looking into past murders in Lucky Cove."

Ariel had the rim of her mug a few inches from her lips. "You're
seriously going to research old murder cases? Wow. You're not playing
around. Let me save you a little time. There haven't been many and, if I
recall correctly, the murders were solved and the murderers were arrested
and sent to prison." Ariel took a drink of her hot beverage.

Kelly slumped. "Maybe in the surrounding towns? Bernadette didn't
identify the man in her vision."

"You're assuming the vision was real, which it wasn't."

Kelly sipped her tea. "I know. But everything started to go south
when Bernadette put the dress on and had a vision."

"It seems like a distraction."

"What do you mean?"

"Think of a magician. Most of their magic tricks are based on
diverting their audience's attention. Look over here while I really do
this thing over here."

"Irene did come in after Bernadette's vision and wanted the dress back."

"She did? Did you give it to her?"

"No, I told her the dress sold."

"But you still have it."

"I do. Something felt off. The day I asked her about the dress, she got
upset, emotional, and told me she never wanted to see the dress again
and then showed up the next day wanting the dress back."

"You're right. It does sound odd. Why would she want the dress back?"

"Because it's connected to a murder?"

"But how?"

Kelly shrugged. "Forensic evidence? No. The dress was dry-cleaned before she consigned it. Or maybe there's a chance a thread of the dress was discovered at the crime scene." Now her binge-watching of crime shows was finally paying off.

Ariel laughed. "Sounds like a stretch but possible."

Proud of herself, Kelly smiled. She might have a knack for sleuthing after all. She finished her tea and accepted the offer of another cup, while Ariel waited for her dad to show up and fix the back door.

Similar to the damage that was done to her granny's rental cottage, Kelly considered it could have been the same person who broke into both homes. A shiver shot through her at the unsettling thought.

Kelly stayed with Ariel until her dad arrived to survey the damage to the back door. Lucky for Kelly, she hadn't had to deal with fixing the cottage's door. The landlady took care of the repair. Mr. Barnes welcomed Kelly back to Lucky Cove in a big bear hug and insisted she join the Barnes family for dinner soon. Ariel cautioned her dad not to crush Kelly, and that was when he let her go and headed to the back door to assess the damage. Ariel assured Kelly she was okay and her dad would make sure no one else would be able to break into the house. As Kelly left, she overheard Mr. Barnes on the phone with a security alarm service.

There was a good chance Ariel could've been hurt if she was present when the intruder entered her house, and Kelly couldn't shake the feeling the intruder was connected to Maxine's death and to Bernadette's vision. She was supposed to head back to the boutique, but she decided to take the long way. Eleven years ago, Kelly hadn't been able to protect Ariel, but now she could, and she was going to start with Mr. Brown.

The man, whether he wanted to or not, was going to tell her everything he knew about the day Maxine was killed, and he wasn't going to slam the door in her face again.

She arrived at DJ's house and turned into his driveway. As she shifted into park, her gaze flicked over to Dorothy Mueller's house next door. To think she went out of her way to deliver the chair Dorothy was now suing her over. She'd struggled to get it into the cargo section of the SUV and carried the big, awkward piece of furniture not only through Dorothy's front door but into the living room and moved it three times before Dorothy decided after all she wanted it in the small entry hall. Kelly lifted the chair a fourth time and lugged it back out to the foyer. And how was her hard labor rewarded? A lawsuit, thank you very much. She was tempted to pay Mrs. Mueller a visit after she was done with DJ Brown. Shutting off the ignition, she glanced out the passenger window and noticed a familiar car. What on earth was Bernadette doing there? She pushed open the car door and stepped out into the damp, raw day. The rain had eased up to a light shower. She tugged her coat closer to her body as she walked along the concrete path to the open front door.

Not again.

The last time she let herself into a house, she found a dead body, and her whole world was turned upside down. Every fiber of her body screamed for her to turn and get the hell out of there, so why were her feet taking her over the threshold into the house?

Déjà vu all over again.

Turn. Run. Get out now!

The hairs on the back of her neck rose. Before taking another step, she debated calling for help but wasn't certain she needed it. Yet. She heard a whimper. And then another. She continued forward in the hall until she came to the opening to the living room, and she stopped dead in her tracks.

Two bent khaki-covered legs stuck out from behind the sofa, and a familiar blonde stood over the prone form of DJ Brown.

Bernadette backed away from the body. She held her hands out and stared at them. She looked disgusted at the sight of them.

"What happened here?" Kelly's words were clipped. She was fighting back a wave of nausea.

"I didn't kill him. I swear! I didn't!"

"Oh, God, I'm going to be sick." Kelly's stomach flip-flopped violently, and she covered her mouth with her hand as she dashed out of the room. She'd caught sight of a powder room across the hall and ran into it, closing the door behind her. With just moments to spare, she vomited. Her whole body contracted with each heave until there was nothing left inside of her. She slowly straightened up with her hands gripping the pedestal sink. She stared into the mirror.

What was going on? How could she find another body? A second murder, and both times Bernadette was present. She knew for certain she wasn't the murderer, so that left...

A loud thump on the door startled Kelly, and she jumped.

"I swear, I didn't kill him. I found him dead," Bernadette pleaded through the door.

"Call 9-1-1. Get some help!" Trapped in a bathroom with a possible murderer banging on the door wasn't how Kelly envisioned her visit to

DJ Brown going. Another strike to the door ratcheted up Kelly's fear to downright terror. Her heart pumped so hard she was certain it would burst out, and her head was on overload with indecision.

If Bernadette refused to call 9-1-1, then Kelly would. Her phone. She shoved her hands into her coat pockets. No phone. Where was it? Her eyes closed as she berated herself for not bringing her tote bag into the house with her, because her phone was in the bag. She needed to rethink her accessories because suede bags weren't the most practical accessory in rainy weather or when there was a possible murderer trying to get access to you.

"Please, Kelly, you have to believe me. I'm not a murderer. I couldn't hurt anyone. I got a message from Mr. Brown to come over, and I found him dead!" Bernadette's voice was thick with sorrow, and she dissolved into deep sobs.

Kelly's resolve weakened as she chewed on her lower lip. There was the possibility Bernadette was telling the truth. Someone could've been trying to frame her. Maybe that was why she was almost run down yesterday. Maybe the murderer didn't think the police were acting swiftly enough to arrest her, forcing the perpetrator to take matters into his own hands. When the attempt on her life failed, he then decided to murder DJ Brown and set Bernadette up to take the fall.

The theory was out there, way out there, but plausible.

"I don't know why this is happening to me." Bernadette's voice had drifted away. "Why bother?" Her last two words were barely audible, but Kelly, pressed against the door, heard them.

Knowing she couldn't hide in the bathroom forever—she needed to get help—Kelly unlocked the door and pulled it open. Her breath caught at the sight of streaks of blood on the white door from where Bernadette had pounded her fists.

Before Kelly could react, Bernadette grabbed her by the wrist with her bloodied hand. Her long golden curls were now wild and uncontrolled, and her normally empathetic eyes were ablaze with fury.

Kelly screamed and tried to pull away from Bernadette, but her grip was too tight.

"We have to leave!" Bernadette dragged Kelly from the bathroom.

Kelly struggled. She wasn't going anywhere with the psychic. "We have to call the police." She was starting to sound like a broken record.

"No! They'll think I did it."

"The man has been murdered."

"We're in grave danger."

"We? Or do you mean me?"

Bernadette's head snapped up, and she looked as if she'd been slapped in the face. "I wouldn't hurt you. I haven't hurt anyone. You have to believe me." She yanked on Kelly's arm again.

Kelly put all of her weight into her heels to make it harder for Bernadette to drag her. "What about all those people who pay you money to communicate with their deceased loved ones or ask for guidance based on your gift? Maxine was about to be arrested in Chicago because she scammed people."

Bernadette ceased trying to pull Kelly to the front door. "You know?"

"Yes."

"She never had the gift. She lied to people."

"I'm calling the police. Give me your phone."

"Please don't. I beg of you. They'll arrest me."

"This isn't up for discussion." Kelly extricated her wrist from Bernadette's grasp and turned it palm side up. She willed her hand to stop trembling, but it was no use. "Your phone."

"I'm sorry, Kelly. No."

"Fine. I'll get my phone." Kelly stepped forward, intent on passing psychic girl and heading out the front door, when she was unexpectedly shoved by Bernadette. Shocked by the attack, Kelly stumbled backward and lost her balance. She landed on the hardwood floor. Her head struck the floor, and mini-lights, like fireworks, went off as a shot of pain zipped through her head. *"I'm sorry, Kelly,"* echoed in her mind.

Bernadette became blurry, and then everything went black.

* * * *

"Kelly, can you hear me?"

Kelly stirred at the sound of her name. "What?" she mumbled as her eyes slit open. Light hit her baby blues hard, and she cringed. "What happened?"

"We're hoping you can tell us."

Kelly's eyes opened completely. Her vision was blurry, but she was able to make out Gabe. He was beside her, his hand on her shoulder. There was someone behind him. Sharply creased navy pants. Kelly blinked a few more times, and her vision cleared up. The blurriness was gone, a good thing, she thought. What wasn't good was when Kelly's gaze traveled upward and she saw Detective Wolman frowning at her.

Kelly looked around the entry hall. Where was she? This wasn't her home. How did she end up on the floor?

"There's an ambulance on the way for you." Detective Wolman squatted next to Kelly and Gabe. "What are you doing here?"

"I don't know. Where am I?"

There were snippets of memory, but they kept slipping away.

"DJ Brown's rental house," Gabe answered.

DJ Brown? Kelly pushed herself up against Gabe's protest. "I came to see him? Why?" She searched her memory, and a few pieces of it connected. "The break-in." She was now seated upright, and her head throbbed. She instinctively rubbed the back of her head, which did nothing to make her feel any better.

"What break-in?" Gabe asked.

"What are you talking about, Miss Quinn?" The detective flipped open her notepad.

"The break-in at Ariel's house. On my way home from East Hampton, I drove by Ariel's house, and there was a police car there. I went to see what had happened. Someone broke into her house and stole her files. When I left her house, I decided to come here and to talk to DJ Brown. I wanted to find out exactly what he knew about the day Maxine was murdered. And to see if he's the one who broke into Ariel's house."

"You expected him to confess if he was the killer or the burglar?" Wolman didn't bother to hide her skepticism.

Kelly shrugged. "It was worth a try. I arrived and..." A flood of memories came back. "Ohmigod, he's dead. He was stabbed!" She pointed in the direction of the living room, where she caught a glimpse of uniformed police officers. "I found him with Bernadette standing over his body. Her hands were bloodied! I got sick and ran to the bathroom." She pointed toward the open bathroom door. "She followed me. She pounded on the door until I came out. She said she didn't kill him. I didn't have my phone! I couldn't call for help. I came out because...I had to get help...She grabbed me." Kelly looked at her arm and the sleeve of her camel-colored coat smeared with dry blood. DJ Brown's blood. Her body trembled, and she fought back a scream.

Gabe squeezed her shoulder. He must've seen the panic building in her. "You're safe now."

Kelly nodded and struggled to maintain her calmness; her heart raced, and her breathing was becoming shallow. "She wanted me to go with her."

"Where?" Detective Wolman asked.

Kelly dragged in a deep breath and let it exhale slowly. She needed to calm down or she feared she'd pass out. "I don't know. She didn't say. She just wanted us to leave. When I refused to go with her, she pushed me and I fell. I must have hit my head." Kelly looked around at the small space they occupied. She remembered falling.

"Two murders, and you're at both of them. Somehow I'm not sensing it's only a coincidence." Wolman flipped her notepad closed and straightened up.

"I didn't kill him. I had no reason to." Kelly rubbed her temple. She'd landed on the side of her head when she fell. She didn't doubt the throbbing pain that spread across and around her head would last well into the next day.

"We'll see about that. The ambulance will take you to the hospital to be examined. Expect to be questioned again, and you may want to have a lawyer present." Wolman turned and exited the hall and then disappeared into the living room.

The voices of the other officials filtered through the hallway, and Kelly digested everything that had happened. Why couldn't she just have left well enough alone and gone home like a normal person? Why did she insist on confronting DJ Brown?

She made a move to stand up, but Gabe stopped her. "Whoa. You're not moving. And I'll call Caroline for you."

Kelly covered Gabe's hand with hers and squeezed. It was good to have a friend. "Thanks. She did say I should have a lawyer present if I was questioned again. Was what I just said okay?"

"You told the truth. That's always okay."

"What about Bernadette?"

"We'll locate her and bring her in for questioning also."

"You know, DJ Brown had a motive for Maxine's murder. He and his mother were swindled out of thousands of dollars by Maxine. He used a fake name when he booked his appointment with Bernadette the day Maxine was killed."

"How do you know all this?"

"Ariel. She's working on a story for a magazine about psychic scams."

Now it was Gabe's turn to look confused. "I didn't realize you two had reunited."

"We have, and she's been helping me. DJ Brown had a motive to kill Maxine. But who had a motive to kill him? I hate to think this, but Bernadette could have killed him out of revenge if she believed he murdered Maxine."

Sirens approached, Kelly's ride to the county hospital for evaluation. She couldn't believe Bernadette pushed her hard enough to knock her unconscious. How could Bernadette have done such a thing? She never thought the psychic was capable of such a violent act, and now she had to rethink her opinion of whether Bernadette was a killer or not.

Chapter 17

Kelly crawled out of bed slowly and unfolded her achy body one vertebra at a time. Even after a full night's sleep, she was exhausted and sore. A wicked combination for any weekday morning. Back in the city working for someone else, she would have called out sick, dove back into bed, and pulled the covers over her head, but now self-employed, she didn't have the luxury of sick days.

A soft meow from the foot of her bed drew her attention. Howard had unfurled himself from the tight ball he'd contorted into after he joined her last night. He stretched out his long, lean body, and Kelly envied how easy it was for him.

"Show off," she grumbled as she took baby steps to the bathroom, all the while cursing her aching bones.

She turned on the faucet and splashed water on her face, which was in desperate need of concealer, highlighter, and false eyelashes. Where to start? Liv had shown up last night, just as Kelly returned home from the emergency room, with a bag of takeout from the only Chinese restaurant in Lucky Cove. By the time they'd finished dinner, Kelly had gotten some good news and some bad news from Gabe.

The good news was Kelly's fingerprints weren't a match for the prints on the knife used to kill DJ Brown. The bad news was Bernadette hadn't been located and Detective Wolman had more questions for Kelly. Kelly drowned her sorrows in extra servings of chicken lo mein and beef with broccoli and was now suffering the puffiness of her indulgence.

She pulled open a drawer in the vanity and took out a packet of anti-puffiness smoothing eye patches and applied them under her eyes. The box of six packets that cost over a hundred dollars, which used to be offset by her Bishop's employee discount, was a splurge, but the eye patches did work miracles. And really, could you put a price tag on miracles?

The eye patches took ten minutes to work their magic, then Kelly padded to the kitchen to make a pot of coffee. Howard joined her and rubbed his body along her leg.

"You're hungry?" Another rub and a loud meow told her she was right. She filled his bowl with food and bent over to set the bowl down for him. Every muscle fiber in her body hurt, making the movement slow and painful.

Howard groused an urgent meow. He apparently didn't understand the condition his new owner was in.

"Impatient, much?" She finally put the bowl on the floor, and the return to straighten up was just as slow and painful.

It was going to be a long, torturous day.

Her cell phone dinged and alerted her to a new email. She snatched up the phone from her nightstand. Heather from *Budget Chic.* She swiped open the correspondence and read. Heather wanted another article. Kelly wanted to jump up and scream, but all she could muster was a smile. Smiling didn't hurt. Two articles didn't make a freelance writing career, but it was a start.

She headed back to the bathroom and, after a hot shower, she felt a little better, but her mood was still dark. Her move back to Lucky Cove seemed to have been mired in death. First, her grandmother's passing, and then two murders days apart. Maybe she should accept her uncle's offer and move back to the city. At her closet, she perused her clothing, looking for something easy to wear. In the shower she'd decided on a dress, and now she had to choose which one to put on. Her fingertips landed on a gray wool godet-flounce sheath dress.

Her next choice was footwear, and that was easy—a pair of black ballet flats. The only thing she had to wrangle herself into was a pair of tights.

Dressed, the cat fed, and her travel mug filled to the brim with pumpkin spice coffee, Kelly made her way down the staircase to open the boutique with a small sense of accomplishment. The events of the day before still weighed heavily on her shoulders, but she had a business to run and an employee to make sure had a job come the next week. After a drink of her coffee, she set the mug on the sales counter and went to the front door to unlock. She flipped over the open sign.

Back at the sales counter, she read through a note Pepper had left when she closed the shop yesterday. Two women had come in to consign clothing, and the merchandise was hung on the rolling garment rack.

Kelly perked up at the good news. In light of recent events, even a sliver of good news was welcome. She went to the rack and found a dozen items hanging. Among the garments, there was a sequined bomber jacket and a long velvet skirt that together would be a cool, fashionable New Year's Eve outfit paired with some sparkly jewelry. She continued to browse and liked what she saw. Back at the counter, she reviewed the deposit from yesterday and found it was a healthy amount. Maybe things were starting to look up for the business.

When she was done with the deposit, she made a note to buy some fall decorations for outside the boutique at some point during the day. She also had to check out what Christmas decorations were on hand for the boutique. The bell over the door chimed, and Liv entered carrying yet another box from her bakery. Kelly's first inclination was to refuse whatever muffin or pastry Liv offered but, considering what she'd been through, she shouldn't be so hard on herself.

"Apple walnut muffins hot out of the oven." Liv placed the box on the counter and opened its lid.

"You're killing me." Kelly plucked a muffin out of the box.

"You deserve a treat after what you've been through."

"I know!" Kelly took a bite and chewed. "I had a near-death experience."

Liv cocked her head sideways. "A little too dramatic. I'll take these to the staff room." She swiped the box off of the counter just as the bell over the door chimed again. She looked over her shoulder.

Pepper had pushed the door open and walked into the boutique.

"What the..." Liv's voice trailed off.

"I...don't..." Kelly almost dropped her muffin as her eyes nearly popped out of their sockets. Her grandmother's best friend had morphed from oh-so-casual-bordering-on-bland to WOW!

Pepper's color-treated blond hair had been straightened and then styled into soft waves, and she'd traded in her straight-legged dress pants for snake-print leggings and topped them with a wine-colored tunic and pulled on a pair of over-the-knee black suede boots. She'd slid on a pair of black sunglasses that instantly gave her a cool vibe.

"Good morning, girls." Pepper continued to the counter, where she dropped her black leather-studded hobo purse. "Feeling better this morning, Kelly?"

All Kelly could do was stare at Pepper, who looked ten years younger. Just the day before, after returning from the hospital, Pepper looked like her old self. When did the transformation happen? That morning? Pepper just happened to have a pair of snake-print leggings hanging around?

"Kelly, maybe you shouldn't be working today." Pepper took off her sunglasses. Her makeup had been revamped as well. Gone was the barely there eyeshadow and too-pink lipstick. In their place were perfect smoky eyes and shiny rose-colored lips.

"No...no...I'm fine. Forget about me. You...you look amazing," Kelly was finally able to say.

"You do! You look freakin' awesome!" Liv put the pastry box down again and dashed around the counter. She twirled Pepper to get a full look at her. "Freakin' awesome!"

Pepper blushed. "Thank you."

"When did all this happen?" Kelly was still wrapping her mind around the makeover. She had no idea Pepper wanted to have one done. She thought it was a great idea, but a little twinge of sadness hit her because she would've loved to have been a part of it.

"I've been thinking about it for a few days. If I'm going to work at a hip, trendy boutique, then I need to be as cool as the shop. You kids do still say 'cool,' right?"

Kelly and Liv nodded in unison.

"Great. So, I look okay? Not too cougarish?"

"No, no you don't look like a cougar at all. You made a smart choice with the flat over-the-knee boots. If you'd chosen a heel, you'd be too *Pretty Woman*," Kelly said.

"Oh, dear, that wouldn't look good on me at all." Pepper laughed. "I really like these boots." She lifted a leg and straightened it to admire her footwear. "They're comfortable."

"And so fashionable. Looks like I've got some competition." Kelly smiled and wrapped an arm around Pepper's shoulders.

Pepper was finally coming around to the changes in the boutique and, after a few very disastrous days, Kelly was finally smiling.

Pepper gently patted Kelly on the cheek. "Never. You're my inspiration." She looked to Liv and reached out for her hand. "You too. Being around such beautiful, young women is good for this old lady."

They shared a moment of silence before Pepper disengaged from Kelly and Liv.

"Enough of this. I'm gonna cry. It's time to get to work."

For the next few hours, the boutique was steady with customers, so Pepper's husband, Earl, offered to pick up the decorations for outside the boutique. Kelly was grateful because she didn't think her body was in any shape to lift a bale of hay or a pumpkin. By lunch, the sales numbers were good, even though about half of the ladies who came into the boutique wanted to ask questions about the most recent murder. When Kelly picked up on the trend, she disappeared into the staff room and told Pepper to get her if it got too busy.

Settled at the desk, she worked on the new article for *Budget Chic,* inspired by Pepper's change of appearance and attitude. The article was about doing a makeover on a budget. Kelly brainstormed some ideas, visited some websites for items, and started writing.

A ding alerted her to an incoming text.

NEED YOU OUT HERE NOW!

Oh boy.

Kelly saved her work on the computer and stood, cursing her achy body. When she arrived at the sales counter, she found both Frankie and Summer.

Double oh boy.

Summer's injected plump lips were pursed as she tapped her acrylic nails on the counter. Kelly guessed her step-aunt was perturbed because her fancy brochures weren't displayed where she left them. She lifted her head and fixed an irritated gaze on Kelly.

Kelly didn't think Summer would come back into the *thrift* store so soon after her last visit. She wasn't even sure what Pepper did with the brochures.

"What's up?" Kelly asked in her most even-toned voice as she braced herself for whatever onslaught Summer was about to unleash.

"What's up? Is that all you have to say?" Summer pulled her hands off of the counter and propped them on her hips.

"I just wanted to check on my cousin. I heard what happened." Frankie dashed to Kelly's side. He pulled his hands from the front pockets of his dark-rinse slim jeans and hugged Kelly. "You could've been killed."

Kelly grimaced. Frankie's hold around her torso was crushing. "I. Can't. Breathe."

"Sorry." Frankie let go of Kelly quickly. "My bad."

"Thanks. I'm okay. Sore, but I'll survive."

"Good to hear." Summer approached next and stood by her stepson. "Now, you can explain this." Summer held her blinged-out phone to Kelly.

As much as Kelly wanted to be annoyed with Summer for shoving the phone in her face, she couldn't summon up the outrage because she was distracted by the pair of tribal earrings adorning Summer's earlobes.

Kelly drooled over those iconic Dior earrings whenever she saw them in a magazine, but they were out of her price range—forever.

"Well, what do you have to say for yourself?"

Summer's sharp voice snapped Kelly out of her thoughts. Kelly focused her eyes on the phone.

Lulu Loves Long Island. *Not again.* Kelly read as much of the text as she needed to understand what Summer was trying to show her. Lulu had breaking news about Dorothy Mueller's lawsuit against Kelly's boutique.

"You sold her a haunted chair?" Summer lowered the phone and shoved it into the angled pocket of her red fitted double-breasted wool jacket. The pockets had exposed zippers, which gave the classic jacket a modern feel while the epaulets paid homage to tradition. In the neckline of the jacket, Summer had tucked a black faux-fur scarf.

"Get out!" Frankie shouted, turning a few heads from customers in their direction.

"Lower your voice," Kelly said in a hushed tone. She wasn't about to have another scene in her boutique. "Of course I didn't. There's no such thing."

Frankie raised a hand. "You don't know for sure."

"I know for sure none of the merchandise in this boutique is haunted. That includes the chair Dorothy purchased. Good grief. I can't believe we're right back where we started. How did this Lulu chick find out?"

"Probably the court." Pepper returned to the counter with a handful of hangers.

Summer did a double take at Pepper. "Pepper? You look...different."

Pepper touched her hair. "I gave myself a makeover."

"Good for you, Pep!" Frankie turned back to his cousin. "Are you sure you're okay? You could have a concussion."

Summer was still checking Pepper out while Frankie started to wrap his arm around Kelly again. Summer turned her attention back to her stepson and step-niece. She waved a dismissive hand at Kelly. "Look at her, she's fine."

"What medical school did you graduate from?" Frankie challenged.

Summer rolled her eyes. "If she wasn't okay, she wouldn't have been released from the hospital."

"Must be nice to live in a bubble." Frankie's tone deepened, and his easy smile was slipping away fast.

"What's that supposed to mean?" Summer asked.

Frankie put up a palm at Summer. "Never mind. I should get going. I have to go to the market. Call me if you need anything." He gave Kelly a light kiss on the cheek and breezed by his stepmother without a goodbye.

Summer squared her shoulders. "It's been a long time since you lived full-time in Lucky Cove. Let me give you the lay of the land. *Our* family is prominent here. We have a reputation to uphold and you being connected in any way to two murders and this haunting nonsense is not acceptable. It's time you get your act together, Kelly. You're not a kid anymore."

Pepper rushed around to Kelly's side and was about to say something when Kelly grabbed her friend's wrist. She didn't want a scene. There were a few customers in the boutique, and she didn't want to lose any more business.

"Goodbye, Summer." Kelly turned, prompting Pepper to join her, and together they returned to the other side of the sales counter.

Summer huffed. Then she swung around and stalked out of the boutique.

"You know she invited me to Thanksgiving dinner," Kelly said.

"It'll be a bloodbath," Pepper warned.

"Yes, it would be." Kelly leaned on the counter. "Who is this Lulu chick, anyway?"

Pepper shrugged. "No one knows." She stepped away from the sales counter when a customer approached with three dresses in her arms looking for the changing room.

"I'm going to run out for a few minutes." At the end of her rope with all the haunting craziness swirling around the boutique, Kelly was going to do the only thing that wouldn't cost her money—plead her case to Dorothy's lawyer.

While she was at her desk earlier, she'd reviewed the legal document she was served and realized Mark Lambert's office was just down the street. She dashed back into the staff room and grabbed the box of muffins Liv had delivered earlier. Since she'd eaten one, the muffins looked uneven. She took out one and set it aside. Now there were four muffins, and it didn't look like she was regifting baked goods. She closed the box, grabbed her leather jacket and tote bag, and headed out, fingers crossed she could convince the lawyer to convince his client she was crazy for suing her over a haunted chair.

Yeah, she'd have to rephrase her request.

Kelly pulled open the boutique's front door and stepped outside. She was greeted first by a cold wind and then a lovely autumnal vignette consisting of a bale of hay, three pumpkins in various sizes, and three potted mums. Earl had not only picked up the decorations, he actually decorated the exterior of the boutique.

She was falling more in debt to the Donovans each day.

As Kelly speed-walked along Main Street, she wondered how Earl felt about Pepper's makeover. How did he feel when he woke up and found a whole new woman kissing him goodbye as she headed out the door?

What was Gabe going to think about his mom wearing snakeskin leggings? Though, she had good legs and rocked those leggings like no other sixty-something Kelly ever knew.

Within a few minutes, she arrived at the location of the Lambert Law Office above Tease, Lucky Cove's stylish hair salon. Kelly peered into the window of the salon, and nearly every chair was occupied. She caught a reflection of herself. She was due for a trim. She'd have to find time for an appointment, but first, she had a lawyer to visit.

She pulled open the door next to the entrance of the salon and climbed the flight of stairs to the second floor. There were two offices, one for an accountant and the other for Mark Lambert.

She knocked as she pushed the door open and was greeted by a bland reception area, much different than the same space back at her sister's office. The desk was unmanned and, by the look of it, she doubted anyone had ever worked at the desk. There was another door, and it was closed.

"Hello!" she called out, and a moment later she heard footsteps. The interior office door opened, and a man appeared, presumably Mark Lambert.

"Can I help you?" he asked.

Kelly's words caught in her throat. If the man standing in front of her was Mark Lambert, then little old Mrs. Mueller had hired Smokin' McHottie, Esq. to represent her. Tall with wavy black hair just begging to have her fingers run through it. Whoa! Kelly had to quickly regroup, corralling her hormones.

"You can if you're Mark Lambert."

"I am. Who are you?"

"The woman you had papers served on yesterday. Kelly Quinn."

He frowned. "I don't think it's a good idea for you to be here."

"Probably not. But since I'm here, we're doing this." Kelly was surprised by her sudden brazenness, but she decided to go with it and breezed past Mark Lambert and entered the inner office.

"Doing this? What are you talking about?" He followed her into his office.

Kelly dropped her tote bag on one of the two chairs set in front of Mark's cluttered desk and placed the box of muffins on the desk, on top of a pile of file folders. "I bought you muffins. Apple walnut."

"I'm allergic to nuts." He crossed his arms over his chest.

"Then you may not want to eat them." She lifted the box off of his desk.

"What are you doing here, Miss Quinn?"

"I'm here to ask you to try and talk some sense into your client. The chair Dorothy purchased wasn't haunted. I don't have a hundred thousand dollars or the money to defend myself in this ridiculous lawsuit."

"Mrs. Mueller doesn't feel it's ridiculous."

"And neither do you? What are you, some kind of ambulance chaser? You're taking money from an elderly woman for a lawsuit involving a haunted piece of furniture. Doesn't the Bar have standards or something?"

"I thought you came here for my help?"

"I did."

"And you're going about that by insulting me?"

"It's only insulting if it's true. Are you an ambulance chaser?"

Mark uncrossed his arms and walked behind his desk. "Have a seat."

Kelly placed the box of muffins next to her tote bag on the chair and perched on the edge of the other chair. "I'm serious. I don't have the money to defend myself. Especially since I'm probably going to need a criminal defense attorney now that I'm a suspect in two murders. Not just one. Two." She huffed as she shook her head in disbelief.

"Two murders? What are you, a serial killer?" The serious look on Mark Lambert's chiseled face was betrayed by the hint of mirth in his voice. He pulled out his leather chair and sat.

"No. I'm not. I'm being wrongfully accused. But that's a conversation for another lawyer." She leaned forward. "You're not also a criminal defense attorney, are you?"

Mark shook his head. "Besides, I couldn't defend you. It would be a conflict of interest. Back to the reason why you came here."

"Right. The chair isn't haunted. I think Mrs. Mueller is confused and scared. She was present the day Bernadette Rydell had a so-called vision when she tried on a dress, about a man being murdered, and then when a medium held a séance and said there were items in my shop that were haunted. Mrs. Mueller had just purchased the chair."

"Your shop has been busy."

Kelly nodded. "It would be nice if I were actually making sales rather than feeding Lucky Cove's gossip mill. Will you help me?"

"I'm limited in what I can tell you."

"I know. My sister is a lawyer. I'm aware of all that lawyer-client privilege."

"Couldn't she represent you?"

Kelly shrugged. "Our relationship is complicated."

"I see." Mark leaned back. "I'll tell you what, I'll speak to Mrs. Mueller. Perhaps a drawn-out legal action may not be in her best interest."

Kelly dipped her head. Finally, a small glimmer of hope. She'd take it. She lifted her chin and met Mark's intense gaze. "I'm happy to refund Mrs. Mueller for the chair. I'll even pick it up for her. I've already practically carried it around her house like four times, what's one more time? I'll do whatever she'd like." Kelly stood and swiped up her tote bag and box of muffins.

"Thank you for the offer of the muffins. I love the bakery." He rose from his chair.

"Sorry they could have killed you."

"Sure you're not a serial killer?" His grin sent Kelly's pulse racing.

"I'm sure." She laughed and stepped away from the chairs. As she turned, she noticed a bookcase along a wall was a collection of framed photographs. Fishing trips. "You fish?"

Mark walked around his desk and joined Kelly at the bookcase. "I do. How about you?"

"No, not really. Looks like you have a regular fishing group." There was one photograph that caught her attention. One of the six men in the photo looked vaguely familiar. She didn't know why. "Who's that?" she pointed to the familiar man.

"Eddie Singer. That was our last fishing trip in Mexico. We all went at least once a year. This year we went twice, which probably was a good thing since he died unexpectedly."

"Car accident up in Maine, I heard."

"Tragic." He shook his head. "Life can turn on a dime. I try to tell that to all my clients. As much as I love arguing a case in court, sometimes it's better to move past things. Litigation brings out the worse in people."

"Tell me about it."

"I'll talk to Mrs. Mueller and see if I can work out an agreement regarding the alleged haunted chair."

"Much appreciated." Kelly looked at Mark. "Thank you again." She walked to the door and, just before she reached the outer office door, she looked over her shoulder. "I have one more question."

Mark's brows arched and he half smiled. "What?"

"Since you were friends with Eddie, do you think his wife could have had her husband murdered?"

His half smile faded as he slipped his hands into his pants pockets and stared at Kelly for a long moment. "That's one hell of a question."

Kelly nodded. "I know."

"The one thing I've learned is that people are capable of anything." He pulled his hands out of his pocket as he walked to the door. "I'll be in touch." He closed the door.

Chapter 18

A half mile down the road, StoreIt Storage Facility came into Kelly's view. After leaving the lawyer's office, she returned to the boutique to get Pepper's SUV. She wanted to check out her granny's storage unit and see if there were any holiday decorations.

Kelly had Mark Lambert's promise to talk to Mrs. Mueller about the ridiculous lawsuit. She also had the image of his sexy grin burned into her brain. Without question, she was losing her mind. How could she explain thinking the opposing counsel was sexy? Kelly made the turn onto Dolphin Lane and wondered if Caroline ever had those types of feelings for lawyers she went up against in court. Probably not. Caroline was zipped up tight. She followed the rules, regulations, and policies, and she was a heck of a hall monitor back in the day.

It was a miracle he'd been agreeable to talking with Dorothy. Not only had Kelly offered him something that could have possibly killed him, but she accused him of being an ambulance chaser. Her visit to his office wasn't exactly her finest hour. She sighed.

She passed through the main entry and got a better look at the sprawling one-story building. Lucky Cove's answer to overconsumption. Packed, piled, and shoved behind heavy rolling doors was the overflow of people's lives. Old furniture no longer used, clothing that no longer fit, and hobbies long forgotten. To think, storing stuff was a billion-dollar industry. Maybe Kelly was in the wrong business.

She drove past the main office, and the sign above the front door seemed familiar. She'd seen that sign somewhere recently. Then she remembered. The article she read on the Lulu Loves Long Island website mentioned the name of the company Eddie Singer owned. StoreIt Storage.

Would she run into Irene?

That thought didn't make Kelly feel good. A feeling of foreboding spread in the pit of her stomach. Nothing good was going to come out of this trip. Just like the visit to Bernadette's house and DJ Brown's house. She had an urge to turn the car around and drive away.

There wouldn't be any turning around. Not when Lucky Cove shop owners and residents went all out for Christmas decorating. She couldn't have her boutique undecorated for the most important holiday of the year. The residents expected a postcard quality Main Street, and customers liked shops that were festive. Even though there wasn't an ounce of festiveness in her at the moment, she pressed down on the gas pedal and drove forward and then made a turn. She drove by the row of units until she came to her granny's unit.

She parked and grabbed the lone key on a gigantic key ring. She guessed her granny didn't want to lose it. She climbed out of the vehicle. She wasn't sure what to expect when she unlocked the dark green door. Had Granny been a secret hoarder? Why else would someone need to rent a storage unit? Or maybe Granny had too many decorations to be stored in the boutique.

She walked to the storage space and noticed how quiet it was. There wasn't anyone else around. A chill skittered through her body. Given what had happened recently, quietness and isolation were a little unnerving. But she bucked up. She had a mission. Find some Christmas decorations or else she'd have to buy new ones, and she didn't have the money for the expense. She unlocked the door and yanked it up. The movement made her cringe with discomfort, especially in the neck area and shoulders. She wondered how long she'd be feeling the effects of Bernadette's surprise assault.

With the door open, she peered into the dark space. Luckily the day was bright and that let a ray of light into the cavernous space filled with cardboard boxes and bits and pieces of household items. At first glance, it was all junk. But Kelly needed to make sure before she filled the dumpster just a few yards away.

She entered the unit and began to peek through her granny's hidden stash. There were boxes of clothes, dishes, and books. After opening what was the third box of clothing, Kelly straightened and sighed. No decorations. Behind a three-shelf bookcase, the corner of a clear plastic container caught her eye. She pushed aside the out-of-style clothes to reach the container and found the sought-after Christmas decorations. Next to the container was another bin with more decorations. It looked like she was all set and wouldn't need to lay out any more cash. She grabbed one container and turned to head out of the unit when she noticed a medium-sized box labeled "garland" next to an old air-conditioning unit. Her little search was yielding quite a bounty. She'd take all three bins back to the boutique and then figure out what to do with all the other items in the unit later. After she'd loaded both plastic containers, she came back for the box of garland. She lifted it up, and its bottom broke open, and all of the garland and lights fell out.

"Shoot." She dropped the now-empty box. Nothing was going to be easy. She squatted down and surveyed the mess. She could carry all the garland and lights out, but it would be easier to have them in a box. She spied another box labeled "ornaments," but it didn't look much sturdier than the one she just tried to pick up. There was a sign on the main office that boxes were for sale. Problem solved. She'd buy a couple of boxes.

She stepped out of the storage unit and looked around. Since she was alone, she didn't think she needed to close the door. She grabbed her tote bag and walked along the building.

She came to the corner and made the turn. Maybe she should have driven to the office. She'd walk for blocks in the city, but she was almost winded making the trek to the main office. Her thoughts about her declining fitness ended as she stopped short.

Up ahead she spotted Irene Singer leaning against the wall, talking on a cell phone.

Kelly wasn't sure what to do. Walk by her and say "hi" or turn around and take what she'd already packed into the SUV or stay and eavesdrop, but, in order to do that, she needed to get a little closer.

"Why are you calling? You know I'm at the office." Irene's voice was harsh. "I know... I miss you too." Her voice softened. "It's not going to be much longer." She ran the fingers of her free hand through her hair.

Curiosity buzzed through Kelly. Who did Irene miss? Her lover? The person who killed her husband? Was Kelly right?

Kelly inched a little closer, staying as quiet as possible.

"There have been some bumps, but we've come this far. Let's not panic." Irene pushed herself off of the wall and took a step forward. "I can't believe that psychic might be the real deal. Why on earth did she have to try on that dress?"

"Irene! Where are you?" a loud male voice called out from around the corner of the building. Kelly inched back quietly.

"Gotta go. Don't call me again." Irene pulled the phone from her ear and shook her head.

"Irene!" the voice called again.

Irene rushed forward. "I'm here. What is it?" She made the turn around the corner and disappeared.

Kelly stood in place for a moment, not sure what to do next. She didn't think going to the main office was a good idea since Irene was there. She'd have to come back for the decorations. She turned and hurried back to the storage unit. Halfway to her vehicle, her cell phone rang, and she pulled the phone from her tote. The caller ID said it was Liv. She swiped the phone on.

"You won't believe what I just overheard!" Continuing back to her vehicle, Kelly recapped the conversation she'd eavesdropped on.

"Get out! Do you really think she has a boyfriend?"

"You mean looover," Kelly said in her best impersonation of Carrie Bradshaw.

"This isn't *Sex and the City.*"

No, it was more like *Murder and the Burbs.* "Sorry, I couldn't resist. This is serious stuff, I know." At the SUV, Kelly plopped her tote bag on the passenger seat and pulled her nude patent Filofax planner from her tote and flipped it open.

"Did she see you?"

"No. Look, I need to get out of here. I'll talk to you later."

"Kell, I'm worried. If she did have something to do with Eddie's death, you just overheard something that could incriminate her. Be careful."

"I will." Kelly ended the call and quickly jotted down what she'd just overheard and then closed and locked the unit's door. Back in her vehicle, she shoved her planner and phone back into her tote bag. Her cell phone rang, and when she pulled the phone out of the bag, she saw Gabe's name and tapped on the speaker, which let her drive hands-free.

"What's up?" Kelly began her drive back to the boutique. When she reached the front of the facility, she sped up a little so that if Irene had looked out the large front window, she wouldn't get a good look at Kelly. Though, by speeding, she'd probably drawn unwanted attention from Irene and her staff.

"Just wanted to let you know we found all Ariel's files when we searched Bernadette's house."

"Oh, no. That's not good news."

"There's a warrant out for Bernadette's arrest."

"I just can't wrap my brain around Bernadette being a killer. Or her breaking into Ariel's house." Kelly stopped at a four-way intersection and then proceeded through.

"I know, but all the evidence is pointing in Bernadette's direction. Look, I'm glad it's not pointing at you."

"Aw, thanks." A warm fuzzy feeling swirled through Kelly.

She and Gabe were like siblings. While they teased each other mercilessly when they were teenagers and it still continued into their adulthood, he always was protective of her. He even got suspended for three days from high school when he defended her to Ariel's then-boyfriend after the accident. The two of them threw punches, resulting in a bloody nose and a black eye, but now Kelly couldn't remember who sustained which injuries. She just remembered looking on in horror as the boys rolled around on the ground.

"You still there?"

"Yes, yes, I am. I'm heading back to the boutique."

"From where?" Gabe didn't bother to hide the wariness in his voice.

Kelly debated telling Gabe what she'd just overheard between Irene and her unknown caller, but she didn't want a lecture and she didn't have proof Irene was talking to a co-conspirator. She just had a strong hunch.

"I went to see Mark Lambert about Dorothy Mueller's lawsuit. And, before you tell me it wasn't a good idea, he did agree to explore other options with Mrs. Mueller to settle the case." Kelly approached an intersection not too far from the boutique.

"Hopefully it will work out for you. I can't imagine the lawsuit going very far."

"Have you seen your mom today?"

"No, why?"

"Just wondering. Thanks for updating me. Bye." She waited until she came to a stoplight to drop her phone back into her tote bag. She really wanted to see Gabe's face when he got a look at his mom's new look. Now, that would be priceless.

Kelly arrived back at the boutique with some of the Christmas decorations and a plan to go back to the storage unit later in the week with new boxes and bring back the remaining decorations. Even though she wouldn't be decorating for Christmas yet—Halloween was just a few days away—she didn't want to be scrambling at the last minute if the boutique was still in business by then.

She locked the SUV and walked from the rear parking lot to the front of the boutique to take another look at the decorations Earl set out earlier in the day now that she was feeling a little better. She glanced at the shop's sign. Pepper was right, it'd been the Lucky Cove Consignment Shop since Granny opened her business. Could she really change the name now? On the other hand, she needed to revamp the business, and the name needed to reflect the change.

Then it hit her. When her granny opened the business, she was making a huge change in her life from wife and mother to widow and mother. Now, over twenty years later, Kelly was making a huge change in her life. The question was—who was she changing into?

A chorus of chatter drew her attention from the sign to a group of women approaching her direction, and she noticed one of the women pointing to her boutique. Customers? She bustled inside to prepare to greet them.

The rest of the afternoon was steady with customers. Maybe having some decorations outside the shop drew people's attention and led them inside to browse and eventually buy, but when Kelly prepared the day's deposit, it still wasn't anywhere near what she needed it to be. As she climbed the staircase to her apartment, she tried to look on the bright side, just like Ariel would do, and reminded herself only a couple of days ago she barely made a deposit. Regardless of how great she believed her ideas for the boutique were, she wasn't going to be an overnight success.

At the top of the stairs, she was greeted by an empty hall with drab paint. Granny had converted the second floor from four bedrooms to a one-bedroom apartment on a shoestring budget and hadn't refreshed the space since then. The carpet was equally drab and worn. While a new carpet wasn't in her budget, maybe she could buy a couple gallons of paint to liven up the space and maybe add a plant or two and hang some artwork. She unlocked the apartment door and tossed her key onto the small, round table beside the door.

"Howard, here kitty, kitty." She tossed her tote bag on the sofa and slipped out of her shoes then made her way to her bedroom and found her roommate curled up in a tight ball on the bed. "There you are. Not much of a greeter, huh?" She approached him, and his head slightly lifted.

His cool eyes appraised her, and then he yawned.

"Exhausting day?" She scratched his head, and he gently purred. The small sound was comforting, and she realized she'd been looking forward to seeing the cat all day long. She was getting used to the little jerk, and she liked his company. Go figure.

Howard lifted his body and stretched. Guess he'd had enough petting.

"No problem." She walked over to the chest of drawers and pulled out her favorite pair of ripped skinny jeans and a chunky ivory turtleneck sweater. She changed and slipped barefoot into her beloved suede boots cuffed with a thick cable knit. Her toes wiggled in the lushness of the boot's plush lining. She padded to the kitchen, and Howard followed.

She needed to make something for dinner, though she didn't feel up to cooking, and luckily she had the leftovers from last night's Chinese dinner. Before she could pull out the containers, her phone buzzed, and she retrieved it from her bag.

The caller ID told her Mrs. Franklin, the owner of her granny's rental cottage, was on the line.

"Hello, Mrs. Franklin." Kelly went back to the kitchen.

"Kelly, dear, I'm sorry to do this to you. I've unexpectedly rented the cottage. I need for you to move out your grandmother's belongings."

Kelly sank to the chair at the kitchen table. She'd been told she didn't have to rush to move out her grandmother's stuff, and now, listening to Mrs. Franklin continue to explain the sudden change of events, she had less than two days. She ended the call with a promise to take what belonged to Granny out of the cottage and return the key.

Howard had strolled into the kitchen and sat staring at Kelly. "Dinner's going to be a little late. I have to go out." She stood and grabbed a jacket from the hall closet and her tote bag then headed out to the cottage.

Chapter 19

"Do you still think your uncle is behind all this vision, haunting stuff?" Liv asked as she followed Kelly into the cottage.

Kelly pocketed the house key. "I'm not yet ready to rule him out. I mean, what other explanation could there be for the uptick in all things paranormal all of a sudden?" She walked through the living room to the fireplace mantel. In her hand, she carried an LL Bean canvas tote bag filled with tissue paper to wrap Granny's framed photographs. She set the tote bag down and pulled out the thick sheath of tissue and began wrapping the photographs. "There isn't much to take out. The cottage came rented with furniture. I just have to take out this stuff, her clothes, and her toiletries."

"Why don't I get started with the closet?" Liv spun around and dashed out of the foyer before Kelly could respond.

"Good idea." With all of the photographs placed into the bag, she carried it to the foyer. Beside the door were three hooks, and on one of them hung Granny's blue rain jacket. Kelly grabbed the jacket off the hook and laid it on top of the bag.

"What do you want to do with the toiletries?" Liv called out from the bedroom.

Since the phone call from Pepper informing Kelly about her granny's death, she'd been making decisions. She expected by now she'd be used to it, but she wasn't. There was a time in her life in the not so distant past she could go a whole hour without having to make a decision.

"I guess we can toss them. I'll get a garbage bag from the kitchen." She looked in the direction of the kitchen. A chill shimmied through her body.

"Want me to go with you?"

Kelly glanced over her shoulder in the direction of the bedroom. "No. It's not like the would-be intruder is in there waiting for me. I'm a big girl. I can handle going into the kitchen alone." She pushed off into the direction of the kitchen, but halfway there, a knock at the door had her trekking back to the foyer. There was another knock, louder. "We have company." She doubted the burglar had returned and decided to be polite.

"Maybe it's Gabe. I texted him we'd be here. Just in case." Liv came out of the bedroom with an armful of dresses. "Your granny sure squeezed a lot into that small closet."

"That's why she was my idol." Kelly opened the door.

Bernadette stood on the front step.

"What are you doing here?"

Bernadette hurried in and shoved Kelly's hand off the doorknob and slammed the door shut. "We need to talk."

"No, we don't. The last time we were together, you pushed me. I got a concussion," Kelly said.

"I'm really sorry. I didn't mean to hurt you." Bernadette reached out and grabbed Kelly's wrists. "You have to believe me."

"What we have to do is call the police." Liv marched toward Kelly and dropped the dresses on top of the canvas bag. "There's a warrant out for your arrest."

"What? Why?"

"Why?" Kelly and Liv asked in unison.

"I didn't do anything." Bernadette looked confused and tired. Her face was drawn, with bags under her eyes, and her hair was unkempt. She wore the same dress as the day before. "I'm being framed."

"By who?" Kelly released herself from Bernadette's hold. She wasn't afraid of the woman. She actually felt sorry for her. And that was how she got tangled up in this whole mess.

"I don't know. All of this started when I tried on the dress at your shop. Do you still have it?" Bernadette asked.

"Yes. Do you want to see it again?"

"I do. I want to see if I'll have another vision."

"Are you insane?" Liv whispered in Kelly's ear. "She's wanted for murder."

Kelly looked at her friend. "True." Her gaze traveled back to Bernadette. "You are wanted for murder. Taking you back to the boutique wouldn't be the smartest thing to do."

Liv nodded in agreement as a small, triumphant smile touched her lips.

"You'll need to sneak over there," Kelly said to Bernadette as Liv's smile disappeared. "The dress is in the office. Go around to the back of the boutique." Kelly grabbed Liv's wrist and led her to the front door.

"I'll meet you over there." Bernadette turned and opened the front door.

"This isn't a good idea." Liv's sneakers dragged on the polished wood floor.

"We don't have much of a choice." Kelly dug out her car key from her jeans pocket.

"I have a bad feeling about this." Liv followed Kelly out of the cottage.

"We don't have a choice. We'll come back for Granny's stuff later." Kelly pulled the door closed and, with Liv, she walked back to the boutique.

* * * *

Kelly opened the back door of the boutique to let Bernadette inside. She craned her neck farther out to take a look around in the night to make sure no one had followed Bernadette, namely the police, and didn't see anyone. She closed and locked the door and led the psychic into the office.

"This isn't a good idea, Kell." Liv paced the length of the staff room. Her laced suede walking shoes were getting a workout.

Kelly ignored her friend's warning—again—and headed for the file cabinet. She pulled open the bottom drawer and retrieved the black lace dress.

"Do you need to try it on or can you just...touch it?" Kelly wasn't familiar with the process for a psychic to have a vision.

"Let me try holding it." Bernadette held out both hands and took the dress and then folded it close to her chest.

"This isn't a good idea, Kell," Liv whispered as she passed by Kelly.

"Would you stop pacing?" Kelly grabbed hold of Liv's arm to stop her friend.

"Would you stop harboring a fugitive?" Liv retorted.

"We'll be done in a few minutes. Now, stay still." Kelly returned her attention back to Bernadette, whose eyes were closed.

Her frazzledness from earlier had disappeared and, in its place, a tranquility seemed to have overtaken her body. Her facial expressions changed rapidly, from calm to tense to horror as her eyelids opened and stared out to nowhere in particular. Kelly followed Bernadette's gaze to the wall.

"What's she doing?" Liv asked.

"She must be having a vision." Kelly began to second-guess her decision to let Bernadette have the dress. "Hopefully she won't pass out like she did last time."

"This isn't a good idea, Kell."

"I heard you the four other times." Kelly glanced over at her friend, who was chewing on her lower lip and wringing her hands together.

She was nervous, and Kelly couldn't blame her. As much as Kelly was curious and determined to get to the truth of the dress and the murders, her insides were all twisted up. Maybe she'd made a bad decision.

"He was murdered…a car…no, pickup truck… She got the news… but…but…" Bernadette's eyes fluttered closed and then finally opened, and she looked at Kelly. "A man was definitely murdered, and the person responsible was wearing this dress."

"Did you see who the man was?"

Bernadette shook her head. "Not yet. Visions sometimes come in pieces, fragments." She handed the dress back to Kelly. "I'm sorry. I thought I'd see more."

"You didn't see the face of the woman wearing the dress?" Liv stopped chewing on her lip and walked to the table and sat.

"No. Just her body in the dress. She was talking." Bernadette joined Liv at the table. "But no one was with her."

"She was talking on the phone?" Kelly returned the dress to the file drawer. "She had a partner?" Kelly surmised Irene's partner was the person she was talking to in secret and placating on the phone earlier.

"Possibly. I didn't hear another voice." Bernadette leaned forward on the table. "Seeing visions can be frustrating. I'm sorry. But now I've held the dress, there's a chance I may see more."

A loud banging on the back door sent all three women jumping. Startled, their heads swung around to the mud room.

"Police! Open up!"

Liv shot up from her chair. "I told you this was a bad idea!"

"Nobody likes a know-it-all!" Kelly raced to the back door before the police knocked it down. She didn't need another repair bill to pay. After she unlocked the door, two uniformed police officers, one of which was Gabe, entered the staff room followed by Detective Wolman.

"Miss Rydell, we've been looking for you." Wolman walked to her suspect and whipped out a pair of handcuffs. "We have a warrant for your arrest."

Bernadette looked at the detective, and she was on the verge of tears. "I didn't kill anyone. I'm being framed. You must believe me."

"You can tell it to a jury. Stand up, please. Please turn around, Miss Rydell." Wolman cuffed Bernadette and told her what her rights were. "Do you understand your rights?"

"Detective, you're making a mistake." Kelly went to step forward, but Gabe grabbed her by the arm and gave her a warning nod.

"Cuff her too, Officer Donovan," Wolman instructed. "Officer Byrd, cuff Miss Moretti."

"What? Why?" Kelly and Liv wailed in unison.

"Interfering with an official investigation and harboring a fugitive." Wolman escorted Bernadette out of the staff room.

"She can't be serious." Kelly looked to Gabe for reassurance she was right. None was forthcoming. Rather, he pulled out his handcuffs from his utility belt, as did the other officer.

"She's serious. Sorry, Kell." With a deep frown, Gabe handcuffed Kelly.

"We weren't interfering!" Liv was prompted by the other officer to stand. He placed the handcuffs on her wrists. "Handcuffing is just grandstanding. We're not criminals."

"Just come along quietly, and I'm sure we can work something out once we arrive at PD." Gabe led Kelly out of the staff room, and the other officer followed with Liv.

"I'm sorry, Liv." Kelly stepped out into the cold night and walked with Gabe to his waiting patrol car, while her friend was led off to another car. Her insides twisted tighter. There'd been a chance she'd be arrested because of her presence at both murder scenes, but she never thought in a million years Liv would get arrested too. The cold air pricked at her—she hadn't had a chance to grab a coat—as tears welled up in her eyes. She'd have to find some way to make this whole mess right. At the patrol car, Gabe guided her into the back seat. As the door closed, she wondered if Liv would ever forgive her.

* * * *

"When my nona hears about tonight, she's going to freak out. She'll be yelling in Italian, blaming my mom for not sending me to parochial school, and dragging me to confession." Liv rubbed her wrists as she passed through the open door with Gabe behind her. "I can't believe Wolman had us handcuffed and hauled down here just to let us go."

"You're both lucky Wolman's letting you go. She could make a case easily against you two. What were you thinking taking Bernadette to the shop? You should've called us right away when she showed up at the cottage." Gabe walked around Liv and Kelly and in the direction of the dispatcher.

Kelly followed Liv out to the lobby of the police department, where they'd been detained, separately, and asked questions about Bernadette. When Kelly told Detective Wolman Bernadette had come to the shop to see the black lace dress again and had a vision, a smirk appeared on the detective's face. Clearly she didn't believe in psychics or their visions. "I wonder who convinced her not to charge us."

"That would be me!" Ralph's voice boomed in the lobby.

"You've gotta be kidding me," Kelly muttered as she came to a fast halt. Did she owe her freedom to her uncle? It was official. Her life couldn't possibly get any worse.

"Olivia Therese Moretti!" a high-pitched, anxious voice called out from the waiting area.

"Oh boy. All three names. This isn't good." Liv passed Kelly and approached her mother. After a quick scolding in Italian, which was loud enough for the entire building to hear, Geovanna Moretti enveloped her daughter in a loving embrace.

Kelly looked at her uncle. There'd be no loving embrace from him. "Thanks for springing us." She walked past him, heading for the exit to walk home.

"That's all you have to say, young lady?" Ralph's tone was sharp and irritated.

Kelly halted and glanced over her shoulder. "Good night?"

"You've never considered the consequences of your actions. Not when you were fifteen and not now." He crossed his chubby arms over his chest and was about to say something when Mrs. Moretti swooped in and got into Kelly's face.

"I can't believe my daughter ended up here tonight because of you." Mrs. Moretti wagged a finger at Kelly. "Kelly Marie Quinn, you're a bad influence on my Olivia."

"Mama, please, it's not really Kelly's fault." Liv tugged on her mother's arm. "Come on, let's go home."

Mrs. Moretti batted at her daughter's hand. "You should listen to your uncle, Kelly. You drag my daughter out in the middle of the night and you welcome a suspected killer into your business with my daughter present? How irresponsible can you be?"

"Mama, please! You're making a scene," Liv pleaded.

Mrs. Moretti threw her hands up in the air. "I'm making a scene? You get arrested and I'm the one making a scene. Wait until your nona hears about this. Maybe I should have sent you to St. Mary's like your cousins. None of them have been arrested."

Liv dipped her head, and Kelly's heart ached for her friend. Liv would be forever the Moretti who got arrested. Sure, she wasn't being charged, but that little fact would be a minor footnote in the Moretti family history.

"Let's go tell your papa and break his heart. His baby girl arrested." Mrs. Moretti turned and headed for the exit. Liv followed. She cast a quick glance over her shoulder, and her expression was unreadable. It was late, and they all were tired and rattled from the night's events.

"Maybe your mother should have sent you to Catholic school too. There you would've learned some discipline." Ralph uncrossed his arms. "I'll drive you home."

Kelly didn't want to be indebted to her uncle for anything more than she already was. "Thanks for the offer, but I'll walk home. I need some fresh air."

"You need to figure out your life. It's becoming more clear that coming back to Lucky Cove wasn't such a good idea. When you're ready to accept that, let me know. I'm still willing to help you get settled back in New York City."

Kelly nodded. Even though her uncle never offered to help someone unless he benefited somehow, she had to admit he might have a point. Did she honestly believe she could settle back in Lucky Cove so easily? There was a reason why she left and barely came back to visit.

Chapter 20

"Just what did you think you were doing last night?"

Gabe and his big mouth. He must've filled Pepper in on what happened last night first thing this morning. The sharp edge in Pepper's voice had Kelly looking up from the almost-filled box of candlestick holders. She'd opened the boutique an hour earlier and then settled in the home accents room to pack up the remaining home accents for the flea market. She'd been listening for the bell over the front door to jingle. So far it hadn't. It looked like it would be another slow day.

"I don't want to discuss last night." Kelly wanted to forget about the whole disaster of an evening and the one bad decision that led to her and Liv being handcuffed and hauled to the police department. She should've called the police the moment Bernadette showed up at the cottage.

"Is that all you're going to say?" Pepper challenged.

"I need to get all this merchandise ready for the flea market." She'd set up a packing station on the oak table, where Valeria Leigh held a séance a few days ago. "I got a booth for Saturday." She continued wrapping the candlestick holders in bubble wrap. She'd found a large roll tucked into a corner of the storage room. She'd only gotten approval for a booth last night. It wasn't much notice, but she wasn't going to pass it up and had immediately started packing the small items.

Pepper marched over to Kelly and propped both hands on her waist. She wore a gray sheath dress with black tights and pumps with a kitten heel. Her blond hair was pushed back in a velvet headband. She was still rocking her makeover.

"Not talking about last night isn't an option. Do you know how close you were to having a mug shot taken and waking up in a cell this morning."

Kelly was very aware of how close she'd come to standing in front of a judge rather than opening up the boutique. She didn't need Pepper or anyone else to remind her. "Please, there's a lot to do today. Let's focus on work, okay?"

Pepper took a step forward. "No, it's not okay. There is a lot of work to do here, and you running around Lucky Cove playing Nancy Drew isn't helping *your* business. You have responsibilities here. You have no responsibility to Bernadette Rydell."

"Don't you think I know that? It's just that I don't believe she's guilty of the murders. The more I think about it, the more convinced I am she's being set up." Kelly placed the wrapped candlestick holder in the box and grabbed another length of bubble wrap and proceeded to wrap the matching candlestick holder. She didn't know why someone would want to set Bernadette up for murder. She'd like to think the justice system would sort it out and discover the reason and the person behind the murders, but then again, she was being sued over a supposedly haunted chair. Understandably, her faith in the justice system wasn't very strong at the moment.

Pepper shook her head. "I don't believe what I'm hearing. You're not a police detective. You're the owner of a consignment shop. Your grandmother, my best friend, left you her legacy, and you've done nothing but try to destroy it since coming back to Lucky Cove. This may not be as glamorous as the shops you're used to in the city, but your grandmother made an honest living selling the merchandise, and she was beloved by this community."

Kelly inhaled a ragged breath. "I'm not trying to destroy this shop."

"Could've fooled me. The name change, the uppity decision to eliminate this section of the shop just because you think it's beneath you to sell tchotchkes."

Kelly's eyes widened. "I don't think selling these items is beneath me."

"Well, let me tell you something, missy. People need tchotchkes."

Kelly's temples began to throb. Anger pulsed through her body, and she struggled to keep her mouth shut so she wouldn't say something she'd regret later.

"You were given a second chance to start your life over again after you made a mess of it in the city. All these years, people have said a lot of bad things about you, and I can't believe I'm about to right now. But I am." She pointed her finger. "Kelly Marie Quinn, you're an ungrateful young woman. And I can no longer work here. I quit."

Kelly's mouth gaped open, but there were no words as a look of shock covered Pepper's face. Kelly guessed Pepper hadn't intended on quitting right then and there. The older woman spun around and dashed out of the room.

Pepper's harsh words replayed in Kelly's mind. One of her few allies in Lucky Cove was gone. Her shoulders sagged, and hurt replaced anger. Everyone and their mother had an opinion of Kelly. It wasn't something new to her. But she never believed Pepper would think so little of her.

"Hey, everything okay? I just saw Pepper run out of the shop." Liv appeared in the doorway, holding a tray of coffee and muffins from the bakery.

"She quit." Kelly dropped the candlestick holder into the box. "She told me I was ungrateful and she quit."

Liv walked into the room and set the tray on the table amongst the bubble wrap and knickknacks. She reached out and gently rubbed Kelly's back in a comforting way. "She's upset. Last night rattled us all."

"No, no. She unloaded on me full-force. Boy, she told me exactly what she'd been thinking all this time." Kelly looked at the table and then back to her friend. Her friend who she got arrested last night. "I'm sorry. Last night was totally my fault. I should've never let you get involved." She inhaled a deep breath and looked to Liv and dissolved into tears.

Liv pulled her in close for a hug.

"I'm sorry. Really, really, sorry."

"I could've left at any time," Liv whispered.

"I put you in danger and got you arrested." Kelly pulled out of the hug and, with the back of her hand, wiped away the tears.

"Yes, you did. You also got me into hot water with my mother. Which, by the way, is far worse than getting arrested." Liv unbuttoned her black wool-blend jacket and removed her gloves.

Kelly grimaced. "Can you ever forgive me?" She waited on pins and needles for Liv's reply. She couldn't bear to lose her dearest and closest friend since grade school.

"I'm here, aren't I, with muffins? All's forgiven. Besides, like I said, I could've left at any time."

Liv's reassurance lifted a heavy weight off of Kelly's shoulders, but there was still the matter of Pepper. Kelly didn't want her friendship with Pepper to end, especially not the way they'd left it just a few moments ago.

"Pepper will come around. You'll see," Liv said.

Kelly looked around the room, scanning every nook and cranny. "Maybe she's right. Maybe I've been ungrateful, but I never asked for this shop. I'm not my grandmother. This was her dream."

"You're right. It isn't fair for anyone to live someone else's dream."

Kelly swallowed hard. Pepper's words still stung because there was some truth to them. "It's time to let go. I'll sell to my uncle and go back to the city. It's where I belong."

"Kell, are you sure you're not giving up because it's too hard?"

Kelly wiped away a tear and pulled away from Liv. "You think that's what I'm doing? I may be a little flighty and easily distracted by shiny objects, but I had a four-point-oh in college and, trust me, I studied more than just how to buy blouses. I also managed somehow to live through Ariel's accident, when everyone blamed me for it. Do you have any idea of how many nights I wished it was me in the car instead of her? How many times I prayed God would take me so I wouldn't have to live with the guilt? I'm not giving up because it's too hard. I'm leaving because I don't belong here." She squared her shoulders and walked past Liv to the front of the shop where she turned over the sign on the door to closed.

After closing the boutique, Kelly went upstairs to her apartment and plodded straight into her bedroom. She pulled off her saddle-brown ankle boots and threw herself on the bed and cried. Pepper's harsh, but truthful, words continued to replay in her mind as if they were in a loop. The events of the night before flashed in her mind, too, along with all of the bad decisions she'd ever made, and the anger of feeling sorry for herself came out in deep sobs.

In a nutshell—her life was a mess.

When did I become so pathetic?

She wiped her eyes with the back of her hand and, through blurry eyes, she caught a glimpse of a streak of mascara on her hand. She could imagine how awful she looked. Crying as long as she had no doubt resulted in red, puffy eyes and creases alongside her face from how she was lying.

Howard jumped on the bed and walked over her back to get to the other side.

"Sorry...I'm...in...your way," she said between sobs and sniffles.

The cat butted his head against hers and purred.

"Great. I'm a messed up, unemployed cat lady." She reached out and scratched Howard's head, and he purred louder. "At least someone doesn't think I'm a walking disaster."

She struggled to sit up. The position she'd landed in on the mattress wasn't the most comfortable position, and her head hurt from crying.

Howard protested at being jostled but curled up on her lap after she pulled herself upright against her pillow. She stroked his head.

"I'll have to find an apartment in the city that allows cats. It's not going to be easy. I may end up in one of the boroughs to find a place I can afford and takes animals." She reached to the nightstand and grabbed a tissue from the box. She blew her nose, drawing a glare from Howard. "Sorry." *Great. I'm apologizing to the cat.*

Her cell phone dinged. She contorted to reach her jeans back pocket without disturbing Howard too much and slid out her phone. It was an appointment reminder for a meeting with the boutique's insurance agent. It was going to be a short appointment because she didn't need any insurance since she was selling the business.

Selling was the sensible thing to do. She had no experience running a business. Owning a consignment shop wasn't her dream, and Lucky Cove was her past, not her future. Selling and going back to the city was the smartest thing she could do.

And it was about time she did something smart.

She set the phone down on the bed and stared at Howard. "The bright side to this decision is no one will be surprised or any more disappointed in me for leaving again."

* * * *

Kelly pushed open the door of the Lucky Cove Insurance Agency. There wasn't a bell to greet her, rather a perky blonde barely out of high school. She stood, revealing a crisp, V-neck striped shirt half tucked into a pair of gray skinny ankle pants. Kelly couldn't help but lean forward ever so slightly to catch a glimpse of the young woman's ankle-strap block-heeled pumps in black suede. Or, more likely faux suede. Just an educated guess she had based on the girl's probable income.

"Welcome! I'm Mandy. How can I help you today?" She stretched out her hand and pumped a firm handshake.

"I have an appointment with Anderson. I'm Kelly Quinn."

"Hi, Kelly." Mandy's bright smile turned downward into a frown. "I'm sorry. I was just about to call you. Anderson had a family emergency and had to leave. We apologize for the inconvenience. Let me reschedule you." She sat down and tapped on her computer's keyboard.

"Maybe it's for the best. I don't think I need to review the store's policy. I'm going to sell." Saying the words out loud was harder than Kelly expected. A pang of guilt stabbed at her.

Mandy's frown deepened as she nodded and looked up from her computer. "Most new businesses, especially retail clothing stores, don't survive. The market is challenging."

In more ways than one.

Kelly forced her smile, which came nowhere close to the one Mandy flashed a couple of minutes ago. "When the sale is finalized, I'll touch base with Anderson."

"Of course. But before you go, would you like to chat about life insurance?" Mandy perked up again, and she gestured to the seat in front of her desk. "I'm studying to be an agent. I like to take the opportunity to chat with clients about their insurance needs. I don't actually sell the policies. *Yet.* Anderson takes care of that aspect. A woman your age could get a nice policy at a good price. Please have a seat."

Kelly wasn't in the market for life insurance, or any insurance, for that matter, but Mandy looked so eager to practice her sales pitch, so how could she refuse? "I don't think I need life insurance." Kelly settled on the chair with her tote bag square on her lap.

"Nice bag," Mandy cooed, her professional persona slipping, but she quickly got back into character. "A lot of people don't think they need life insurance, but we never know what could happen. Life changes at the drop of a hat. One day we're all healthy and living life to its fullest, and then we're gone." She snapped her fingers for emphasis. "Just like that."

Kelly was very aware of that fact since she'd found two dead bodies in a matter of days. "Life is unpredictable."

"But insurance isn't. It's a comfort to have it, knowing your loved ones won't have to bear the financial burden we ultimately leave in the wake of our death."

Interesting sales pitch.

Mandy leaned forward. "I'm not one to gossip, but we recently witnessed a similar scenario. A local business owner died unexpectedly in a car accident way up in Maine, and his wife is now a widow. She didn't wake up that morning a widow. She had no idea it was coming her way. One phone call changed her life completely."

Kelly's ears perked up. The wannabe insurance agent was talking about the Singers. "You don't say?"

"Now, could you imagine what it would have been like for the widow if her husband didn't have a life insurance policy?"

"I imagine it would have been difficult for Irene."

Mandy's eyes clouded, and she chewed on her lips. "I really can't divulge client names."

"I understand. But we both know he's the only local business owner to die up in Maine." Kelly leaned forward. "I don't mean to be nosey, but how big was Eddie's policy? I mean, I'm only asking to get a rough idea of how much I should have."

"I'm sorry. I can't divulge that information. It's confidential. You understand? Besides, your policy would be significantly different than Eddie's. It's all very individual. We pride ourselves in bringing that often-overlooked aspect to each one of our clients. It allows us to provide the best possible policy at the most affordable price."

Kelly had to hand it to Mandy. The girl had her buzzwords down pat. "I do understand. If I did have a policy and I died, how long would it take to pay out?"

Mandy didn't miss a beat, nor did she attempt to assure her would-be client death wouldn't come for a long time. Maybe not true, since no one really knew, but it would've been a nice thing to add. "Not very long. After the death certificate is submitted to the insurance company, payment happens rather quickly. Eddie's policy has already paid out." Mandy's hand flew up to cover her lips, and her eyes bulged. "Oops. I shouldn't have shared that. My bad."

"No worries. I won't tell anyone." Kelly couldn't help but wonder how big of an insurance policy Eddie Singer had. Was it enough for Irene to murder her husband? "I'm sure you've heard about the *murder dress* in my boutique."

Mandy's head bobbed up and down. "Who hasn't?"

Good question.

"Can I tell you something in confidence?" Kelly asked.

"Of course you can."

"The infamous dress belonged to Irene Singer." A little bit of guilt worked its way through Kelly. She hated using Mandy's young age and inexperience to pump her for information. Information Kelly wasn't sure would lead anywhere.

Mandy gasped. "You don't say? Do you think she killed her husband? If she did, she's not entitled to the insurance money."

"I'm not saying she killed her husband. It just seems odd that the psychic had a vision of a man being murdered, and Irene's husband died unexpectedly and she got an insurance payout. Odd, right?"

"Definitely. But I still can't reveal anything about the policy...except..." Mandy seemed to be battling an internal conflict of what to say and what not to say.

"Except what?" Kelly had no internal conflict about snooping, because she believed Bernadette was innocent of the murders. There wasn't any proof of her belief, and she probably wouldn't find any, but she was still curious what Mandy had to say.

Mandy shrugged. "It's probably nothing. Irene just changed her address to a PO box. She mentioned something about selling her house. It's not unusual to downsize after the loss of a spouse." The office telephone rang, and Mandy gestured she needed to answer the call.

Kelly took her cue and excused herself from the office. Outside, she shivered. A swirl of leaves swept by her feet, prompting her to look up. The trees were almost completely bare. One more good wind storm and the last holdouts of fall foliage would be gone. Kelly tightened the cashmere scarf around her neck and buttoned her barn jacket, which wasn't warm enough now. Luckily, she had a short walk back to the boutique. She slung her tote bag over her shoulder as she walked away from the insurance agency. She wasn't in any particular hurry to get back to her apartment. Or the new tasks that now waited for her.

Rather than finish unpacking and settling in, she'd be boxing up her belongings for a move back to the city. She'd also be making decisions about all of Granny's possessions. Most of them couldn't be moved along with her stuff. She'd have to figure out a way to get her stuff and Howard back to the city. She doubted Pepper would be offering her SUV for the return trip.

"Kelly! Wait up!"

Kelly stopped and looked over her shoulder. Gabe jogged down the sidewalk, carefully passing other pedestrians. Dressed in a pair of baggy jeans and an unzipped jacket over his college sweatshirt, he looked grim.

"Glad I saw you. What the hell happened between you and my mom?" Gabe shoved his hands into the pockets of his jacket.

"I wish I knew. She came into the boutique this morning all worked up, telling me how irresponsible I am and that I'm ungrateful." Saying the words had Kelly tearing up. She quickly wiped away the tears before they fell and composed herself because she didn't want another weepy episode. She'd already had to redo her eye makeup once. "She's right. Everything is a mess."

"She's worried about you. She loves you like a daughter. And she treated you like one." A crooked smile touched Gabe's lips. "You've heard her go off on me."

"I know. I know. It's what she didn't say that has me feeling really bad." She saw the confusion on his face. "I've disappointed her." The emotion was too overwhelming for her. The tears burst like a dam, and she fell forward into Gabe's solid chest and cried. She never wanted to disappoint Pepper, because it would be like letting her granny down. "I'm sorry. Really, I am."

Gabe wrapped his arms around her and gently rubbed her back. His comfort was welcome and exactly what she needed. "You were trying to help Bernadette, and you got in over your head."

Kelly nodded. "I'm in way over my head with more than just Bernadette."

"What are you talking about?"

Kelly pulled away from Gabe's broad chest. A gust of wind hit, sweeping her hair up, and she pushed back locks of hair from her face. "The boutique. I'm not ready for the responsibility. I'm not even sure I want to own a used clothing store. It's just not my thing."

He pushed back a wayward lock of hair off her face. "Not your thing? Kell, you may not have noticed. But I've seen how much you light up when you're in your boutique or when you talk about the changes you see happening in there."

Kelly wiped away her tears with the back of her hand. She was going to have to redo her makeup again. She must look like a raccoon. "I was just dreaming. I can't build a life on a dream."

"Why not? Your grandmother did. What are you going to do?" His voice was deep with concern.

Her guess was he knew what she planned on doing.

"Sell to Ralph." Her uncle was her best option for a quick sale.

"You can't sell to him. He'll bulldoze the building and everything your granny worked for will be gone."

"Gabe, I can't live my life in the shadow of my granny."

"You're right. From where I sit, I think she gave you a perfect way to shine in your own life...that is, if you're willing to take the risk and go for it."

Kelly's breath caught. Granny didn't leave her the consignment shop to be run exactly how she managed it, because she knew Kelly would want to make it her own. She never expected her granddaughter to live her life, rather, she gave Kelly a foundation to build her own on. "When did you become so smart?"

Gabe tilted his head sideways. "I've always been smart. You've never appreciated my genius. Or my words of wisdom." Gabe laughed and grasped both of Kelly's shoulders and held his gaze on her. "Seriously. Running away again isn't the answer. Stay. Fight. Then decide." He glanced at his watch. "Gotta go. Don't make any rash decisions today. Okay? Promise me."

"I promise." She said goodbye to Gabe and continued along Main Street at a fast pace, because she was freezing, to her building. But a window display in a neighboring shop caught her attention, and she dashed inside to buy the new little orange man in her life a gift.

Chapter 21

Kelly entered by the back door and walked through the staff room into the boutique. When the house was converted to retail space, there wasn't enough in the budget to create a separate entrance to the second-floor apartment. Instead, the staircase was enclosed with a door for access upstairs. Kelly reached the locked interior door and went to pull out the key, but a loud knock at the boutique's front door had her setting her tote bag down and walking to the front of the store. Delivering Howard's gift would have to wait.

On the other side of the front door was Breena Collins. Her face was pressed against the glass, and her hands were cupped around her head as she peered inside the boutique.

Kelly unlocked and opened the door. "Breena, what are you doing here?"

"I'm here to see you. May I come in? Why is your shop closed?"

"Long story. Yes, please come in." Kelly stepped aside to allow Breena to enter and then closed the door. "What can I do for you?"

"I have a confession to make." Breena's eyes cast downward for a nanosecond. When she looked back at Kelly, her amber eyes were remorseful. "I kinda didn't tell you all of the truth the other day about Eddie Singer."

From what Kelly remembered of the conversation, Breena hadn't said much about him. Only that he was in debt to Leo Manning, was desperate, and eventually stopped coming around to the Thirsty Turtle. "You didn't?"

Breena unzipped her olive-colored puffer jacket to reveal a berry sweater with a plunging V-neckline. Her bootleg bleached jeans were skintight, and her platform wedged boots were scuffed. Breena's style hadn't changed much since high school. In fact, Kelly was almost certain the outfit looked familiar.

"I don't want any trouble. I've been working really hard on making something of my life." Breena drifted toward a circular rack of blouses and mindlessly browsed through them. "You're really lucky to have come back home with a future. I came back with a kid and a whole lot of regret."

Kelly joined Breena at the clothing rack. "What's going on?"

"Can you keep a secret?"

Kelly nodded. "I can."

Breena shifted to be face-to-face with Kelly. "When I left home to move to the city to be an actress, I ended up waiting tables instead. I got plenty of auditions, but I wasn't prepared for all of the competition. Sure, I had lead roles in our school plays, but I quickly saw I didn't have the talent that was needed to make it big."

"I think we all had inflated egos back then. I was certain I'd be the toast of the fashion world if I could just get them to see my genius." Kelly laughed at the memories of her eighteen-year-old self. Oh, the things she'd tell her younger self now if she could. "I quickly got knocked down a couple of pegs in fashion school."

"At least you went to college. I waited tables, which didn't pay much. Still doesn't, but it's a paycheck. I had to find other work while I waited for my big break." Breena's eyes lit up, and then the light faded. "Not really reputable work. But it paid good."

"Oh." Kelly understood having to pay dues. She'd worked the sales floor of Bishop's while studying fashion merchandising. For a struggling actress like Breena, waiting tables was a normal stepping stone, and then sometimes actresses had to take other roles. "You mean you were a p...p...po..."

"No! No! Nothing like that. Oh my gosh. I wouldn't ever be able to show my face back here in Lucky Cove if I did *those* types of movies." Breena giggled.

"Thank goodness. I mean, I wouldn't judge you if you had."

Breena smiled. "I know. I worked for one of those nine hundred numbers and talked to men. As I said, it paid well. But, after my shift, I always needed a hot shower. Those guys were pigs. Well, most of them. There were a few guys who called because they were lonely. Like Eddie Singer."

"He was lonely?"

"Yeah. He owed a lot of money to Leo Manning, and he was having problems at home. He'd nurse a beer for hours just to avoid going home."

Breena moved over to a spiral display rack Kelly had merchandised with short cocktail dresses perfect for holiday parties.

"He sounds like he was a sad man. Why didn't he get help with his gambling?"

Breena shrugged. "I don't know. Guess he wasn't ready." She tapped one dress. An emerald-green short-sleeved faux-wrap dress with a surplice neckline and gathered at the waist with a jeweled ring. She checked out the price tag. "I love this!" She took the dress from the rack and, holding it in front of her, she raced to the full-length mirror to take a look. "What do you think?"

"I think it'll look lovely on you. It flatters your figure."

"And it's the right price."

"Is there any more about Eddie you want to tell me?"

Breena pulled her gaze from the mirror. "Sorry. He started to open up to me. People like to talk to me. Guess that's why I did so good as a telephone operator. Anyway, on slow nights at the bar, I had more of a chance to talk to him. Remember I told you how he stopped coming around? Well, before he did, he told me he was really scared of Leo Manning. Deathly scared."

"He owed that much money?"

"He never said how much he was in for, and I never asked. See, the one thing I learned a long time ago was not to ask too many questions about men like Leo Manning. Look, I like you. I think we have a lot in common, so I'm here to warn you."

"Warn me?"

Breena's head bobbed up and down. "You came to the bar the other day looking for him. What did you think would happen if Leo was there?"

"I just wanted to ask a few questions about Eddie."

"Bad idea. Eddie is dead. Don't come back to the bar, and don't go nosing around Leo Manning's business. Just leave it alone."

"Breena, do you think Irene could have killed Eddie?"

"You think Irene killed him? Where are you coming up with this stuff?" Breena folded the dress over her arm.

"I have a theory. Do you think Irene could have killed Eddie?"

"From what he told me, she was really angry with him. Though, I don't think I could blame her. If my husband owed money to a bookie, I'd be peeved. But Eddie died up in Maine and, at the time, Irene was here in Lucky Cove."

"She could've had a partner. Did Eddie ever mention if he thought Irene was also having an affair?"

"No. You think she had a lover and he followed Eddie up to Maine?"

"It's a possibility," Kelly said.

The last vision Bernadette had was of Irene talking to someone when her husband was murdered, and then Kelly overheard Irene's call at the storage facility. As crazy as it sounded, she was starting to believe in the psychic's visions.

"Thank you for coming here and telling me this. Now you need to tell the police everything you told me."

"The police? Why?"

"Eddie could have been murdered. And I think someone is trying to kill Bernadette because of the vision she had."

"This is crazy. If the police suspected foul play in Eddie's death, they would have investigated. Besides, I'm not going to risk my job at the bar. I have tuition to pay and a kid to take care of. If Cody finds out I'm talking out of school to you, or worse, to the police, I'll be out of a job."

"I understand your position, but there have been three murders I feel are connected. Eddie, Maxine, and DJ Brown."

"Eddie wasn't murdered! I can't believe I came here."

"Then why did you?"

"To tell you to mind your own business. Leo is bad news. Look, I don't want to get on his bad side, so keep me out of whatever you're doing." Breena shoved the dress into Kelly's hands and then spun around and stormed out of the boutique, slamming the door behind her.

Kelly went to follow Breena, but her former classmate was fast on her feet and already heading down the street. Kelly discarded the green dress and darted to the staff room, snatching up her tote bag on the way. In the staff room, she pulled open the file drawer. She retrieved the black lace dress and shoved it into her bag. Bernadette needed to see the dress again. Kelly had to figure out who Irene was talking to. She wasn't going to let Irene get away with murder, if she indeed was the murderer.

On her way to the staircase, she heard footsteps in the front of the boutique. She peered out and found a redhead eyeing one of the tunics Regina Green consigned and Kelly had dressed the display torsos with. She'd forgotten to lock the door after Breena left, and the redhead must not have noticed the closed sign.

The woman seemed particularly interested in the eggplant-colored tunic draped with an infinity scarf. Kelly couldn't very well leave the customer all alone. She dropped her tote bag and stepped out onto the sales floor.

"You have a good eye. That tunic would look lovely on you with your coloring." Kelly had approached the display table with her best cheery voice and smile in place.

"Really? It seems like a risk. I usually go for greens or black, like every other woman." The woman laughed. Yes, New York women loved their black fashions. "I'm Jo. You must be Kelly, Martha's granddaughter." Jo extended her hand to Kelly.

Kelly shook Jo's hand. "Yes, I am. And, yes, I think this top would look fabulous on you. You should try it on. The changing room is that way." Kelly pointed.

"I think I will." Jo headed to the changing room while Kelly removed the tunic from the display torso. Twenty minutes later, and with a shopping bag full of clothing, Jo was pocketing her wallet. "Maybe I shouldn't say this, but the few times I came in here, I never found anything I wanted to buy. Martha was a wonderful woman, so kind and welcoming, but the merchandise wasn't my taste. And today, I thought I'd just browse to see what you've done to the shop." She lifted the shopping bag. "I can't believe I found all of this, and I love everything, especially the price."

"You have no idea what it means to me to hear you say that." Kelly was on the verge of tears again, but this time for a good reason.

"You have a gift for this." Jo took in a sweeping glance of the boutique. "You're going to do very well. I should get going. Thank you for your help!" As she exited, Kelly couldn't help but notice the spring in Jo's step. It was amazing how something as simple as a new top or dress or even a pair of earrings could lift a gal's spirit.

What just happened with Jo was what Kelly loved the most about being in the fashion industry—styling and helping a woman feel good about herself. If she returned to the city and managed somehow to get another job in a buying office, she wouldn't be able to work one-on-one with customers. To do that, she'd have to get a job in sales at a boutique and work for someone else and earn barely enough to pay rent. She walked to the door and locked it. She needed some time to think about what to do next with her life. And she needed a glass, or two, of wine.

Chapter 22

Kelly filled her glass with a generous amount of wine and then topped it off with a little extra for good measure. She'd earned every ounce. She set the bottle down, which she considered drinking from rather than a glass for a nanosecond.

She inhaled the fragrance of the red wine from her glass after she swirled it. She wasn't a connoisseur, but she felt less like a lush if she didn't gulp the wine down right away.

She savored her first sip. She definitely needed the wine, between Pepper ripping her a new one and then quitting and Gabe's unexpected but insightful pep talk.

Her plan to visit Bernadette didn't happen because, when she called the police department, she was informed Bernadette had been transferred to the county jail and, since she was being held without bail, visitors weren't permitted. Even if Kelly was allowed to visit, she doubted they'd allow Bernadette to handle the dress. So much for trying to get another vision out of the psychic.

Howard approached stealthily from the bedroom and wove his body between Kelly's legs, rubbing against her. Startled at first, she relaxed as he pushed his long, lean body into her ankle.

She'd done a little research and found when Howard rubbed against her he was marking his territory. The article also said she should take it as a compliment but, deep down, she wondered if he was just another possessive male. She'd dated a couple of those over the years. The breakups weren't pretty. Howard followed up with a tiny meow that she interpreted, thanks to the extensive article on cat behavior, as a "hello." Though she'd been home at least twenty minutes, enough time to change into a pair of yoga pants with a T-shirt, slip her feet into her Ugg slippers, and pour a glass of wine, it appeared Howard was too busy sleeping to welcome her right away.

"Hello to you. Did you do anything besides sleep today?"

Howard gazed at her. He had no comment.

"Didn't think so. Want to hear about my whole day?"

Howard rubbed her leg one last time before strolling out of the living room and disappearing into the bedroom.

"He's still a jerk." With her wineglass in hand, she walked over to the sofa and set the glass on the coffee table. A *whoosh* of wind assaulted the house and rattled the old windows. She walked over to the windows and peered out. The majestic oak tree's limbs swayed in the cold, night wind and were precariously close to the power lines. Her spot on Long Island wasn't a stranger to power outages caused by storms. Darn. She hadn't had time to get the generator serviced because she'd been busy chasing down a killer. More proof Pepper was right about her.

She couldn't keep dwelling on the choices she'd made, since she couldn't change them. All she could do was move forward and earnestly make better decisions.

She wrapped her arms around herself. It was a good night for soup. If she remembered correctly, there were a couple of cans in the kitchen cupboard. She turned away from the window and propped both hands on her hips and looked around at the space that combined both dining and living areas. There was a lot of furniture crammed into the space, like the oversized hutch by the table. It used to display her granny's heirloom dish set downstairs in the formal dining room. Now it was overpowering the small dining area. It needed to go into storage. She'd seen a glass-door cabinet sideboard on Ikea's website, and it would be perfect in the hutch's spot. More streamlined and contemporary. It was more Kelly's style.

She smiled. She was decorating the apartment. She was going to stay in Lucky Cove and keep the boutique. Granny had given her an opportunity to do what she loved doing, albeit in a place where she never thought she'd be. Whether or not the decision was a bad one or possibly the best one she could make was a toss-up.

The one thing she knew for certain was she was done running. Granny left the shop to her for a reason. Was it to give Kelly the opportunity to come home and start over? Granny knew Kelly wouldn't have re-rooted in Lucky Cove for any other reason.

First order of business was to pack up the collection of Granny's knickknacks. For now, they'd be stored in the storage room downstairs, along with the stuff she'd pick up tomorrow at the cottage. Later in the week, she'd figure out how to get the hutch out of the apartment. She was definitely going to need Liv's brother and Gabe.

Next thing on her to-do list was a biggie. Call Pepper after dinner. They hadn't talked since their argument, and she'd come to the conclusion she needed to be the one to reach out and apologize for behaving like a spoiled, ungrateful child. She swallowed the lump in her throat. She didn't completely agree with Pepper's assessment. A lot had been thrown at her in just a few months, and most days she felt like she was struggling to breathe, but there were a few instances she could have handled better. And she would. Going forward.

She assembled a box and taped its bottom then reached for a few sheets of tissue paper and then grabbed a colorful bird statuette. She wrapped the statuette carefully and placed it in the box and continued to repeat the motion again for six more birds. Granny must have gone through a phase at some point. Because after the birds, there were dolphin statuettes.

The packing was a mindless activity that allowed her thoughts to drift. And drift they did. From ideas of personalized shopping bags to further branding her boutique to contacting the town about the cracks in the parking lot behind the boutique to Bernadette.

She huffed. All roads led back to Bernadette and the murders.

She grabbed another handful of tissue paper and wrapped a flower vase. Granny had more knickknacks than any one person ever needed. There were dozens hidden away in cabinets and the linen closet, along with the five on the server. Funny thing was, on her visits over the years, she'd never noticed how many things her granny collected. She never paid attention to the little things. A pang of guilt stabbed at her heart. She guessed each knickknack held a story for Granny. Stories she would never know because she never thought to ask.

More tears fell from her eyes. "Oh boy. Why am I always crying?" She set the wrapped vase down and walked over to the sofa. She swiped up the wineglass and took a long drink. With the glass in hand, she walked back to the table and sat down at the end of the table where her laptop was set out. Next to the laptop were the copies of Ariel's file on her psychic investigation. She pressed the ON button of the computer and, within a few seconds, she had her browser opened.

She should've been letting go of the murders. Since she was no longer a suspect, she had no business sticking her nose into the investigation.

She had a boutique to run, or rather, a boutique to keep from the brink of failure. Playing Nancy Drew didn't help her with her responsibilities to the boutique or to Pepper. Even though Pepper quit, Kelly was confident she'd come back once Kelly apologized.

No matter how chaotic her personal life was with her friends and family, her thoughts kept coming back to Bernadette being held in a cell for murders she probably didn't commit.

The look in Bernadette's eyes the day she discovered Maxine's body wasn't a look of someone who was responsible for the death. Or the day DJ Brown was murdered. Bernadette was confused and scared, and that was why she acted in such an irrational way. She wasn't trying to hurt Kelly. She was trying to save herself. She's wasn't a killer.

Kelly shivered and reached for the cardigan draped on the chair to slip on. The apartment, like the downstairs, was drafty. At some point, she needed to address the heating issue, but she was scared what would be uncovered. An out-of-date furnace, no doubt. She bet the insulation wasn't energy efficient any longer, and probably the windows too. Dollar signs floated in her mind.

Kelly opened the file folder and sorted through the documents, which included some newspaper clippings from the Chicago area stating Bernadette's visions were crazy. There was a lot of information proving Maxine was a fraud. So, it made sense her cousin was one also.

Besides, Eddie's death had been ruled an accident, and there was no way the police would reopen the case based on Bernadette's vision. And the vision was sketchy at best. Bernadette had no details, other than the dress Irene was wearing and she was talking to someone.

Who was the man? Maybe if Kelly could confirm Irene was having an affair, then the police might consider reopening the case. She'd have to tell Detective Wolman.

But she'd have to do it soon, because it appeared Irene was moving. Irene opened a PO box, and the packing peanuts on her sofa that she claimed Buster had been playing with were probably for Irene's move. The widow wasn't downsizing. She was leaving Lucky Cove with the insurance payout.

Kelly sprawled out the copies of Ariel's notes, and one had a few handwritten notations. Ariel had scribbled the name of Maxine's brother. Marco. The police's theory was he tried to kill Bernadette out of revenge for his sister's death.

All nice and tidy.

Detective Wolman had an answer for everything.

Kelly had caught a glimpse of the driver. The incident happened so fast that she didn't think she could've officially identified him in a lineup. Maybe she could. She did a quick internet search for Marco Lemoyne and got quite a few results. To say the guy was shady would be an understatement. She found one article from a Detroit newspaper that Ariel didn't have in her file, and the article included a photograph of Marco. Kelly leaned into the chair. Marco's hair was a light shade of brown. "He's not the driver."

At that moment, the lights went out in the apartment. She'd lost power. *Great. Just great.* She pushed her chair back and stood. It was time to break out the candles and find a flashlight. She remembered seeing one in the coat closet. Another thing she needed to do was to prepare an emergency kit.

She hurried to the closet but stopped short when she bumped into the front door of the apartment. She cursed. As she began to close the door, her breath caught. She'd shut it when she arrived home. And Howard couldn't open a door.

Could he?

"You're right about Marco not being the driver. I was the driver."

The unfamiliar male voice from behind sent Kelly jumping away from the door and back against the wall. Her body was pressed rigidly against the almond-colored wall, and her hands were balled into fists. Her heart raced so fast she thought she'd pass out.

"Who...who are you? What...what are you doing here?" Kelly swallowed hard as fear rippled through her. How did the man enter her apartment and she not know it? Her first guess would be, because she was absorbed in tracking down the killer, everything else was tuned out. Apparently that was a pattern these past weeks.

He stepped forward. She couldn't get a good look at his face because of the darkness.

"You've been sticking your nose where it doesn't belong. And because of that, other people are asking questions." He took another step forward. "I don't like questions."

"No...no... I understand. If you don't want to tell me who you are, you can leave and I won't say anything. I swear. No one will know."

She saw a flash of white. He must've been smiling. He probably found her terror amusing. Her entire body shook, from the roots of her highlighted blond hair to her toes, which hadn't seen a proper pedicure since she left the city.

"I don't have any money...but I'll give you my credit cards and my ATM card... Anything... Please just go."

The stranger took another step forward and then pulled out a mini-flashlight from his belt and switched it on, illuminating his face. Kelly gasped. She recognized him from the photograph online and from Mark Lambert's group photograph of his fishing buddies.

"No can do. At least, not without you, Miss Quinn."

Eddie Singer's chilling words reverberated through Kelly's body, and her knees went weak. They buckled, but Eddie grabbed her by the arm before she landed on the floor.

She struggled to break free of his grip, but it was too tight. "I'm not going anywhere with you!"

"You don't have a choice."

She yanked her arm hard and was able to slip it from his hold and spun around. She needed to get to her cell phone. Where did she leave it? In her tote bag?

She didn't get very far. Eddie grabbed her shoulder and pulled her back toward him, knocking her off balance. He caught her, wrapping his arm around her midsection.

The flashlight dropped, and he cursed. "You're not going to make this easy, are you?"

"You're supposed to be dead!"

"Yeah. That was the idea. Until you and that damn psychic started raising questions."

Eddie's hold around her stomach tightened, so she lifted one foot and, with all of her might, she stomped on his foot. He cursed again but didn't let go of her. All it got her was an angry tug around her midsection. She guessed the move would have been more effective if she'd had on boots like he did.

"You're a fighter. Let's see how that works for you."

His body shifted, and then she heard the click before she saw the gun out of the corner of her eye. Her heart sank, and her body froze.

"Not so feisty now, huh? Here's what we're going to do. We're going downstairs and out back to my truck. You make any funny moves, and I will shoot you."

"You're going to kill me anyway."

"Yeah, but do you really want to bleed out on the staircase?"

She shook her head. She didn't want to. The thought of Pepper or Liv discovering her body sent a wave of nausea rolling through her. Besides, going along with Eddie for a little while would buy her some time. Time she'd use to figure out a way to escape.

Chapter 23

Eddie shoved Kelly out the back door, and she stumbled but remained upright due to his tight hold on her. She quickly regained her balance; all the while fear coursed through her body. She glanced at him, standing several inches taller than her. His gaze was focused ahead. The only sound was the big, sweeping gusts of wind that swayed the overhead tree limbs. She scanned the area. A chain-link fence enclosed the long stretch of deserted parking lot. Not a soul was around. How could a parking lot on Lucky Cove's Main Street be so desolate?

He yanked her forward, and she stumbled again. She glanced down and saw the cement stopper. She was being dragged to the spot where she used to park her loaned SUV. Now the space was empty, just like the parking lot.

Another tug of her arm jerked her head around, and then she saw the van, the one that tried to run Bernadette down, parked just outside of the cast of light from a tall lamppost. It looked like Eddie cut the power to her building to get an advantage over her.

Kelly swallowed a hard lump in her throat. There wasn't anyone around to help her. She was on her own.

"You'll never get away with this," she said. Though, once the words escaped her lips, she realized they weren't very convincing. So far Eddie had gotten away with murder and, once he disposed of Kelly, he'd be free and clear.

Eddie responded with only a grunt.

"You faked your death? How'd you manage that?" Kelly thought talking to and engaging the psychopath in conversation might buy her some time. Slow down his stride to the waiting truck.

"Yeah. It was a good plan," he boasted.

"Not really, or else you wouldn't be here now." *Good going, Kell. Antagonize the murderer.*

His grip tightened on her arm so hard that she yelped.

"Shut up, already!"

Kelly pressed her lips together as her mind raced. All the pieces started to come together for Kelly. "Irene knew! She was in on it too. The phone call. You called her after the accident! She was wearing the dress when you called her to tell her your truck went off the road."

Bernadette had been right all along. A man had been murdered.

"Yeah, you've got it all figured out. Lot of good it'll do you now." He picked up his pace and dragged Kelly to the truck. They arrived at the passenger side, and he reached out for the door handle.

"Why? Why fake your death?"

Eddie shook his head. "You're asking a lot of questions. Guess you haven't learned your lesson yet."

"Don't you think I have a right to know why you've done all this and why you're going to kill me?" Saying those words out loud caused her stomach to roll. She didn't want to die. She finally had something to live for, a reason to wake up every day. She glanced at the boutique. Her granny's legacy would be bulldozed by Ralph in a matter of weeks, just like Gabe said earlier. And who would take Howard? He was kind of a jerk, but she'd fallen in love with him nonetheless.

"Five hundred thousand reasons. That's what I owed Leo Manning. I don't have that kind of money. If I didn't fake my death, he would've killed me."

"Who died in the car crash?"

Eddie shrugged. "Some homeless guy. I offered him a coffee and a ride. Long story short, I sent the truck off the road and it exploded into a big ball of fire. Small town with just a handful of cops. They were eager to close the case quickly. Left them just enough evidence for them to assume Eddie Singer died that rainy afternoon."

"What about Maxine?"

"Yeah, my bad. I thought she was Bernadette. Those chicks looked alike from behind. I never believed in all that psychic stuff, but after you told Irene about the vision, she panicked and called me. I didn't have a choice. I had to make sure she didn't keep repeating the story. Then the police were looking at you as the murderer. I really needed to make sure no one believed Bernadette."

"That's why you killed DJ Brown."

"Again, no choice. Now, the psychic is arrested and you'll be dead. Irene and I can leave for Mexico tonight. Get in!" Eddie yanked open the passenger door.

"Not so fast!"

A man's voice startled Kelly. Finally, someone had arrived to discover she was being abducted at gunpoint. Hopefully, the person was calling the police on his cell phone. The sense of relief she experienced was short-lived. The stranger was holding a bigger gun than Eddie's on them. Then it hit her, the Good Samaritan was either in law enforcement or just an average Joe coming to the aid of a gal in big trouble.

Eddie's eyes widened in terror as his body turned to face the stranger. "Leo..."

Leo Manning? As in the not-so-nice bookie who threatened to kill Eddie? Any relief Kelly had was gone. She wasn't being rescued. The likelihood Manning would let her go was pretty low, in her opinion, because she was what was called a witness.

"It's over, Eddie. Drop your gun," Leo commanded. A sliver of light from the tall lamp cast down on Leo. Short, pudgy, with a receding hairline, he didn't look too scary. It was the gun in his hand and his unforgiving tone that scared the daylights out of Kelly.

Eddie glanced at Kelly and then at Leo. He looked torn between surrendering or shooting. Kelly wasn't keen on being in the middle of a shootout.

"I was going to come and see you next, Leo." Eddie's voice suddenly became uneven. Gone was the bravado he'd displayed just moments earlier.

Leo laughed, and not in a funny ha-ha kind of way. His laugh was sinister, and if Kelly wasn't already shaking between being held at gunpoint and being outside in a wind storm without a coat, she would've been trembling right down to her core by the pure evilness of Leo's laugh.

"Is that a fact?" He lifted his gun just a little bit higher. "I heard you say you were heading to Mexico tonight with the wife. And all that insurance money she collected. Not to worry. I have it now." His thin lips stretched into a grim smile.

"What? What did you do to Irene?" Eddie let go of Kelly and raised his gun higher, aiming right at Leo's head.

"What do you think?" Leo challenged just before a flash of light coming from behind Leo caught Kelly's attention.

Kelly cocked her head sideways. What was the light? It was coming closer to them at a really fast speed.

Her eyes widened as Ariel and her motorized wheelchair came into view. She couldn't believe what she was seeing. Ariel's hair was blowing in the wind, and she was aiming right for Leo, who turned in Ariel's direction too late. Her chair banged into his body, plunging him forward and, as he went down, he dropped his gun. Kelly's eyes squeezed shut for a second, preparing for the weapon to discharge, but it didn't. When she opened her eyes, she saw Eddie was momentarily stunned, giving her the chance to take the bold, risky move, and lunged for the gun. Scrambling, she reached the weapon and grabbed it. Her hands shook uncontrollably, but she managed to clamp a firm grip on the gun, which she pointed at Eddie.

"It's over, Eddie. Put down your gun." Kelly glanced over at Ariel, who was on her cell phone telling the 9-1-1 dispatcher where she was. "The police are on their way. Don't make this any worse."

Eddie grinned. "Be careful, or you'll hurt yourself, little girl. You don't even know how to use a gun."

Kelly had an urge to wipe the cocky grin off of Eddie's face. He'd killed three innocent people and planned on making her his fourth victim. No way in hell was he leaving before the cops arrived to slap handcuffs on him.

She raised the gun higher and steadied her hand. "I'm a fast learner." Her gaze darted to the weapon. "The safety is off." She looked back to Eddie. "And my finger just needs to pull back the trigger. Then it goes *bang,* right? Should I give it a try since you've threatened my life?"

"Do what she says. The police will be here any minute." Ariel navigated her wheelchair over to Kelly.

Sirens approached, and police vehicles came racing into the parking lot. Their strobe lights lit up the darkness. The three cruisers came to a hard stop.

"Ah, hell." Eddie carefully squatted down and set his gun on the ground and then stood with his hands in the air.

"That was pretty impressive with the wheelchair move." Kelly looked at Ariel. The light was coming from Ariel's head. "Is that a flashlight on your head?"

"Yeah." Ariel nodded. "A flashlight headband. Neat, huh? I got it last year for Christmas."

"Best gift ever!"

"Right?" Ariel's face turned somber. "What's Leo Manning doing here? Who's the other guy?"

"Eddie Singer." Kelly indicated the man she was pointing a gun at.

Now Ariel looked confused. "Eddie Singer is dead."

"Long story." Kelly's head whipped around as the police officers rushed in her direction.

"Kelly, put down the gun!" Gabe called out as he approached the scene.

"Right." Kelly released the gun onto the ground and then stepped far back as Gabe and two other officers came rushing toward them and arrested Eddie and Leo Manning.

Flashing strobe lights continued to light up the parking lot, and the muffled sounds of radio squawk filled the air as Kelly stood, leaning against Gabe's police car with his jacket wrapped around her. Ariel was beside her and watched the police arrest Leo and Eddie and took copious notes.

"I meant to ask, but with the police and criminals…how did you know something was wrong?" Even though Kelly had Gabe's jacket draped over her shoulders, she was still shaking.

"Well, to be honest, I didn't know anything was wrong. I came to see if you wanted to get dinner. Then I saw him." She pointed to Leo. "Making his way around back here, so I followed him."

"That could have been dangerous."

"I know. But I could easily outrun him in this chair." She smiled brightly as she patted her chair. "The speed on this baby is awesome. As you saw."

"I most certainly did." Kelly's smile faded as the reality of the night continued to sink in. "You saved my life."

Ariel nodded. "I did, didn't I? And you caught a killer."

"Well, I wouldn't exactly say I caught him. He broke into my home and held me at gunpoint."

"Yeah, but when you had the chance to turn the tables on him, you did. You're a real badass."

Kelly dipped her head. She wasn't used to praise and found it a little unsettling accepting it. "We now know the truth." She lifted her head and took in a deep breath. "It looks like Bernadette's vision was correct."

Ariel shrugged. "She might be legit. I'm still skeptical, but I'm willing to keep an open mind about her when I finish my article."

"Sounds fair."

"I hate to break up this moment, but Detective Wolman wants both of you gals down at the department now."

Kelly straightened her arms and lifted them forward. "You gonna handcuff me again?"

"No. Neither of you are under arrest. You'll come with me. Ariel, Officer Parker will drive you."

"Meet you there." Ariel began to turn her wheelchair but stopped. "Kelly, I'm glad I was here for you tonight."

"Me too." Kelly swooped forward and hugged Ariel tightly. "It's good to be home."

"I'm happy you came back. Welcome home," Ariel whispered before Kelly let go of her.

Chapter 24

Kelly checked her phone. No text from Gabe. She fired off a text reminding him to text her when he left then shifted her attention to the boutique. Liv had arrived just after eight to help set everything up for the grand reopening of the boutique. Liv had gone above and beyond the past three weeks to help Kelly realize her vision.

Like the new accessory department.

Once the home accents department of the Lucky Cove Consignment Shop, it now housed fashion jewelry, shoes, handbags, and scarves. Kelly had dusted off her merchandising display skills and kicked up her bargain hunting skills to find budget-friendly fixtures.

In the past few weeks, since Eddie and Irene Singer were arrested for three murders, insurance fraud, and attempted murder, Kelly had been able to focus on the boutique. Business had picked up, which included consignments, which gave her ample inventory for the newly revamped space. The old, cluttered addition was now bright and cheery, thanks to a coat of soft white paint, cleaned lighting fixtures, inexpensive shelving put up by Frankie, and two floor leaning mirrors she snagged at a ridiculously low price at the flea market where she sold the remaining home accents inventory she had.

The mirrors were in bad shape, but, after a Sunday morning of covering the frames with batting and faux black leather and then tufting them with crystal buttons, they were a fun addition to the space. She came across a coordinating ottoman perfect for trying on shoes. An addition of a graphic art print on canvas in silver tone with intertwining initials reminiscent of her favorite designer, Coco Chanel, hung beside one of the leaning mirrors. The room still took her breath away. It was perfect.

"Has he texted yet?" Liv popped her head into the room.

"No. I texted to remind him to text." Kelly spun around and walked toward Liv. "They should be leaving any minute. Right?"

"People are gathering outside. Come on." Liv waved for Kelly to follow her. "This is so exciting. It's official now." She stopped at the sales counter. "This day has been long coming."

"It most certainly has. There were times I didn't think I'd get here."

"You're happy you didn't sell to your uncle?"

Kelly nodded. "Definitely."

"Hey, I'm not late, am I?" Frankie dashed in from the staff room and gave Kelly a quick hug. "I got the champagne and orange juice. I'll make the mimosas when you open up."

"Thanks, Frankie. The mimosas will be a nice touch." Kelly wanted to have drinks available throughout the day, and Frankie had offered to take care of the task. He had not only planned three cocktails, but he also created a menu for appetizers he'd serve throughout the day.

"Oh, heads up. I didn't come alone," Frankie said in a dry tone.

Kelly heard footsteps coming from the staff room and then heard voices. "Why did you bring them?"

"I didn't. They arrived when I did." Frankie scooted over next to Liv.

"Kelly, looks like you made some headway with this old place," Ralph boomed as he entered the front of the boutique.

"Everyone is gathering outside for the opening." Kelly hoped to get her uncle and his wife to turn around and leave.

"We know. We saw the little group as we pulled into the parking lot." Summer held Juniper, and the baby cooed, melting Kelly's heart.

"She's adorable." Kelly walked over to Summer and Juniper and gently stroked the baby's small, chubby hand. "Good morning, Juniper. You were adorable on Halloween. You were the cutest little pumpkin ever. Yes, you were."

"I love this baby." Liv rushed over to join Kelly in swooning over Juniper. "Hi there, pretty girl."

Juniper smiled, and her face lit up. Her blue eyes twinkled.

Kelly wanted to scoop her up and snuggle with her, but she had a grand opening to attend to. "I'm glad you brought her today. I love seeing her."

"Everyone does. Looks like you made some changes. It's nice you're trying." Summer drifted away from Kelly and Liv, who looked at each other and rolled their eyes.

"I hope you didn't sink too much money into this grand opening or paid too much for that roof repair, because the likelihood of you staying

in business is doubtful. Tourists don't want to shop in thrift shops."
Ralph shoved his thick hands into his pants pockets, brushing back
his navy blazer.

Kelly was about to reply but caught Summer eyeing a nutmeg-colored
sleeveless suede dress with a drawstring waist. She smiled and looked
at her uncle. "You don't have to worry. I've got this." She breezed past
him and joined Liv and Frankie at the counter. "Any word from Gabe?"

Liv and Frankie shook their heads.

"We have to open in a few minutes." Kelly tapped her fingers
on the counter.

"Frankie, I set up the glasses on the tray for you." Breena joined them
at the counter from the staff room. She'd arrived just after Liv and got
to work finalizing the boutique for the opening.

The day after Eddie was arrested, Breena came back to the boutique
and apologized to Kelly for her behavior. They hugged it out and, over
coffee, she offered Breena a part-time position at the boutique. Kelly didn't
want her former French classmate waiting tables at the Thirsty Turtle any
longer, though she wasn't sure if she could match the salary the bar paid.
Breena accepted the job and said she was going to pick up some hours
at Doug's Variety Store so she'd be able to quit waitressing at the bar.

Liv let out a little happy scream that had all heads turning.

"What?" they all said in unison.

Liv looked up from her phone. "Lulu Loves Long Island posted about
today's re-grand opening."

"Really? What does she say?" Frankie asked.

"Today Lucky Cove's consignment shop on Main Street reopens under
the new management of Kelly Quinn, former assistant women's fashion
buyer at Bishop's Department Store and most recently a named suspect
in two murders." Liv's smile faded.

A collective letdown was heard in the boutique.

"Sorry. I thought it was going to be good." Liv set down her phone.

"Today is good. I don't care what Lulu writes." Kelly's phone buzzed,
and she looked at the message. "Okay. Gabe just texted. He's a couple
minutes away. Let's go outside and wait for them." Kelly ushered everyone
out the front door.

It'd been three weeks since Eddie Singer broke into the boutique and
held a gun on her. The thought of the incident still sent shivers down
her spine and had her double-checking her locks at night. The following
morning after Eddie was arrested, Pepper came by to see Kelly. They'd
had a long talk and both of them apologized and decided to start fresh.

Since then they'd worked side by side in revamping the shop into Kelly's vision. And as a reward for her hard work, Kelly gave Pepper yesterday off with pay. She instructed Pepper to stay away from the boutique and to relax. Reports from Gabe since yesterday reassured Kelly her employee was doing just that—relaxing by the fire, curled up with a good book. Kelly even arranged for Frankie to deliver a gourmet lunch to make sure Pepper didn't venture out and ruin the surprise.

A loud round of applause greeted Kelly once outside. Familiar faces were in the crowd, including Ariel.

"I'm happy you're here today to celebrate with me." Kelly hugged Ariel.

"I wouldn't miss this for the world. Is that your uncle and Summer?" Ariel asked.

Kelly nodded as she let go of the embrace. "They snuck in the back."

"You need a better lock." Ariel laughed.

"Gabe's here!" Liv rushed to Kelly's side.

Frankie and Breena joined them while Ralph and Summer faded into the crowd.

They all watched as Gabe parked his truck in the reserved parking space right outside of the boutique and dashed around the passenger side to open his mom's door. Together they stepped up to the curb, and Pepper beamed. She'd first scanned the crowd and then followed Kelly's gesture to look up at the new sign.

Pepper looked confused. "Lucky Cove Resale Boutique? But…the shop's name is Curated by Kelly."

Kelly had canceled the Curated by Kelly sign and ordered another sign with the business's new name. "You were right. It's always been Lucky Cove. I just tweaked it a little bit."

Pepper teared up. "It's perfect. It really is, Kelly. Martha would be so proud of you." She threw her arms around Kelly and hugged her tightly, and the crowd erupted with more applause and cheers. "I couldn't be prouder of you if you were my own daughter."

It was Kelly's turn to tear up. Overwhelmed by emotion, she held on to Pepper tightly. Until she was tapped on the shoulder.

Liv cleared her throat. "We should go inside. It's cold."

Kelly loosened her hold on Pepper. She swung around to face everyone. "Welcome to the new Lucky Cove Resale Boutique! Come on inside and have a look and have a mimosa! Welcome!"

She gestured for everyone to start filing into the shop. Once everyone was inside, she followed and found they'd dispersed throughout the boutique.

"Great turnout." Liv approached Kelly, carrying two flutes of mimosa. She handed one to Kelly.

"Exactly what I'd hope for. They seem to like the changes?"

"They do. You've done a great job curating merchandise and displaying it. You're pretty good at this stuff." Liv gently bumped Kelly with her shoulder.

"I am." Kelly took a satisfying drink of the mimosa. Drinking champagne in the morning felt decadent. She took another sip and savored it.

"Congratulations, Miss Quinn." Detective Wolman entered the boutique and stopped next to Kelly. "Nice turnout."

"Thank you, Detective Wolman. I'm glad you've stopped by."

"Are you?"

"No hard feelings. You were just doing your job when you questioned me as if I were the killer and when you had me arrested for harboring a suspect, who actually wasn't the killer." Kelly lifted her half-empty glass and tipped it slightly before taking another sip.

"Very generous of you, Miss Quinn."

"I just can't believe the Singers thought they'd get away with faking Eddie's death."

"It's not an easy thing to accomplish. Mistakes are bound to happen, and that's how they got caught."

"If there's anything else I can do to help, please let me know."

"You've done quite a bit, Miss Quinn."

It seemed unlikely Kelly would receive a thank-you from the detective for helping bring two murderers to justice. "Well, then, if you're off duty, please help yourself to a mimosa. They're delicious."

"I am off duty. I thought I'd browse."

Kelly arched an eyebrow. Off duty and the detective was still wearing her bland uniform of a pantsuit and button-down shirt. The woman desperately needed a fashion intervention.

"Please do." Kelly swept her hand in the direction of the sales floor. "Let me know if you need any assistance."

Detective Wolman nodded and then continued into the boutique and disappeared into the crowd.

"She could've at least said 'I'm sorry.'" Liv took a drink of her mimosa.

"In her own way, she did." While hearing the words would have been nice, Kelly realized the detective showing up at the grand reopening was her way of apologizing. "Besides, it was her job to investigate everyone."

"Kel, this is fabulous." Frankie rushed to his cousin's side with a mimosa in hand. "Breena could use some help at the changing rooms."

"I'm on it." Liv dashed away in the direction of the changing rooms.

"You're going to need more of them, you know," Frankie said.

"I do. Eventually. I think today is the exception. There probably won't be this many people here again at once until I do a Black Friday sale."

"Well, I'll be…" Frankie's gaze shifted to the front door, and Kelly looked over her shoulder.

"Caroline?" Kelly stepped away from Frankie and met her sister at the door. "What are you doing here?"

"I came to see what you've done to Granny's shop. And to congratulate you."

"I'm glad you came." Kelly's hand covered her heart. The roller-coaster of emotions continued. Having her sister show up was more than she'd dreamed possible. "Ariel is here too."

"Great. I'd love to catch up with her."

"Come on. Let's go find her." Kelly went to turn, but Caroline reached out for her hand. "What's wrong?"

"Nothing. It's not going to be easy."

"I know."

"Do you have any plans for Thanksgiving?"

The holiday was a week away, and she hadn't even thought about it. Kelly had been so busy with the boutique after clearing her name in the murder investigations that she didn't even think about what to do on Thanksgiving. Her focus was on Black Friday.

"No, I don't." She remembered Summer's invitation a few weeks earlier. She'd rather eat a frozen turkey dinner with Howard than spend the day with her uncle and Summer.

"Good. Come to my house. I'm hosting this year." Caroline looked hopeful and sounded sincere.

"I'd love that. I'll be there." She reached out and hugged her sister. The day couldn't get any better. There were no psychic visions, no séances, no murders, and no arrests. There wasn't any way the day could get any better.

The bell over the front door jingled and drew Kelly's attention. As fast as her mood brightened, it plummeted at the sight of Mark Lambert, Dorothy Mueller's lawyer.

"Miss Quinn." The handsome lawyer looked good, real good, in a pair of worn jeans and a fisherman sweater. "Do you have a moment?"

Dread welled up in her stomach as she pulled away from Caroline and sent her off to take a look around. Her walk to the lawyer was like a pirate walking the gangplank. She braced herself for bad news.

"Congratulations on your grand reopening and for being cleared as a murder suspect." He flashed a bright smile, and Kelly noticed he had dimples. He was getting sexier by the minute.

"Thank you. What brings you by today? I don't think you're interested in buying any dresses."

"No, I'm not. I'm here concerning Mrs. Mueller's lawsuit." He shoved his hands into his jeans front pockets. "I've discussed the case with my client, and she's willing to drop the lawsuit in exchange—"

Kelly threw her arms around Mark Lambert and hugged him. "That's such good news! Thank you! Thank you! Thank you!"

"You're welcome, Miss Quinn. But there's a condition."

"What?" Kelly pulled back from Mark. "I'm sorry. I shouldn't have hugged you. That was completely unprofessional."

Mark smiled. "No need to apologize."

Kelly composed herself. She was now a local merchant in Lucky Cove and needed to maintain some level of professionalism. "What's the condition?"

"Mrs. Mueller would like a store discount."

"Okay. I can do that. Done."

"Lifetime discount."

Kelly pressed her lips together. Of course Mrs. Mueller wanted a lifetime discount. "How about I extend to her the employee discount? Do you think that would be acceptable?" The lawsuit and wondering how she'd pay to defend herself had dogged her for weeks, so agreeing to a discount was a no-brainer.

"I think she'll be agreeable to that offer."

"This means the lawsuit is officially dropped?"

"Well, I'm afraid I added a codicil to the offer."

"Codicil?"

"That's lawyer talk for adding another condition to the original condition."

"What's the codicil you added?"

Mark took a step forward. "Dinner with the lawyer."

She'd fortified herself for some unrealistic requirement she couldn't possibly afford to agree to, and then Mark's last words processed in her mind. A date? He was asking her to go on a date? She smiled and nodded.

"I can accommodate that codicil."

Mark's grin got wider. "Glad to hear that. How about seven?"

"Sounds good."

"Kelly!" Pepper called out from the sales counter. "A little help, please!"

"Looks like you have work to do. I'll see you later." Mark turned and walked out of the boutique.

After she watched Mark leave, Kelly turned around to face the sales floor and the line that formed at the sales counter, where Pepper was bagging merchandise. She let out a deep breath. The last few months had been rocky, and she wasn't sure where she was going to land, but never in a million years did she think she'd land back in the place where she began. You could take the girl out of Lucky Cove, but you couldn't take Lucky Cove out of the girl. But, for now, this girl was staying put. She was home.

Meet the Author

Debra Sennefelder is an avid reader who reads across a range of genres, but mystery fiction is her obsession. Her interest in people and relationships is channeled into her novels against a backdrop of crime and mystery. When she's not reading, she enjoys cooking and baking and as a former food blogger, she is constantly taking photographs of her food. Yeah, she's that person.

Born and raised in New York City, she majored in her hobby of fashion buying before working in retail. Today she lives and writes in Connecticut with her family. Her writing companions are her adorable and slightly spoiled Shih-Tzus, Susie and Billy.

You can learn more at www.DebraSennefelder.com